BLOOD STANDARD

BLOOD STANDARD

LAIRD BARRON

G. P. PUTNAM'S SONS | NEW YORK

G. P. PUTNAM'S SONS
Publishers Since 1838
An imprint of Penguin Random House LLC
375 Hudson Street
New York, New York 10014

Copyright © 2018 by Laird Barron
Penguin supports copyright. Copyright fuels creativity, encourages diverse voices,
promotes free speech, and creates a vibrant culture. Thank you for buying an authorized
edition of this book and for complying with copyright laws by not reproducing, scanning,
or distributing any part of it in any form without permission. You are supporting writers
and allowing Penguin to continue to publish books for every reader.

Library of Congress Cataloging-in-Publication Data

Names: Barron, Laird, author.
Title: Blood standard / Laird Barron.
Description: New York : G. P. Putnam's Sons, 2018.
Identifiers: LCCN 2016053622 (print) | LCCN 2017012173 (ebook) |
ISBN 9780735212886 (epub) | ISBN 9780735212879 (hardcover)
Subjects: LCSH: Missing persons—Investigation—Fiction. | GSAFD: Noir fiction.
Classification: LCC PS3602.A83725 (ebook) | LCC PS3602.A83725 B56 2018
(print) | DDC 813/.6—dc23
LC record available at https://lccn.loc.gov/2016053622

Printed in the United States of America
1   3   5   7   9   10   8   6   4   2

Book design by Gretchen Achilles

For Jessica M

. . . the woman with the dog's eyes would not close my eyes . . .

—HOMER

A thousand thousand slimy things lived on;
And so did I.

—SAMUEL TAYLOR COLERIDGE

PART I

KISS OFF

ONE

As a boy, I admired Humphrey Bogart in a big way. I coveted the homburg and trench coat. I wanted to pack heat and smoke unfiltered cigarettes and give them long-legged dames in mink stoles the squinty-eyed once-over. I longed to chase villains, right wrongs, and restore the peace.

Upon surviving into manhood, I discovered the black and comedic irony that is every gumshoe's existential plight, the secret that dime novels and black-and-white movies always elide: each clue our intrepid detective deciphers, each mystery he unravels, each crime he solves, makes the world an unhappier place. I got smart and became a gangster instead. More money, more women, and better clothes. Much less in the way of mystery. As for the misery quotient? Basically a wash.

Became a gangster. There's a mouthful. How I wound up hitting for the far north division of the Outfit is a woeful saga. The story of how I escaped that life is no less grim, but it's a hell of a lot shorter.

THE OUTFIT FLEW ME FIRST CLASS from Anchorage to Nome on a working vacation.

Boss had wrapped his arm around my shoulder.

"Isaiah," he said. "Do me a favor, son? Take in the frozen vistas, photograph the northern lights, maybe crack a few heads. See ya in a couple months."

Perhaps not those exact words, but close. What he really meant was snoop around and make sure everything was copacetic behind the scenes.

The gig didn't appeal to my sensibilities. Nome isn't a premier post by any means. In fact, the suits in Anchorage and Chicago treat the town like a Mafia penal colony. Two types get sent to the deep freeze—guys with specialist talent and ne'er-do-wells. We're talking malcontents, sadists, and screwups. No, I didn't relish the assignment, short-term or not. However, I understood my place. A polite request from the headman was no request at all.

Upon landing, I reported to Vitale Night, a local mob potentate in charge of tundra as far as the eye could see. A medium-built guy; angular, from his hawkish nose and bony hands to his sharp knees. Shiny, graying hair and tailored duds—a Sinatra wannabe.

Night had risen through the ranks in Chicago as the premier button man of the generation prior to my own. Quick on the draw as a Wild West gunfighter with a pile of bodies to his credit. I witnessed him in action at the shooting range. Fast wasn't really an adequate description. The pistol seemed to teleport from its holster to his hand as he emptied a magazine through a bull's-eye the diameter of a nickel.

A man without compunction was the book on Vitale Night. It's difficult to come by a higher compliment in the mob. Why the powers that be shipped him to Alaska presented a mystery. Rumors abounded—he'd whacked somebody without permission; he'd stolen the wrong captain's mistress; he'd looked funny at a boss. Could have been any of those trespasses, or none.

Lately, Night handled various rackets between Nome and Prudhoe Bay. Drugs, guns, gambling, prostitution; anything to improve the morale of lonely commercial fishermen and oil field roughnecks as they toiled in the Land of the Midnight Sun. The Outfit loved Alaska—wide-open shipping lanes, among the finest weed in North America, and a never-ending glut of petroleum money that eventually flowed into their pockets. Maintaining a successful Alaska operation was a matter of identifying men who could handle extremes of light and dark and perpetually savage weather.

My task? Intimidate a few of Night's underperforming subordinates so he didn't need to lower himself or muck around with hurt feelings. Family relationships are petty and complicated—doesn't matter what family you're talking about.

When you needed a whip hand, you sent Isaiah Coleridge. I'd set the gold standard. Those movies by Albert Broccoli about the world-famous spy? In every flick there's a sinister, powerfully built dude in a nice suit lurking at the margins. He kills people who annoy his boss, the archvillian. I was that dude.

The first few weeks in Nome were smooth. The bozos I'd come to frighten took a gander at my game face and straightened their acts out in a hurry. Easy money. Mostly, we played cards and spent a sizable chunk of our evenings boozing at one of a dozen taverns. I got close to the crew, especially Night's second fiddle, Tony Becchi (aka Tony Flowers), a potbellied old-school gangster. Old-school as in Dark Ages.

Like myself, Tony Flowers guest-starred in this particular drama. Chicago had decided Night required the talents of an older, stable gangster; not permanently, just for a year or two. Originally from Florida, Tony F hated Illinois weather. Well, he hated Alaska winter a damned sight worse. I allowed him to believe the two of us shared this sentiment. He made the assumption due to me being half Maori. We established a running gag:

What the fuck is a Maori doing in Alaska? he'd say.

Freezing my ass off, I'd reply. *What's the forecast?*

Partly shitty this morning, intermittently shitty this afternoon, and mostly shitty tonight.

Funny thing, I'd come to ask myself the same question with increasing frequency: what was I doing here? Instead of heeding that instinct, which I came to acknowledge as the angel on my right shoulder, I downed another shot and waited for it to leave me in peace.

Kept right on that way until it was too late.

TWO

The universe went sideways on a skiff in the Chukchi Sea. My increasingly changeable nature had given plenty of signs. I should've seen it coming, should've been wise to the demands of my soul.

The whole charade began to fall apart the day Vitale Night decreed a handful of his crew would accompany him on a short flight to a private lodge near Kotzebue. He refused to explain the occasion and merely smirked when I inquired. You don't ask a captain twice; you keep mum and wait to see what happens next.

What happened next is we got into a twin-prop passenger plane and zipped north to a rustic hunting lodge on an isolated shore. I found it spartan, albeit classy enough. Log construction as one would expect, and decorated with polar bear heads and photographs of various Popes and the Rat Pack.

Vitale Night threw a righteous bash. He'd brought a case of champagne and plenty of blow. Several snow bunnies entertained the company of hard cases. I brooded in a corner and drank far too much. In the morning I staggered downstairs to witness Night and Tony F unpacking rifles and an array of skinning knives. The men grinned at me and nudged each other as they laid their implements on a bunting cloth spread across the dining room table. They wore wool shirts, wool pants, and heavy-duty snow boots. Their sneers foretold impending awfulness. It remained to be seen what form that awfulness would assume.

Vitale Night checked the scope on a rifle.

"Coleridge. I hear you're a hunter." He centered the bore on my head and dry-fired. "Christ, don't scowl like that. You're scarin' the womenfolk. I'm just yankin' your chain." He and Tony F shared a belly laugh.

I walked over to the bar, grabbed a bottle of Knob Creek, and poured myself a tall glass for breakfast. The bottle got dangerously low before the all-terrain vehicle arrived.

A half dozen of us bundled into the cramped compartment and were driven out onto the fast ice. The ATV clanged along on metal treads that chewed through blue-white pressure ridges. Clouds gathered, low and heavy, and merged with lighter fog. Eventually, pack ice began to separate in open water. A long wooden skiff piloted by a local awaited our arrival. Everybody pulled anoraks over their winter coats and piled aboard the skiff. Twin Evinrude motors barked and the pilot sailed us into the briny mist.

"What's waiting for us?" I said to Tony Flowers.

"Herd a walrus," he yelled over the motors' roar. "They winter on icebergs near the coast. Gonna bag us a shitpot of ivory!"

The sun ate through the clouds.

IMAGES FROM THAT AFTERNOON will score my memory until death sweeps the slate bare: the iceberg, stepped like an abstract sculpture of a ziggurat and dotted with drowsy walruses who had no fear of approaching humans; Night, Tony F, and two other shooters blazing away as the skiff rocked and rolled; another hunter gathering a brace of machetes in anticipation of the mass beheadings; the squalls of dying animals; and streams of hot red blood hissing over the edge of the berg and into black seawater. The stench of terror and shit and smoke as if that piece of the wilderness had become a portable abattoir.

One of the men filmed the slaughter with a Handycam. He whooped narratively.

I did not consciously decide to act. Had that been the case, I might have hesitated—Vitale Night was too fast and too mad. To defy him was to risk a hideous death. I did what I did out of instinct, a sympathetic response from the animal in my hindbrain.

Vitale Night and I stood side by side near the bow. He gestured to me for a fresh magazine. In retrospect, I believe he meant to demonstrate dominance by reducing my status to that of his personal spear-carrier. He reloaded slowly and deliberately, feet braced against the rocking of the boat. Completely vulnerable. He raised his head to survey the action and I chopped his throat with the edge of my hand. Night's tinted glasses flew. He made a sound like steam whistling in the flue of a kettle and dropped to his knees. Take a man's air, you take all the fight right out of him and I don't care if he jumps into both pant legs at the same time in the morning.

I picked up his rifle and pointed it in the general direction of Tony Flowers.

"Hey, Tony. Better call it a day and head home. Vitale needs a doctor."

None of the crew knew which way to jump. Night's men were as confused as the bawling walruses flopping around the iceberg. The *Mafia Handbook* doesn't cover the situation.

Tony Flowers carefully set his weapon aside and defused what might've escalated into a shoot-out in the middle of the Chukchi Sea.

"Yeah, yeah. He don't look so hot." He smiled a sickly, hateful smile.

After we reached shore, I rode in the plane back to Nome with him and Vitale Night. Night slumped in a rear seat, eyes squeezed shut, face gone gray. He gurgled the way a baby does. Tony F clasped his hand and whispered what I assume were promises of vengeance.

As we taxied into the Nome airport, a bitter wind howled off Norton Sound. Snow fell thick and fast. Right before he climbed into the ambulance with his boss, Tony F finally made eye contact.

"Isaiah . . . You just fucked yourself royal. Why?"

I had no answer for him. How could I explain in words he'd remotely understand? Despite everything, despite the evil in my heart, I never was a hunter of dumb beasts.

THREE

It was me in the chair this time.

Vitale Night's boys took no chances. A guy with my reputation? You didn't screw around. Nope, you hired a sexy cocktail waitress to slip under my guard and deliver the sting. Horse tranquilizer mixed into a scotch and soda followed by a midnight ride to the old Nome cannery district. If you were smart, you hog-tied me, beat me, bled me, softened me up for the main event. No surprises, no opportunities to turn the tables, no second act. Curtains, baby.

I took a measure of morbid pride in their professionalism and their fear. Tony Flowers and a couple of goons stripped me to my boxers. They chained me in the center of a ten-by-twenty concrete subbasement cell. I'm a big man, so the fellows used a lot of chain.

The chair was solid wrought iron and looked as if it had been unbolted from the deck of a trawler. Dirty fluorescent bulbs pulsed overhead. The chamber reeked of bleach and mildew. The faint muddy stench of seawater seeped through the foundation. Mid-winter and meat locker chilly, although I'd stopped noticing the finer details after Tony F and his sidekicks traded turns dealing blows to my jaw.

Goon number one was a broad-shouldered lad with fists like bricks. Not quite my size, but ripped from pumping iron at the fire-house rec center. An indefatigable brute—his umpteenth punch struck with the same bone-crushing force as the first had. I figured he'd be going places if he lived long enough. I winked through the gore at the kid to remind him that nothing in this life is guaranteed. Me being Exhibit A.

He said, "Dude's still got jokes."

"Everybody's a hard case until you get to their balls," Tony Flowers said.

A special word about Tony F. He didn't look like much in his patented cardinal red tracksuit and wire-rimmed glasses. He'd killed plenty of people, however. His specialty lay with knives, drills, and similar toys. His birth name was Tony Becchi. He came to be known as Tony Flowers because once upon a time if you saw Tony in his professional capacity it meant flowers on your grave. He'd matured into a shrewd businessman. Few wiseguys knew more about gam-bling or coke than Tony F. That's why he could afford to hump a procession of trophy girlfriends, drive last year's model Jag, and blow so much dough at the bar every weekend.

And here he stood in a frozen cell orchestrating a beating that would bring him neither fame nor fortune. He had to assume it would be his turn one day.

Reversals of fortune happen fast. Meteor streaking from the sky fast. Two days ago, I'd eaten New York steak, sipped Cristal, and taken my brothers in crime to the cleaners at our weekly poker game in the back room of the clubhouse. Two days ago, I was a man of status. Respected and feared by friends and enemies; doted upon by lackeys and subordinates. Not the king, nowhere near, yet significantly more than a mere supernumerary in the venerable blood opera.

Tonight, I was a prisoner: drugged, stripped, tortured, and well on the way to becoming a corpse. I intended to face my approaching doom with a smidgen of equanimity. Fortune and ruin, life and death, all the important things, are balanced upon the razor's edge. Yes, the chickens had come home to roost. In this business they always do. Actions have consequences and my fate could be put down to physics. I regretted nothing. Nothing except the perpetual bad weather that had socked in all the flights out of town and kept me stranded, vulnerable to reprisal.

Sweat peeled the duct tape from my mouth. The tape was a formality, stage dressing for a ritual as old as crime itself; that ritual concerning the purification of traitors. I could yell all I wanted. Nobody would hear me except the rest of the thugs keeping watch upstairs. We were in the underworld, that spot on the map marked with skulls and crossbones and dragons. Tape, pliers, and ball-peen hammer were meant to satisfy tradition as much as anything else. The goons understood that trying to frighten me was a waste of effort.

Well, the hammer served a purpose. Tony F had busted several ribs and squashed the little finger of my left hand with it. He'd be working his way up the arm soon. I knew the routine; I'd been the one with the hammer in my fist often enough. Our destination held no mystery. By evening's end it would be big bad Isaiah Coleridge's head on the mantel.

I spat out the tape and said in a voice scarcely my own, "How's Vitale?"

Night loomed conspicuous in his absence. I guessed he wasn't feeling well.

Tony Flowers said, "Ain't gonna sing karaoke no more. Can't even talk. He really, really wanted to be here to see you off."

"How could you tell? They hang one of those whiteboards around his neck?"

My wit earned me a smack on the left wrist and I went to the hot white void for a while. Angelic figures on winged horses saluted my hovering soul, celestial music trumpeted, and thunder boomed from Mount Olympus. That sort of thing.

I crashed to earth, disappointed to find myself still chained, still hurting. Tony Flowers and his goons stared down at my sorry bulk. They'd held a conference, from what I gathered.

"Y'know what I say, Tony?" The kid hefted a pair of garden shears with industrial rubber grips. He glanced toward the vicinity of my crotch. "I say we skip the pleasantries."

Tony Flowers let the hammer clank onto the floor. He took his fancy glasses out of his pocket and pushed them onto the bridge of his nose. He seemed abruptly eager to get this filthy business done. Doubtless, a stewardess or college-age stripper was keeping the sheets warm back at his hotel.

"Okay, kid. Have at it."

The kid tipped me a wink of his own as he knelt between my thighs. The shears snicked wide. I flexed every muscle in my body, but the chains didn't burst. Mama, your son is about to be made a eunuch.

Thank God the phone rang.

WORD CAME DOWN FROM ON HIGH that I'd been pulled from the job. No more fun for my tormentors.

The goon reluctantly put his shears away.

"Hey, let's do this again."

"See ya around, pineapple." Tony Flowers spat on my face. The others did too.

They loaded me onto a cargo plane bound for Anchorage, where I did a stint at Providence Hospital. My catalog of injuries was modestly impressive. Mashed nose, broken ribs, broken fingers, hairline fracture of the wrist, and a partially collapsed lung. Contusions from head to toe. Small potatoes, really. Nothing some righteous dope and a few weeks of proper R & R wouldn't fix.

Cops came around and were sent away counting out the crisp C-notes that'd been pressed into their sweaty palms. I expected a visit from Vitale Night or one of his favorite henchmen. Had I awakened to Tony Flowers cutting my throat, it would have seemed the most natural thing in the world.

Except, that's not how it went.

FOUR

When the latest morphine buzz faded, I opened my eyes. The Outfit's headman in Anchorage, Mr. Lucius Apollo, sat at my bedside like the world's most sinister uncle. I've known him forever. He befriended my father twenty-five years ago. This had been during my teens when the Coleridges settled in Anchorage permanently. No idea where they first crossed paths or what bonded them—probably a mutual interest in hunting and drinking and whoring around.

Whatever the case, the men were thick as thieves for a while, and not long after Dad and I had our great parting of the ways, Mr. Apollo took me in and saw to my education. I called him Uncle Lucius. He saw talent beneath my surly exterior; talent wasted on petty crime and petty violence. Uncle Lucius became Boss and Boss introduced me to the life. There are those who'd say I should hate him for making me into an instrument of destruction, for ruthlessly exploiting my anger and loyalty to achieve his nefarious ends. I don't, because, at its worst, manipulation was better than living with a father who had no use for his son at all.

Only Boss would dress for the tropics while residing in the Arctic. Decked out, as ever, in his finest white Panama suit and a straw-weave hat that shaded his expression. I didn't need to see his eyes to get the drift. Boss was unhappy. Boss wanted an explanation. Boss wanted a reason not to finish what Night's friends had started in that basement in Nome.

"Damn it, kid. You were only supposed to observe and report. Now it's a bloody mess."

"And crack a few skulls," I said.

"Not Vitale's. What in God's name happened?"

Obviously, Tony Flowers had already raved at Mr. Apollo over the phone, detailing my infamy. I told him my side of how it went down. Afterward, I clammed up and waited to see whether my tale of woe intrigued him or if he'd simply order an associate to put a pillow over my face.

"Walruses?" Mr. Apollo said. "You putting me on? Walruses?"

Wiseguys and cops alike called the old man the Kingpin of Anchorage. He owned paving companies and contracting companies, a famous strip club, and a swanky restaurant chain where the staff presented you with a loaner jacket if you forgot to bring one. Don't let any of that fool you. The buttoned-down, crimp-mouthed sonofabitch had a claw in every dirty deed from Anchorage to Fairbanks.

"Walruses," I said. "Hand to God. A whole herd."

"Vitale is after ivory."

"There's a shortage of cribbage boards at Ye Olde Nome Gifte Shoppe."

"Ivory is not worth the heat."

"Nope."

"I've told him—I've told all of them up there—to stay away from ivory and polar bear hide."

"My impression is he doesn't give a shit."

"Can you prove anything?" The question implied that he was still deciding whether or not to have me dumped in the bay.

"The whole kill is on candid camera. One of Night's idiot thugs filmed the operation. I, ah, appropriated the camera when I left. The reason Tony was tenderizing my parts—he wanted the footage."

"The Feds will tack Vitale's hide to the wall if he isn't careful," Mr. Apollo said.

"Better him than us. Thus goes my reasoning."

"The bastard isn't even cutting me in. That's what really hurts."

I didn't tell him my suspicions about Night's arrangements with the Nome black-market ivory dealers. A few weeks monitoring the situation had given me a world of insight. You shoot the breeze with your fellow lowlifes and soon learn who's screwing whose old lady, who's skimming the till, and who's in debt to whom. The Nome crew had a mean dope habit—coke for Night, meth for the rest. Night didn't want money for ivory, he wanted drugs. All pleasure and no business.

Mr. Apollo stared at the ceiling for a bit. I could practically hear the steel ball bearings clicking in his head. Finally, he patted my arm.

"Well, Isaiah, it was a good thought."

"Thanks, Boss."

"Who's got the film, if you don't mind?"

I told him I'd mailed it to my personal P.O. box and where to find the key. No point to holding out on him. Either I'd be pardoned or I'd be crab food. When I'd finished talking, my bedclothes sopped with sweat.

Mr. Apollo removed his hat and set it in his lap. Bald as a turkey vulture, pale blue eyes, a trim silver beard; a Confederate general in his dotage. He leaned so close that I got a whiff of imported cologne, the sweet, dark scents of Cuban cigars, and top-shelf whiskey. For a moment I worried that he intended to give me the kiss of death. Turned out it was only the kiss-off.

"Son, I've always liked you," he said with what resembled genuine fondness.

"Sir, I know that."

"Vitale is mighty vexed over your shenanigans. The troops are referring to your rebellion as the 'Ice Capades.' It's a big problem, Vitale being who he is and whatnot."

"Sorry." I tried not to smile. Mostly because it hurt my face too much.

"Leave it to you to not only piss off a made guy, but a guy who was once upon a time Chicago's go-to hitter."

"I didn't have time to break off his thumbs, more is the pity."

Mr. Apollo sighed. He'd put up with my antics since forever.

Waves of exhaustion crashed over me.

"Send him a fruit basket and a get-well card," I said.

"Your fat head in a Christmas basket would probably be more welcome."

"Sir, is it worth your trouble finding a basket that goddamned big?"

He didn't laugh.

"Chicago called twice today. Second call came from the Chairman himself. He's concerned. Very, very concerned."

I kept my mouth shut. Usually the best policy.

"As it happens, Night hasn't been authorized to make a move on you. And he won't. For now, at least. Sooner or later, though. He wants to pay his respects personally. Claims he's more than happy to wait until your bones knit. A matter of honor."

"A real prince, Vitale is." I regarded the plaster cast on my arm and the one on my leg. The pulleys and cables and IV drips made me depressed and so I stared at the ceiling. "It's going to be the death of him."

"I appreciate what you've done for the Outfit."

Oh boy. Here came the other shoe. I pressed the button again.

"That is why it grieves me deeply to say this."

"Sir—"

"I am afraid we've come to the end of the road."

"Sir—"

"Shut up, son."

"Yes, sir."

He straightened and put his hat on.

"You can't be around here anymore. Not in Anchorage, not Wasilla, not Fairbanks. Not a bloody igloo on Little Diomede. You can't set foot west of Delta Junction again. Ever. If you're smart, you won't even visit the Yukon Territory. Ever. I also advise against vacationing in Chicago. Ever. Do you understand what I'm saying, Isaiah?"

The medicine kicked in. Kicked in like that ball-peen hammer caving my skull in.

I floated on a cotton cloud and beamed at him with the beatific simplemindedness of a newborn calf. Lately, I'd studied Buddhism via 1960s samurai flicks. My composure wasn't solely a function of the lovely, lovely drugs. I emptied my mind the way any good samurai might, chucking the last twenty-odd years out the window.

Mr. Apollo removed a manila envelope from his coat and laid it on the dresser in the shadow of a vase of white roses. Nice and thick too.

"Your severance package. There's another envelope for every year you've served, minus hospital expenses. Cash. Plane tickets. A letter of introduction addressed 'To whom it may concern.'"

"You shouldn't have." My eyelids were heavy.

"Once you're on the mend, I'm sending you all the way east. First class. I arranged a place for you to recuperate with old friends of mine. A horse farm north of New York City. Up in Catskill country."

"What do I know from horses?"

"Don't look one I give you in the mouth, I hope."

"Excellent point, Boss."

"Anyway, you go relax. Recuperate. Hope everybody here forgets your name. My friends at that farm got a soft spot for idiots. Picture it this way—you're getting exiled from Alaska. Heck of a deal, is what I say." Then the vicious bastard dropped the bunker buster he'd saved all along. "Best part is, you'll be closer to your old man."

"Dad? You . . . talked to him?" Six years since last I'd spoken to Mervin Coleridge. Sixty would've pleased me more. I'd even kindled the tiny hope that he might've shuffled into the afterlife. The gods are cruel. As a goon of my recent acquaintance would say, "The gods got jokes."

"I sent him word you were in the hospital. Told him you might not be long for this vale of tears. He's your dad. We must respect that." Mr. Apollo gave me a look that recommended I *best* respect said familial bond or else. "We talked. He bought a spread in the Adirondacks a while back. Gotta be honest with you, son. It's your father who tipped the scales against me whacking you. I owed Mervin a favor from the old days. Doesn't matter what, don't ask. He called in the marker and you get to keep breathing. We're even."

"Ah, Christ," I managed as my heart lurched and the mattress softened into quicksand. Man, I tried to climb out of bed in a sudden panic and got as far as the notion and no further.

Mr. Apollo studied me with worry.

"Isaiah, you okay, boy?"

I wanted to tell him he should've left me in the iron chair, should've let the goons do what goons do best. My complaints came too late. Too late all the way around. The sirens of the void sang to me and I went.

FIVE

ike it or lump it, the Hudson Valley was in my cards. Might as
well follow the advice of that sage Billy Joel and get into a New
York state of mind. We all had roots in the Hudson Valley—the
Coleridges and the Apollos. Dad's family once owned property near
Accord before they scattered on the winds of time and war. My sur-
rogate uncle, Mr. Apollo, like most wiseguys not from Illinois, grew
up in Yonkers.

I chose to roll with the punches despite a searing antipathy toward anything to do with Dad. Antipathy and a not insignificant
measure of fear. Dad's property lay several hours to the north of New
York City, deep in the Adirondacks. Remote, yet entirely too close
for comfort. His longtime girlfriend, Harriet, a sweetly addled ex–B
movie actress, kept in touch with us kids. She'd sent postcards from
their previous abodes in Alaska and California. The pair gravitated
to rural paradises surrounded by forest and streams jumping with
trout. I imagined their latest retreat would be no different.

The sole mitigating factor was, I'd not be likely to see him in the
flesh unless I took the initiative. Dad frequently traveled abroad, and

he relished manipulating events through intermediaries; always had. Mooks and thugs and femmes fatales, I could handle. Too weak to run, too weak to fight, biding my time as a wounded bear would in its cave felt appropriate.

A friend of my father met me at Newark International. I'd balked at the idea; Mr. Apollo insisted I play nice, however. Said to let my father make his gesture and be grateful if Mervin didn't come to be my personal chauffeur. The contact was a middle-aged bruiser by the name of Kline. Crew cut, aviator glasses, bomber jacket. Very likely career military, judging by his brisk comport, the way he held his mouth. Not the talkative sort. That suited me. I wanted to think, despite the fact that for weeks languishing in a hospital bed and thinking was all I'd done.

Kline played Ellington's *Such Sweet Thunder* on the stereo. The docs had busted my cast off and I enjoyed the simple joys of scratching an itch, the warmth of a breeze caressing my arm. I squeezed a squash ball. I didn't use tennis balls because I ruined them too quickly. Two hundred with the left, two hundred with the right. Most guys neglect their hands. They love chest presses and biceps curls and squats, but when the chips are down, a man has to be able to depend upon his grip. If it's a bone crusher, all to the good. Tony was never far from my mind as I throttled that ball.

We entered the Hudson Valley.

I'm comfortable with old, old places, places hostile to evolved life. My longest and best home, Alaska, is such a one: a vast, wind-blasted vista of mountain and river and sea as ancient as the bedrock of the world itself. Large and largely empty. Inhuman, yet aware on some primal frequency. Palpably malevolent in its indifference, Alaska is a land where winter kills off wolves and caribou alike and breeds creeping, deadly cabin fever that does in scores of men and women every year.

But we were quits, Alaska and me.

The Hudson Valley is old and frightening in a different way. Less a matter of deep geological time and more in line with the puny yardstick of man. Nonetheless, it hits you hard on a first encounter—say, as you're wheeling along Route 32 in the back of a black sedan in the spring when the light is all pinks and greens and the geese rise against Van Gogh's *Wheat Field under Clouded Sky*. Squirrels in the trees, bees in the hive, picket fences and gilded parkways, potholed roads winding onward and onward toward the falling sun.

Where the Land of Ten Thousand Smokes strikes you with its austere immensity, New York State is much the opposite. She reveals her length and breadth, her mercurial character, by slow degrees. Reveals herself via the shift of sunbeams through the canopies of forests still wild at the margins, through the soft sweep of the Appalachians and the Catskills, the Hudson and the Rondout curving gently as a mama's arm around her child.

I figured once we got more familiar, we'd get along fine.

Kline ferried me north and east into what city folk consider the wilderness and I beheld a panoply of debauched, gothic America. At my request, he took the scenic route in a big loop around our destination. I wanted to get a feel for the landscape while someone else worried about driving. The outskirts of Newburgh, Poughkeepsie, and Kingston slid past like a dream of ruin—during the revolution *this* town had been burned and *that* town sacked. Brick-and-mortar shops with cracked façades, shuttered warehouses and rusting bridges, moribund churches, tall and sinister upon battle rises, abandoned colonial graveyards, derelict memorials, and overgrown estates of dead-as-dust patrician overseers, all unspooling.

We rolled over the Wallkill, then hard left onto an unpaved country road that meandered into the foothills and their cave tombs.

Hawk Mountain Farm and Center for Symbolic Studies occupied

many acres between the Wallkill Valley Rail Trail and Hawk Mountain. I'd traced the Rail Trail on a map. Its path intersected many a highway and secondary road as it arrowed northwest and toward the borders of the state and transitioned to another trail system. Maybe I'd lace up my hiking boots and go for a wander when my health returned completely. It had been a few moons since my last excursion into the wilds.

We passed through densely wooded draws and bucolic fields tenanted by distant A-frame houses. Nearer our destination where the road doglegged stretched an expanse of cropped turf designated HOUNDS TRAINING GROUNDS. Next door, behind a tall cyclone fence, were rings, swings, and nets and a bunch of other high-wire equipment. A wooden placard said TRAPEZE CLUB.

Acrobats in leotards hung around the parking strip, laughing and passing a water bottle. A woman in green stood apart from the other performers. She smoked a cigarette and watched our sedan trundle past. She didn't smile when I gave her a little wave. She turned away with deliberateness and arched her back and stretched her arms toward the light.

"Wow," Kline said without rotating his head. The only word he'd uttered since climbing behind the wheel.

"Holy smokes," I said.

Three ramshackle turret-style cottages peeped through the trees atop the ridgeline. The stone cottages were surmounted by geodesic domes painted bright green and brighter red. All of this belonged to the Walkers, a family with roots extending back to the Civil War, although white settlers first cleared the land before the nineteenth century. Much of the modern infrastructure went in during the 1950s and '60s. Hard not to imagine the architectural committee sky-high on magic mushrooms during the planning phase.

"What the hell are those?" I said.

Kline drove up a steep hill with washboard ruts.

"Gnome homes," I said to test the sound. "Hobbit houses."

"Probably full of hippies, sir."

We pulled into a long pasture. The main house was a rambler with freshly stained pine siding. The farm was divided into plots by a picket fence and a cabbage patch, then another heavier post-and-wire fence and a slab log bunkhouse, an L-shaped stable-and-barn combo, a woodshed, and an antiquated mill partially blockaded by cedar shavings piled high on the side. Farther away, horses grazed on tufts of weeds in a field. Ducks floated upon a muddy pond. Even more distant, and among the bordering forest, crouched another of those wacky gnome huts. This shanty had a yellow Dr. Seuss roof.

As my boots touched gravel I got a snootful of cedar, ripe horse dung, and hickory smoke boiling from the chimney stack. Kline unloaded the three canvas seabags and a dented footlocker that comprised my worldly possessions. We stood there for a moment in a cloud of gnats and flies.

"Good luck, sir," he said, catching himself mid-salute, instead embarrassedly tugging his ear.

"*Sayonara*, and thanks for the lift. Tell my old man to piss up a rope, if you see him."

Kline nodded as if taking a mental note. He drove away without another word.

SIX

An elderly couple approached from the direction of the barn. The man could've doubled for Sidney Poitier if the lighting were right. The lady had piled her white hair in a severe bun. Her wrinkles dug to the bone. They wore wool sweaters and lace-up work boots.

"Welcome to the farm. I'm Virgil Walker. And this is my wife, Jade." Virgil Walker grabbed my hand and shook it. "Hey, honey, this young fella is big enough to slap a saddle on."

"The farm is saved, hurrah!" Jade said without enthusiasm. She looked me over, pursing her lips at my sallow complexion and gimpy leg. Her expression made me thankful I wasn't an injured horse. They scowled at my shaggy hair and thickening beard; nor were they pleased by my leather jacket, slacks, and scuffed Doc Martens. Tin-horn, city slicker, ne'er-do-well, is what my Big & Tall duds said about me. How much did they know of my background? No telling what lies Mr. Apollo had fed them, no telling what manner of bargain he'd struck.

"So, you drink like a fish, huh?" Virgil said, dispelling part of the mystery. "Well, mister, we got a cure for that. It's called honest labor."

"Honest labor?" I said, no doubt reinforcing my first impression of a great lummox. They were right about the drinking, although I sort of thought I drank precisely enough.

"What my husband means is, you'll be bucking so much hay and mucking so many stalls you won't have time to drink. Or go around wrecking motorcycles."

I smiled toothily and cursed Mr. Apollo and his choice of back-story.

"How do you know Mr. Apollo?"

Jade examined her nails.

"Our families go back a long way. Mr. Apollo has sponsored the farm since we opened. He's been kind."

"You're awfully peaked." Virgil said it *pee-kid*. "We don't wanna break you the first few days."

"I'm grateful, Mr. Walker. I'll take it slow."

"D'you like horses?" He unfolded a pocketknife and cut himself a plug of tobacco. He chewed the plug and stared at me with skepticism.

"I like horses fine."

"Is that so? I hope you like horse crap too," Jade said.

I probably would've fallen in love with the dame then and there if she hadn't been a hundred and fifty years old.

"Yes, ma'am."

"Well, Virg, I guess he'll do. Listen, young man. Here are the ground rules: No partying. No tomfoolery. No drugs. Horses get fed at seven a.m."

"Got it."

"Ah, and do try to exercise prudence in the friends you choose to invite to the farm."

"She means ixnay on a parade of whores coming and going from your shack," Virgil said.

"I wish," I said.

A station wagon pulled into the yard and a cadaverous man in a plaid jacket emerged. Virgil introduced him as Norman Coates, manager of the Hawk Mountain Farm.

"Chief cook and bottle washer, mainly," Coates said.

We shook. He had the watery blue eyes of an old sailor who'd seen the worst. His accent, although faint, placed him as a native of the Shetlands.

Virgil hollered, "Gus!" and a lad with a vacant expression eventually toddled over. Gus got tabbed to haul my bags to an empty cabin catty-corner to the barn. The Walkers then gave me a brief tour of the immediate grounds. They chatted in their laconic fashion, idly brushing aside peahens and chickens as we crossed the yard. I tried not to limp too noticeably, nor wheeze, nor lag. The trip had taken its toll.

Along the way, I discovered a few things. The Walkers both possessed doctorates in literature and sociology. Suckers jetted in from around the world to partake of drum circles, sweat lodges, and "incense"-fueled seminars at the Center. Bottom line: numerous people came and went from the property. In addition to relatives and hangers-on who dropped in at all hours, one had to contend with volunteers and random visitors. Festival season lay around the corner, and tourists would flood in to attend the Beltane ceremonies. The veterinarian, farrier, and accountant paid regular house calls.

"What's the Beltane celebration like?"

"Heard of it?" Jade arched her brow.

"I've seen *The Wicker Man*," I hedged.

"Oh, then you get the gist. Rivers of beer. Great, ruddy fires. Topless lasses. Dancing around the maypole and fornicating in the rows."

"Really?"

"Not really," Virgil said glumly.

Next I met Lionel Robard, the farm's other full-time employee. He proved an acerbic towheaded man a few years younger than myself. Lean and weathered and handsome like a guy who should've made it onto the silver screen but never did. Definitely an ex-soldier. Something in the flick of his cold glance, how he appraised me without seeming to, hinted at Special Forces. He was pitching hay when we came across him.

"Hi, I'm Lionel." He left it at that. He tucked a hideout pistol into his boot, and I bet nobody else had noticed it yet. He didn't seem to care for my demeanor, but he also didn't hate me on sight, which I get a lot, being so handsome and whatnot. There's a warm place in my heart for shifty dudes who stash deadly weapons on their person for apparently no sane reason. Maybe we could be friends.

"This is our granddaughter, Reba." Jade gestured toward a skinny girl in an orange T-shirt and cargo shorts as she skulked past us.

I pegged her for seventeen, maybe eighteen, going on forty. Lighter of complexion than either grandparent, with a suggestion of Egyptian heritage in the shape of her eyes and cheekbones. Reba didn't shake my hand, didn't acknowledge me, beyond a sharp, contemptuous glare on her way to join Lionel in the loft. I recognized that would-be badass stare.

"She's standoffish," Virgil said as the girl disappeared up the ladder. "Getting over some troubles in the city."

"Wild child," Jade said.

I'd figured as much. The *13* tattooed on her calf was a declaration of sovereignty or a cry for attention. It required twelve jurors and one judge to send an original G to the pen. Everybody knows that, though; real criminals and aspiring delinquents alike. She'd forgotten the ½, which meant "half a chance." It didn't mean anything except I should keep one eye open and my hand on my wallet.

Reformed hippies with dubious business schemes, a paranoid war vet, and a gangster in the making. Gnome huts and the Black Forest in the backyard. Yeah, this already felt like home.

LE CHÂTEAU DE COLERIDGE comprised a rustic main room and tiny bathroom. Pine floors and walls and low timber beams, sooty and dusty from benign neglect. Toilet, shower, and a double bed. Electricity, but no phone line, no television, no space for anything more than the sparse handmade furniture, a record player in an oak armoire, an empty gun rack, and a fireplace. Some tenant left behind an oil painting of naked Hercules slashing the Hydra with a gladius while a peasant cowered, his upraised torch a tongue of red fire. I had a chuckle at the serendipity of that particular image. Outside, moss crusted the shake roof. Bats and songbirds nested in the eaves.

A hairy spider scuttled under the bed at my approach. I collapsed on the mattress and lay in an exhausted sweat. Everything on me hurt, so I swallowed some Vicodin and closed my eyes until the spinning stopped.

"What are you doing here?" Reba stood in the open door. The sun sank behind her shoulder and cast her face in shadow.

I lifted my head.

"Admiring the ceiling."

"What are you doing at the *farm?*"

"Same as you, sister. Same as you. Suffering for my sins."

"I'm not your sister, pineapple."

I didn't bother correcting her about my ethnicity.

"You do a mean Eastwood."

"Dude, I know what you are."

A quick study—I didn't even have any ink work to tip her off.

"What am I?"

"Bad news. It's your eyes."

"Eyes without a face," I sang in a creaky falsetto.

She waited, arms folded tight.

A ray of sunlight reflected off a crystal starburst someone had hung from a string in the window. The red light caught at her throat and momentarily illuminated a death's-head. I blinked, and it wasn't a death's-head on a chain around her neck but rather a stylized horse. The afterimage of the human skull revolved in my mind, sent a shiver through me.

"When did you get out?" I said.

"Who says I was in?"

"You were in. Somewhere with locks and bars and a curfew. Or you're fronting."

"Think I'm frontin'?"

"Does it matter? Maybe you are, maybe you aren't. Maybe Grandma and Grandpa have a custody deal with the state. Honestly, I'm more interested in finishing this nap."

"There's only one thing about me you need to know."

"What's that, sister?"

"If you mess with Jade or Virgil, I'll stab you in the heart."

I liked her better already.

"When you put it that way . . ."

SEVEN

I dream of the old days, of childhood and family. I dream of hell.

My father is Mervin Coleridge, son of an English fellow well met and a Kentucky preacher's daughter. Dad fled home and joined the military at the tender age of eighteen. He made full bird Air Force colonel in minimum time thanks to conniving and toil. I've seldom met craftier or more ruthless operators, and considering the company I keep, that's saying a lot. From him I learned how to throw a punch and shoot a rifle.

Dad's first wife hailed from a distinguished lineage of cattle barons and wildcat oilmen. Blonde, refined Clare Sexton, the Texas belle, gave birth to four strapping boys: Wyland, Steven, Hayden, and Hoyte. However, an officer's life was not for her and she soon fled back home to her parents. There may have been other issues. Legend has it she issued her regiment of brothers and cousins orders to shoot Dad on sight.

I've tilted the occasional brew with Wyland and Hoyte when they flew up to Alaska for salmon fishing season. Steven won't speak to the likes of me, and Hayden is too busy with landgrabs and range wars to be bothered. Sadly, I've never met Clare. She remains, by all accounts, the Gila-eyed matriarch of a ranch on the Rio Grande where the water runs clear and the grass is sweet. She hates Dad to this day. I adore her from afar.

Skip forward five years after the blowup of a divorce and Tepora Ulu, my mother, becomes Dad's second wife.

Mom came from a large family that had resided in New Zealand since ancient times. A scandalously beautiful woman whose countenance allegedly launched a thousand bar brawls, Tepora was a girl of nineteen when she married Dad, who by then had gotten long in the tooth. He always cut sharp in his dress uniform, I must admit. How could a girl resist? What could her disgruntled parents do except mutter and shuffle their feet?

The couple initially crossed paths at a bar near the Christchurch air base. She worked as a cocktail waitress. On the spot, Mervin decided he simply had to have the winsome lass. He successfully wooed her and along came baby Isaiah before the ink dried on the marriage certificate. A barn burner of a May-to-mid-October romance, I'd still lay odds that nobody figured it'd last until the leather anniversary.

In quick succession, Mom had Jordan and then Erika. I'm not close with them either. These days, we three exchange Christmas cards and Facebook "likes" and that's the extent of it. I don't blame them. Even the strongest sibling bonds couldn't hope to withstand the stress of coping with a brother who kneecaps fellow gangsters for a living.

The childhood of a military brat isn't a stroll through a rose garden. Compound the customary trials and tribulations if you're a heavy, dark-eyed boy who can't pass for white. Alas for me, I resembled Mom. Neither Caucasian nor Maori, I suffered the slings and arrows of prejudice as mixed bloods ever have.

Dad was moved around a lot. The Philippines, South Korea,

Guam, Germany, Hawaii, Alaska. Everywhere we traveled I met new and interesting people and beat the shit out of them, and, often enough, had them come after me in wolf packs to return the favor. These thick scars on my calf? Bike chain to the leg. The stripes across my shoulders? Got those from being whipped with a radio antenna off a car. The notch above my left eye? Some little bastard with a great pitching arm caught me with a Fanta bottle from across a parking lot. Forget about the puckered bullet holes in my stomach or the patch of glassy, keloid-darkened flesh on my neck that came from a splash of industrial acid—those are long stories that occurred after I emerged from a misspent youth and started a second mortgage on adulthood.

The only good and true constant during those Dark Ages was my dog, Achilles. Dad's status enabled us to transport pets to several of the stations. When that proved impossible, Achilles stayed with Uncle Lucius. I hated those stretches and took it out on my enemies, which meant anyone who looked at me cross-eyed.

Dad had become a big wheel with the Intelligence and Reconnaissance Service. Big wheels got to roll, right? What could dear devoted Mom do but allow herself to be dragged along, babies in tow? Mervin was also a drinker and a taskmaster and an absentee father. Not an easy man to live with, but for a while we kids loved him; loved him like dogs love their master no matter how rough it gets.

Mom wasn't exactly a picnic either. Tepora believed in the merits of the rod. She brooked no nonsense in her house. A kind woman, though. I remember that. She protected us from the worst of the old man's ferocious moods, and comforted us during those endless months he'd be missing in action, reassigned to Timbuktu or jetting off into the wild blue yonder on clandestine missions to save the Free World. I remember that too. Traces of her kindness haunt my soul and that's probably my saving grace.

Everything might've been okay, maybe we would've settled in as a family if we could've held on until the old man retired and relocated us to the islands as he'd always promised. Everybody knows how the gods are when it comes to the plans of mortals.

Dad claimed to love Mom more than sweet life itself. Maybe it's true. Nonetheless, he killed her one summer night as they rowed a skiff across Black Loon Lake. I was fifteen.

EIGHT

Virgil Walker and foreman Coates didn't quite break me that first two weeks on the farm. There were moments I believed they must have been trying. As Jade foretold, I bucked hay and mucked out stalls and swept the stables, mostly under the stern eye of the foreman himself. I stacked cordwood that Coates or Lionel dragged in behind the tractor and unloaded burlap bags of feed from the container van that rumbled in every few days. Acclimating to the weather required some fortitude, as I'm a gloomy-day person. Years of outdoor adventuring in the Arctic had thickened my blood.

Rough, salt-of-the-earth labor. Virgil had constructed a rude sauna of planks and logs on the far side of the main lot. I crawled in every sundown and steamed my blisters and bruises.

After my steam session, I'd eat a plate of whatever Jade left covered in tinfoil on the hood of the broken-down Ford by the woodshed. Vicodin with a Johnnie Walker Black chaser from a bottle I managed to smuggle in via bribing Lionel. Then, lights out, while the owls hooted and the crickets chorused around the cabin. I was so damned tired that plotting my comeback, or at least my next move, remained as remote as the moon.

There were bad moments. My ribs were the worst. Every sneeze or cough felt like a body blow from George Foreman. I endured. Each day I felt a little better, a little more like myself. Virgil, Jade, and Coates treated me with grousing wariness; Gus, the stable hand, loved everybody; Lionel maintained an affable diffidence like a dog who's been kicked; and Reba gave me the stink eye when she wasn't ignoring my existence altogether.

I got acquainted with the horses. Eleven of them; ten, easygoing and peaceable, and Bacchus, a huge piebald gelding who didn't tolerate anyone on God's green earth but Jade and Reba.

"An ornery cuss," Virgil said, and he wasn't kidding. At least once a week, Bacchus kicked down a fence or charged through a gate and escaped into the surrounding countryside. I spent several hours alongside Lionel rounding up the herd that had followed Bacchus in a massive jailbreak. In the end, we came full circle back to the barn to find the gelding placidly eating sugar cubes from Reba's hand. He flicked his ears at me in a decidedly insolent gesture.

"Get used to it." Lionel wiped sweat from his brow. "Damned horse loves to torment us men. He wants revenge because we still got our balls."

There were goats, a gaggle of chickens and peahens, a coal black, snarly barn cat named Titus, and Titus's mortal enemy, Chaucer, a decrepit, deaf Australian shepherd who didn't venture off the front porch of the main house anymore. Chaucer barked at his own shadow.

The place existed in a perpetual state of charming dilapidation. Lionel traveled in my periphery, tending to leaky roofs, busted fence posts, cantankerous machinery, and a hundred other nagging tasks that never ended, mounting ever higher like some hellish version of *Green Acres*. He was, in the vernacular, busier than a one-legged man in an ass-kicking contest. Reba tagged along, carrying buckets, tools, and bags of nails. I suspected she carried a torch for him as well. For his part, he obviously considered her a little sister. Even had she been a few years older, it wouldn't have changed anything. Him being one of those guys who'd never consider dating a woman he actually respected or liked. The old Madonna–whore complex.

Lionel resided in the yellow cottage in the woods and spent his evenings there killing a bottle of Jim Beam, or down at the Golden Eel, a bucket of blood on the Rondout near the 9W bridge in Kingston. He invited me to tag along some night. The bartender laid on the hooch and cute girls from SUNY New Paltz frequently slummed with the locals. A man could do worse than spend a Saturday night knocking down whiskey, listening to Lynyrd Skynyrd on the juke, and ogling skirts. I'm more a Hall & Oates man, but I took his point.

Bit by bit, I settled in to the rhythm of the farm. I straightened the cabin, nailed up shelves and stocked them with hardback encyclopedias and treatises on world mythology and the natural sciences that'd moldered in Virgil's storage shed for decades. A Methuselah-like Vietnam vet named Emmitt Rogers periodically came around in his renovated Consolidated Edison repair truck that he'd plastered with slogans of antiwar and looming apocalypse by the Hand of Almighty Gawd. Bald, bearded, and wild-eyed, he most definitely resembled an Abrahamic prophet.

Emmitt was a local scavenger who lived a nomadic lifestyle, packing his tent camp whenever a farmer or the sheriff's department rousted him. He peddled his treasures for pennies on the dollar. I scored a box freezer and propane fridge, both items previously dumped roadside. A bit of spit and polish and creative rewiring and I got them humming well enough to keep my beer frosty and cold cuts frozen.

Baby steps, baby steps.

Emboldened, I decided to secure a ride. There are two things every man must have—a good dog and a ride. I couldn't bear the thought of getting a dog. A vehicle, yeah. Virgil told me to avail myself of the antique Ford if I could get it running. Mechanics aren't my forte, so I asked Mr. Handyman, Lionel, what it would take to help a brother out.

"A case of Colt 45. Oh, and round up Virgil and Gus to help get the engine in the wagon. I'll rig a block and tackle to set the thing back in the truck." He'd tinkered on the engine and then abandoned it in the workshop last year. His own chariot was a 1975 Monte Carlo, deep green and burnished to a high shine.

"No problemo."

I fetched the wooden wagon we used to tote hay bales around the yard. After some grunting and groaning and colorful language, I loaded the monster block into the wagon and dragged it over to the truck, where Lionel stood, hands in pockets, his eyes shining like quarters.

"Hoss, that weighs six . . . damn, seven hundred pounds."

"Yeah. I may have herniated myself." Too close to the truth. Stars and little birdies flickered through my vision. Definitely a shadow of myself—I'd flipped a compact car onto its side once. Granted, I'd been in a fury, and when I'm raging, best to step aside. Nonetheless, my rehabilitation had miles to go.

He whistled.

"I almost herniated myself watching. Gimme a few days. I'll see if there's any spark left in her. Meanwhile, can you carry that anvil to the barn? There's a boulder stuck in the mudflat by the pond . . . Just kidding. Damn, Hoss. Fucking Hercules done come down to the farm."

"More like Milo."

"Milo?"

"Milo of Croton. The kid in ancient times who carried a calf across the stream every morning on the way to pasture. One day, the kid had grown into a man and he was lugging a bull. Milo, god of Greek wrestling."

"Oh, yeah, that guy."

I removed my shirt and sluiced the grease from my hands and arms with a cold-water hose outside the workshop. Jade leaned against the rail of a nearby corral. She called occasional instructions to Reba, who stood at the center of the ring.

The girl was dressed in a yellow polo helmet, jacket, and long pants. Decals of the band Sublime and Bob Marley decorated the helmet. She lunged Bacchus with a lengthy nylon rope. Bacchus snorted and stamped and flexed his massive muscles, posturing and threatening to bolt. Reba spoke to him softly, praising and cajoling in a precarious dance to keep the piebald on the right side of the razor's edge. She appeared fragile alongside the powerful bulk of the horse. Both were ghosts in the rising dust.

"Beautiful," I said, taking a spot next to Jade.

"They are." She glanced at me while I buttoned my shirt. "Heck of a scar you have on your neck, Isaiah. Or is that a burn?"

"Rode hard and put up wet in my youth."

She'd noticed the light chain necklace.

"Were you in the military? I didn't realize."

"No, ma'am. Rabies tags from an old dog who isn't around anymore."

If she thought it bizarre that I'd made a piece of jewelry from some mutt's tags, she was too decorous to let on. Virgil and Coates had extended the same courtesy. Polite folk here at Hawk Mountain.

She reversed course and came at me from another direction.

"How's the drinking?"

"No problems swallowing."

"Nobody likes a smart aleck."

"History agrees with you."

She snorted.

"Well, you're settling in fine. Maybe we'll get you on a horse before the summer is over. Take you out on the Rail Trail, yondering. It leads through the lower Catskills and keeps on a winding."

"I pity the horse, ma'am."

"Don't worry. They can handle even fatter cabooses than yours. Unless you're scared."

My turn to snort in disdain.

We observed the center ring waltz for a time. I'd picked up on tension between the Walkers and their granddaughter. The couple paid her a small wage for her labor. Reba rented an apartment in Kingston with another girl and spent some evenings and most weekends on the farm. Considering Reba's youth and attraction to the dark side, the wisdom of that setup escaped me. Jade spoke of baby birds and nests.

The girl attracted a procession of suiters and that's where the tension arose. Virgil ran off three guys in a red Suburban who'd come to pay her a courting call. Early to mid-twenties; one Hispanic, one white, another possibly Native American. Some of Reba's hood friends from town, apparently. In any event, the old man gave them the heave-ho, which royally pissed off the girl. *You're ruining my life, I hate you*—sob, scream, sob. The tempest blew over to be replaced by the glacial sulk only a kid can level at the beloved authority figures in his or her life.

Today, tempers had soothed. It's difficult to maintain a proper snit around animals.

Reba patiently reeled in Bacchus and patted his neck. She waited for him to steady, then vaulted atop his back. Bacchus cantered around the ring, stately as you please. From what I gathered, the gelding balked at road crossings and streams and presented a serious danger to his rider. Reba insisted upon riding bareback whenever the chance arose and that caused even more indigestion for the elder Walkers. Lionel ambled over to observe the proceedings. He scowled with worry. Bacchus had kicked the stuffing out of him before.

"Bacchus was a racehorse," Jade said. "Never properly gentled. He bites and kicks. Acts the fool. His previous caretakers neglected the pitiable sod. On his way to the stew factory the day I rescued him. A coincidence. I happened by the feed store for a trifle and heard a man talking about this horse he meant to euthanize."

"There aren't any coincidences, Mrs. Walker," I said. "Only cycles and patterns."

"Buddhist?"

"A superstitious cynic."

"Within every cynic beats the heart of an idealist. I gather that you read. Mythology is integral to our studies at the Center."

"Mythology is my favorite history. The Mahabharata, the Labors of Hercules, the Prose Edda. The Bible, of course. How could I not love Samson?"

"How could you not love Tū of the Maori? Or do you not cleave to your roots?"

"Creation myths are all the same at the core. The Maori gods, the Norse pantheon, the Greeks . . . There are fathers, mothers, nurturers, tricksters, and destroyers. Everybody screws everybody else, in the end, and the joint gets wrecked. Tū, Mars, Apollo. Killers, each."

"What did you do in Alaska?"

I was ready for that one.

"Communications expert."

"Mmm-hmm. Perhaps you'll ply your trade here. Once you get your bearings."

"One can't predict these things."

"That is true. This might be your big chance to start over. Sail home from the wars as Odysseus did."

"Odysseus had a heap of trouble awaiting him, didn't he?"

"An annoyed wife."

"Yeah, the Penelope situation. A houseful of enemies too. I'm more the Hercules type." I flexed my biceps.

"For your sake, I hope not. For everybody's sake, I hope not."

I couldn't take my eyes off the girl or the horse. Perhaps because we'd been speaking of myths I caught that aura from them, a sense they'd merged as a centaur from legend. Dust billowed, golden in the glare.

"Not much on mulligans, Mrs. Walker. Maybe this time is different."

"It's always different. You're a sprout, else you'd know that."

NINE

Money comes and money goes. I've always maintained an account with a national bank in order to establish credit and make certain my plastic works when flashed. The remainder gets hidden in a mattress or a hole in the ground.

When I'm flush, it's with a fat stack. That's fortunate because the stuff tends, like women and hooch, to run through my fingers. I do so love the ponies, boxing, mixed martial arts—you name it, I'll lay odds on it. I tend to put my money where my mouth is. In the end, the house wins. A lesson guys like me don't retain past the next major score.

Mr. Apollo's severance pay included a bonus. I jammed the money into two metal lunch boxes in denominations of fifty- and hundred-dollar bills shrink-wrapped for freshness. Several grand went into a jar in the cupboard, another few hundred I stuffed into my wallet. The majority stayed neatly layered in the boxes, which I buried under a rock by the light of the moon.

Lionel bolted the Ford together in short order. She roared when he stamped the gas pedal. Smoke rolled forth, and maybe a few flames.

The truck was a '59; white and red, with plenty of rust and body damage, and major spiderweb cracks in the windshield. Virgil slapped the tabs on and handed me the title and registration without comment.

I took the day and drove into Kingston on an expeditionary mission to restock the booze and visit the hardware store. Then there was the matter of dropping into Big John's Surplus and selecting two brand spanking new revolvers—a .38 snub, with an ankle holster, and a .357 S&W Magnum. I also nabbed a clean, pre-owned twelve-gauge pump shotgun and a bucket of ammunition. Big John's sexy blonde partner, Arlene, got the paperwork started while I flirted with her. Finally, I ducked into an office supply store and purchased a top-end laptop with onboard Wi-Fi. The Internet made everything easier, especially research, should the need ever arise. I may be a barbarian, but never a Luddite.

I made a triumphant return, laden with beer, whiskey, and miscellaneous supplies. The rest of the long, hot afternoon saw me hammering five treated four-by-four posts into the turf behind my cabin. I poured in quick-set concrete, padded the posts, and wrapped them in all-weather matting. Afterward, I relaxed beneath the shade of an oak tree and sipped from a glass of ice water Virgil brought when he came along to survey my handiwork.

"Striking posts?" The old man jingled ice in his own glass and looked at me.

"Yes, sir."

"Thought so. My boy took karate for years. Had something like 'em in his dojo. You a karate man? You got the moves."

"Not really," I said.

He drained his glass and wiped his mouth and looked at me again before he walked away.

After the concrete hardened, I rose and slipped off my boots and landed a few tentative blows. I played it safe, testing these scarcely healed bones. A kick here, an elbow there, moving from post to post in slow motion. This went on for a while. I gradually increased the tempo, maybe pushed it a little too hard. Sweat poured from me, and I finished by slamming my right fist into the matting with a dull thump that shivered the wood. My blood pumped, my teeth were bared.

I glanced at the crosshatch of shadows and light filtering through the oak branches and witnessed another death's-head, this one as large as a movie screen. A breeze shifted the leaves and the image vanished. Not from my mind, though.

Lifting weights and hitting the post or the bag or grappling with my colleagues had become intrinsic to my identity during adolescence. This felt different, electric. There were forces in motion and I had to be ready. Maybe it's a myth that animals sense earthquakes, are keen to approaching doom; that's a trait I share in regard to intuiting the presence of danger and death. Maybe it has something to do with the fact a man with my baggage is bound to attract attention from the powers that be. Whatever the cause, my hackles were up.

Summoned by my grim thoughts, a storm front rolled over Hawk Mountain. Black-and-blue clouds were announced by stabs of fire and the cymbal clash of thunder. I loved that sound. I feared that sound. The gods were telling me something.

As the wise men say, act and the universe will respond.

Near the witching hour, headlights splashed the window. There came a knock at the door. So much for a low-profile relocation. The peace couldn't last.

"Come on in."

I've owned a greenstone *mere* since age eleven. A rite of passage gift from my maternal grandfather, but that's another story. It's a short, heavy war club the Maori used to crush the skulls of wild boar and to beat their enemies to bloody death. I sat in a rocking chair near the fireplace and laid the *mere* across my thighs and an open 1978 *National Geographic* magazine over that.

Two men came through the door. One was a goon, the other a slick-haired wiseguy flashing a gold Rolex. Both wore custom suits, dripping from the rain, and both were strapped under their coats. The slick one introduced himself, with a New York accent, as Marion Curtis. He didn't acknowledge his partner but instead crossed the floor and made himself comfy on the edge of my bed. The goon guarded the door. Scary pair, yet I felt relief that they'd been sent by one of the New York families and not the Chicago Outfit. I assumed this because they hadn't blasted the cabin with a machine gun or lobbed a grenade through the window.

Curtis shook a Nat Sherman from a pack and lit up with the fanciest Zippo of them all. He smoked, taking a moment to examine the heel of his Gucci for horseshit.

"How you likin' New York?"

"All these trees are freaking me. Can I bum one of those?"

He lit another and leaned way over to pass it to me. I quit cigarettes in my late twenties. On occasion, I had a drag for nostalgia's sake. Meeting Family heavies definitely put me in a nostalgic mood.

"Mr. Deluca sends his regards." That would be Eddy Deluca of the Albany Delucas. A big fish. "Alaska says you're not on the job no more."

Chicago and New York observe certain protocols when it comes to these matters. Etiquette keeps unnecessary bloodshed to a minimum. Apollo had informed Chicago of my relocation. Somebody in the Chicago office then casually mentioned this to New York lest they assume I'd come to do a contract, and here we were. Way, way back in the Capone days, the system was called the bush telegraph.

"I'm out to stud," I said.

"Interestin'. Difficult to believe a man in his prime would up and quit. So, I ask: are you working?"

"You really think I'm in my prime? I'm flattered."

"Yeah, you look good. But, I asked a question."

I stared past Curtis at the goon. The goon stared back. Taller than me, a few pounds lighter. Still, a big boy. Long, luxurious blond hair and the physique of a gym rat or somebody who'd done hard time. Likely both, in his case. He paid too much attention to building his chest and not nearly enough to thickening his legs. A man's strength comes from his thighs, his ass and hips. He also positioned his feet too close together.

"Charles, go wait in the car," Curtis said.

Charles took his sweet time, but he left.

"Okay, he's gone," Curtis said.

"I *know*. This is so exciting. Dear *Penthouse*, I never thought it could happen to me . . ."

He smoked and glanced around the cabin, measuring everything.

"Couldn't get you on the horn, so I decided to make the trip. You're really in the sticks."

"Yeah. No line to the *casa*. Sorry."

"Ever heard a cell phones? They're gettin' big. No problem. Some country air, stretch my legs. Quiet out here. You notice how quiet it is? You like it, huh? Reminds you of the tundra."

"Darned frogs raise a heck of a racket."

"See, this setup confuses me. From what folks say, you're a classy sort a guy. You appreciate the finer things. Long way from the opera house, ain't it?"

"Let's say I've gained an appreciation for Thoreau. The radio works fine, thanks."

He took a business card from his breast pocket and slipped it under my pillow. The odor of his cologne wafted all the way over to me.

"Clive Christian?" I said.

"Clive Christian." He pancaked on a ton of makeup to compensate for a bad complexion. Eye shadow too. He'd probably dusted more than one fool for mocking his appearance. His demeanor suggested that he'd enjoyed squeezing the trigger.

"I'd love a bottle of that for my birthday. It's my favorite."

"See what I can do."

"Your mascara is running." Call me the poker of bees' nests.

He dabbed his face with a silk kerchief. The tiny monogram at the bottom no doubt said PRO KILLER.

"That the hotline to the Don's red phone?" I indicated the pillow.

"Mr. Deluca don't want to talk to you."

"Whose is it, then?"

"Mine."

"We're already talking."

Curtis stood and dropped his cigarette butt on the floor and made a production of grinding it underfoot. I got the association.

"No, Coleridge, we ain't talkin'." He went to the door and glanced outside and tsked. Rainfall magnified barnyard odors to the power of ten. "What do you need cologne for when it smells so sweet around here?"

"Have a swell drive back to the city."

"Any plans for gettin' on your feet? I'll have an opening soon." He gestured with his chin in the direction Charles had gone. "Nice kid, but a royal fuckup. Connected, is the problem. His uncle is Dino the Ax. It's a mess."

"Nobody truly appreciates how you middle management fellas suffer."

"That a no?"

"I'd thought of starting a small business. Be my own man for a change."

"You don't say."

"Yeah. Pony grooming. I'm a natural at braiding manes."

He showed his teeth the way a shark does when it opens its maw to take a bite.

"Small-business taxes can be a bitch around here. Before you jump, call that number."

"I'm not feeling froggy." That might've been a lie. What was I if I wasn't in the life? A man possessed of my temperament doesn't hang up his guns and pitch hay forever. He gets buried with bandoliers across his chest.

"Call that fuckin' number." Curtis cocked his thumb and index finger and pointed at my head. He let the door swing shut behind him.

I checked the window and watched their taillights dwindle into the darkness. I inhaled smoke and reminded myself to peek under my truck for bombs every morning from now on.

Best damned cigarette I'd had in what felt like a hundred years. I finished it and fell into bed. Slept the sleep that only the guileless or the incorrigible can truly know.

ELEVEN

That comic philosopher Bill Hicks once said that life is just a ride. He said a mouthful.

The journey from birth to darkness has its share of plot twists, reversals, and triumphs. Nonetheless, one must never forget it's into the dark that we're hurtling. We all shake hands with King Pluto. Understand, I'm tough as nails. Even so, I've got my limits. You don't need a mallet to take me apart. Let me stew in my own misery. Let me drown in what-ifs and maybes.

Maybe if I hadn't contracted pneumonia, none of what happened next would've happened at all. If I'd been on my feet, it would've turned out different—or so the devil on my left shoulder whispers. Maybe it wouldn't have mattered, as most of my labors haven't mattered in the final analysis, but that doesn't matter either. I like to torment myself. It's what I do second best.

THE BELTANE FIRE CELEBRATION began an hour before dusk on the final evening in April under a cloudless purple sky. A stone's throw past the Trapeze Club rose a steep ridge and on the other side spread a series of fallow pastures hemmed by a treeless drumlin hill where a pile of bonfire wood awaited the torch. These were the festival grounds. The rain had lasted several days and the grass glittered. Mist slithered through the surrounding underbrush as the temperature dropped. The moon lit the horizon with a yellow haze. Werewolf weather on the moors.

We attended as a group: the Walkers, with two mares draped in decorative blankets and flowery bridles; Reba, Lionel, and Gus, alongside to assist; and me, shambling in the wings like the lug I am.

The chaos was all very organized with ticket sellers stamping hands. Areas were cordoned off by flexible plastic fencing that comes on a spindle. Hundreds of guests congregated among a scattering of gaily striped pavilions. This event attracted people in Renaissance Fair costumes. Acres of motley and lederhosen and chicks in corsets and pinned-on swan wings. Every other reveler frolicked as a fox or a stag or a rabbit. The air seethed with clove and cinders, the musk of beer, and sweaty flesh. Speakers broadcast flute-and-drum concertos interspersed with public-service announcements.

Emmitt's ancient Central Hudson truck parked in the grass near the front entrance. Somehow, the coot had finagled the cotton candy racket. It appeared to be a bull market. He unloaded it by the gross upon the teeming masses.

"Hello, Walkers and hangers-on!" He charged Virgil a five-spot for a sticky mass of blue cobwebs. He leered benevolently at Jade and Reba and handed each a bag, gratis. Reba rewarded him with a peck on his grimy cheek and he chortled in joyous embarrassment. Probably wouldn't wash it for a week. Or ever, judging from the rest of him.

A throng of young women, pasted in yellow and blue ochre and nothing more, swept past. Their laughter eddied in accompaniment to the flutes. Fairies? Picts? Damned if I knew, but I was groggily intrigued.

Jade nailed me in my sore ribs with an elbow. She and Reba had chosen ensembles of oak-leaf circlets, linen shifts, and sandals. Lionel and I had stuck with button-up shirts and blue jeans. Lionel clapped on his Stetson and cowboy boots.

"Don't lollygag," Jade said. "Stumble around, all moon-eyed, and one of these pagan chicks will put a bit in your teeth and lead you into the woods."

"That's what happened to me!" Virgil said. He wore antlers and a hemp robe and made it look good. Obviously, his past included a stint of Shakespearean theater.

I wasn't in any shape to chase naked pagan women. Toiling in the mud and the muck and the driving rain that previous week sapped me. I'd pushed my recovery too fast. A nasty cold had settled into my chest. High on cough syrup and a fever, I grinned and tried not to let on that I might be dying.

"I think Mongo's sick," Reba said. A clinical observation rather than a sympathetic one.

"Who let you anywhere near *Blazing Saddles*?"

"Virgil claims Mel Brooks is an essential part of a classical education."

I wiped my brow with my sleeve. We'd bonded a bit earlier in the week. I captured Bacchus after his most recent Great Escape. A thunderstorm walloped Hawk Mountain—one of those epics with howling wind, sizzling strokes of lightning, and buckets of rain. I tracked the horse into the forest along a swollen stream. A handful of sugar cubes allowed me to get close and loop a rope around his neck. He followed me home, both of us muddy, drenched to the bone and shivering. My heroics earned a curt nod from foreman Coates and Reba's amazed skepticism. Her look suggested I might not be completely useless. Downside was, I caught a cold that had progressively worsened since.

"*Shee-it*, dude," Reba said. "Cleavon Little was the hotness."

"Mind your language," Jade said. "Besides, Gene Wilder is the hotness."

"No fair coveting our white men," Lionel said.

"Do I look like Mongo?" I said to no one in particular. "I'm way handsomer than Alex Karras."

"If Mongo was a giant, sinister half Polynesian, half whatever you are—sure, there's a resemblance," Lionel said. "How do you feel about candy?" He'd gotten a running jump on the festivities by demolishing a sixer of Colt 45 before we left the yard. Why didn't the Walkers bust *his* chops about boozing?

The Walkers headed toward the hillside drummers to join a mob that would soon organize itself into the procession of the May Queen. Lionel beelined for the beer garden and I followed and let him shove a plastic cup of bitter microbrew into my hand. We drifted apart after that. I wandered, boggling at the scene while searching for a place to rest my aching bones, found a likely stump and encamped there, head in my hands, watching drops of sweat patter onto the dirt between my shoes.

While I faded in and out, the universe kept moving pieces around the board.

I glanced up and beheld a ghost. The black-haired trapeze artist stood a few feet away amidst a clutch of her acrobat pals. She wore a simple wrap and was caked in white ochre. Her lovely small feet were bare. She eyed me sidelong while sipping from a bottle, so I raised my hand in greeting. Trapeze Girl seemed to glide an inch above the turf as she approached. I manfully resisted vertigo and said, "Hi, my name is—"

She cocked her head, hand on hip.

"You're at the Walker place."

"Meet the new stableboy."

"I'm Meg." A soft voice, kind of throaty. Assured.

"I thought you were a ghost."

"That's what I thought about *you*. Your color is terrible."

"As a matter of fact, I feel terrible."

"Shouldn't you go home and crawl into bed?"

"Probably. Might not be safe to try it alone. What are you doing?"

"Staying out of trouble. *Trying* to stay out of trouble."

I said in a whisper from behind my hand, "FYI, you're blowing it talking to me."

Meg laughed. A nice laugh. Her teeth were white and sharp. One of the guys she'd accompanied called to her and she waved him off. I took this as an excellent sign. She said she was in the procession and did a twirl so I could admire her costume.

I asked her about the procession and she said she was a White Warrior Woman, companion guard of the May Queen. She tapped the hilt of a ceremonial dagger, a paperweight, riding on her sash.

"Right on," I said. "Ready to shiv the Green Man when he gets too fresh with Her Majesty?"

"I'll be in on it." She was really smiling now, full wattage, and the idea she might have a morbid streak made my heart go pitter-pat. O gods above and below, pretty please. The canned music shorted out and the announcer said something that made her put on her serious demeanor again.

"Duty calls?"

"Gotta go. Save the Queen from the Green Man, dance and make merry . . ."

"Gods save the Queen," I said, weakly admiring her as she trotted away, fleet-footed as Atalanta. There I went mixing up mythologies again. My teeth chattered.

The walk back to the farm was a solid mile and that daunted me. I decided to skip the impending spectacle and curl into a ball in the bed of Virgil's pickup. I grabbed my work jacket from the cab and rolled it into a pillow and lay on my back and regarded the gathering stars. Sleep followed within seconds.

Reba's voice snapped me out of dreamland. Sharp and plaintive. An alarm. I sat up fast, vision swimming, thoughts flung far and wide. I'd only been under a few minutes. Dusk had settled in and the light was tricky. I dragged myself out of the pickup and swayed in place, trying to get my bearings, and spotted Reba and another guy slipping through a cluster of pavilions. From where I stood, it appeared he'd helped her along with a shove.

I went after them.

Cheers resounded from the crowd, and a high, thin horn blared to commence the procession. Drum circles boomed in discordant harmony. Everything moved in stop-motion, too fast, too slow. Fire crackled upon the hill as tinder burned and whooshed heavenward, mingling with the crimson sunset. Lights and shadows funneled around me. Fox heads and swan wings and Celtic war paint were grotesquely vivid. Leaping flames and shouts of exultation were the mind-bending special effects in a del Toro flick. The bonfire built into roiling pillar, and in my delirium I imagined sacrifices of squalling babes to Baal and Chemosh and all the jolly old death gods that got it in the neck after the New Testament. Figures rushed inward from the shadows and formed a ring at the base of the hill.

Wild, inchoate panic bloomed in my chest. Drums and horns and the tidal surge of many bodies pressed cheek by jowl conspired to unnerve me. I shouldered through revelers. Somebody cursed and a cup of warm beer splashed across my chest and I lowered my head and blundered forward past a tent, its gaping entrance illuminated by a fire barrel, and into a pasture gone to seed.

There I found her. We'd navigated a semicircle and come back to the road. A red Suburban idled with its lights on. Reba argued with two men I'd glimpsed at the farm—the punks Virgil had run off. One, dark-haired and -skinned, in a polo shirt and baggy shorts; the other, dirty-blond, in a wifebeater tee and jeans and with a chunk of bling hanging around his neck. A shadowy third figure sat behind the wheel. Not far, yet in my state it could've been a mile.

The argument reached its crescendo.

Reba slapped Polo Shirt right across his weasel mug and it must've smarted, judging from his recoil. He shook himself and cocked his fist. The blow struck her in the body and she crumpled halfway to the ground before he jerked her up short by the hair. A real gentleman.

By then, I'd closed most of the gap. My legs were rubber, my throat raw from gasping for air. I bent and drew the .38 from its ankle holster, straightened, and shouted. Both men froze for a couple of beats to take in the wild-eyed bruiser lumbering onto the scene. Neither liked what he saw. The blond kid leaped into the rig. Polo Shirt kept his fistful of Reba's hair and attempted to drag her in after him. He leaned forward for leverage. That saved his life.

My bullet zipped through the headrest instead of his skull. A window shattered on the opposite side. I blame the gloom, my double vision, and the fact it's tough to aim on the run. Polo Shirt dropped her and slammed his door. The Suburban sprayed gravel as it peeled out.

Reba had sagged to her hands and knees. She pitched a rock at the receding taillights. I touched her shoulder and she snarled and slapped my hand aside. Under other circumstances, the cold fury in her glare might've hurt my feelings. I tried to come up with something reassuring to say, something to make it all better.

I threw up on my shoes instead.

TWELVE

Do everything right, or right enough, it should be a case of all's well that ends well. Arrive on the scene in the nick of time, scatter the varmints, and save the day. Do a good deed for once and rescue the girl, surely the gods will smile upon you. Right? Unfortunately, some people won't stay rescued. The gods? A bunch of capricious bastards.

The last time I saw Reba Walker before she disappeared, I lay partly in my bathtub and partly in the Land of the Dead. I was covered in ice and raving about wild boars and Mama. Doubtless, an alarming sight. Fever gripped me in its teeth of fire and I'd gone clean 'round the mountain to where Grandma lived in the darkest, deepest cave. The Cave of the Ancestors. You don't want to go there unless the scoreboard timer reads all zeros.

I couldn't separate the living from the phantasms. What a parade it proved to be: departed Mother waving to me from the edge of a glacier; evil Father, belt wrapped around his sinewy forearm, as he snarled and instructed me how to avoid the worst of the slash from a knife or busted glass; my sweet, dead dog Achilles, tongue lolling joyously; lovers, enemies, and some guys I'd rubbed out along the way. My double with a rifle, my double with a garrote, my double grinning an animal's grin as heads rolled. Exploding cars, a black smoke cloud swallowing the hunter's moon. Bloated faces of kingpins laughed in the smoke. Mocking me, the pissant.

Reba held my hand and apologized for cussing. She thanked me for rescuing her, even though she remained convinced nothing would've happened, the boys came from a different culture, everybody had to understand that. Virgil waited nearby, visage grim as an old stone monument. Reba dematerialized and Jade kept spooning bitter medicine down my throat. Herbal remedies from China, she said. Mainstream doctors were butchers and quacks, she said. I realized for a fleeting moment that everybody thought I was a goner.

Wait, I said in my mind to Reba's departing shadow. *Wait.* And I reached for her, though I didn't know why. Virgil poured more ice into the tub. Jade shushed me and placed a damp cloth over my face. I went under again.

SIX DAYS AND NIGHTS I LAY in my open grave of a bed. Six days and nights of compresses and sponge baths and psychedelic visions and that god-awful Chinese elixir. The Walkers distrusted modern medicine, thus no emergency room trip for their number one tenant. Too weak to argue, I slipped into deep and tormented slumber.

In my nightmares, I was five again. Dad had come home from the barracks drunk, blood on his shirt, scotch on his breath. A beast in a rage. He'd smashed the door and turned his baleful glare upon Mom, had taken a step toward her and I recall, albeit as a blur, hurling myself against his leg, punching ineffectually while yelling at him to leave her alone. I'll kill you, I'll kill you, yada yada. Brother and Sister cried and Dad regarded me blearily, then tousled my hair and wandered into the night, lost. I dreamt of Achilles and how he'd fallen into blue-and-green space, how he looked me in the eye as he floated away, dying so that I might live. I wandered through Elysian Fields and the Boar of the Wood hunted me, his tusks as sharp as spearheads. He felled the tall golden grass with each sideways swipe of his massive head. My grandfather, dressed in skins and a necklace of sharks' teeth, floated always two paces ahead, his gaze serene as a storm cloud. He raised a flint ax and I woke, the blare of a conch horn trailing into the ether.

It was the seventh morning.

THIRTEEN

B elieve it or not, I don't mind cops. The incompetent ones are stupid and about as dangerous as flies buzzing in your hair. The competent ones know what's good for them and keep clear, or you can grift them, or you blackmail them, or you shoot them.

The detectives who dropped in to visit me were on the take. Fancy cologne and nicer shoes told all. The pair were only going through the motions. Rourke and Collins. A heavyset man with hangdog jowls, and a bemused blonde who might've fooled me with her aw-shucks schoolmarm act if I hadn't seen it all before.

Normally, I don't speak to Johnny Law unless my counsel is present. The coppers caught me off guard. Dizzy, weak, disoriented, and vulnerable. I said as little as possible; just lay there, slack-jawed, while they lobbed softballs with nasally northeastern drawls. Their inquiries concerned the three fine gentlemen at whom I may or may not have discharged a firearm during the night of the Fire Festival.

In my wooziness, I didn't comprehend that their interest in those punks might run deeper than our primitive tête-à-tête. I figured a witness had complained and sicced the dogs on me, so to speak. I gave the cops a partial plate on the Suburban and denied firing a pistol. All the usual jazz. I needn't have sweated it—they didn't care.

Collins winked.

"I admire your style, Coleridge," she said. "Sincerely. Any maggots slapping around a sweet young thing deserve what they get."

"You remember anything, let us know, chief," Rourke said.

"Be seeing you, handsome," Collins said.

The detectives showed themselves out the door.

Jade brought my laundry and my meals and I tried to thank her, but she hushed me with a stern glance and hustled off. It wasn't until another two days passed that I could do more than hobble around the cabin. Not one to lie around like a sluggard, I decided to resume my duties—fetching and carrying as per my routine.

Even starting well after noon and moving at drastically reduced speed, I sweated like one of the horses after a lunging. Honest labor had a salutary effect on my well-being. When dusk rolled around and I called it a day, I felt something near to alive once more. I rested on my porch, ate a can of stew, and drank a tall glass of iced tea. The landscape disappeared as the blue-and-orange sunset downshifted to black.

The Walkers' rig pulled into the drive and lights in the house came on. I scraped my plate and scoured it with sand from the horseshoe pit and finished the tea, then made my way up the path to the house.

The funereal aspect permeating the living room halted me in my tracks.

"Reba's gone," Jade said when she saw me. Her eyes were red. "They took her." *They* could only mean her friends in the red Suburban.

"Those goddamned dirtbags," I said and sat on the couch next to her. Felt weird—I wasn't sure whether to put my arm around her or not. She stared at the darkened main window, that portal into the Ancestor Cave, and wrung her hands.

"We don't know if it has anything to do with them." Virgil was behind the kitchen counter. An uncorked bottle of Wild Turkey rested near his hand. "We aren't even certain . . . The police aren't convinced she's missing."

Jade slowly looked at him. They'd been together an eon and it was a cold wind that blew between them in that moment. The liquor wasn't making her happy either.

Virgil said to me, "Like Jade says, the girl is gone."

"How long?"

"Five days."

I covered my face with my hand and tried to organize my thoughts. Five days. Five days equaled deep trouble unless Reba was simply off hitchhiking or shacked up with friends. Otherwise, no news after five days was the worst kind of news.

"Okay. What do we know?"

Reba was last seen by her roommate in her Kingston apartment on the previous Saturday, around midmorning. She'd made plans to go clubbing with friends. Nobody, whoever *nobody* was, recalled seeing her that night. Her car, an old Mazda, remained on the street outside the apartment. She and her purse were gone, vanished from the face of the earth.

Where was the cavalry? I already guessed the answer. No cavalry. Reba had a rap sheet. Reba had a history of running away. Once, she'd hitched a ride with a trucker to New Orleans and was off the radar for two weeks until calling at 3 a.m., broke and hungry. Reba was black. The authorities clucked sympathetically and filed the report, sent a couple of bored detectives out to the farm as a weak gesture to public relations. Meanwhile, somewhere down the Hudson, a blue-eyed blonde girl was late getting home from work and the media were issuing nationwide red alerts.

"Is Reba on probation?" I said.

Virgil shook his head. "She's a good kid. Some scrapes. She once stole her uncle's motorcycle and wrecked it. Played hooky. Got caught with marijuana and beer at a party. That was the incident that pushed things too far. Her parents stuck her in that blasted reformatory, but she never belonged there. Right, honey?"

"Right," Jade said, distant and frail. "Dawn wouldn't have done it. It's Dante's fault. That plonker."

"Honey."

"Mom and Dad?" I said. "Where are they in all of this?"

Virgil poured me a double and Jade crossed her arms and scowled.

He said, "Dante's our boy. He's out of the picture. Been out of the picture for a long time. Postcards-from-the-front bullshit."

"I am familiar with the routine," I said.

"He was in Rikers for a stretch. Gang involvement. Minor league, but enough to ruin his life. He lives in the Bronx. Dawn is an angel. She took a position as an RN in Cleveland last summer. Reba didn't want to leave her friends, so she stayed and we've tried to look after her. She's eighteen and there's only so much we can do."

"The day she disappeared . . . Where was everybody?"

"Lionel and I went to see a farmer on the other side of the valley. Haying's in a few weeks and we helped him get his tractor running. Gus was in the stables later in the afternoon, as usual. Coates and his wife and granddaughters had nipped off to the coast for the weekend. They have a cottage and a fishing boat. Honey, you were with Isaiah, right?"

Jade studied her hands.

"That's about right. I was either here or in the house. Kept my cell on me. Reba never called, if that's what you want to know."

"Can't say I know what I want to know," I said.

I asked a few more questions, treading lightly as possible.

Did Reba do drugs? No, she was clean, although she'd had various prescriptions during her stay at Grove Street Academy, per doctor's orders. Some were to treat mood disorders. She also suffered minor but chronic pain after getting injured in the motorcycle accident.

What were the names of the dudes in the Suburban? Virgil and Jade had no idea because Reba kept mum on the subject. Apparently, she'd also refused to comply when the police asked why I'd allegedly gone berserk that night. Stand-up kid.

Had she dated any of the ghastly trio? Not that the couple was aware. My takeaway was that these guys were bad news. Gang-bangers, drug dealers, real live desperadoes, and Reba had grabbed a tiger by the tail. No doubt they'd acted sweet as pie in the beginning. Once the sugar wore off, she'd come to fear them.

Oh, and had anybody seen Lionel? I thought he must be holed up in his shack.

"You gotta understand, Lionel drinks," Virgil said. "By that, I mean he drinks a lot. When he came here a year and a half ago, he was suffering mightily. Saw some things overseas that shook him to the core, I expect."

"He seldom speaks of his service," Jade said.

"Iraq or Afghanistan?" I said.

"Both. And some other places. He's on the mend. There *are* rough patches. He disappears for a while. Comes home beat to hell like a tomcat that got in a tussle with every rival in the neighborhood. Scared us the first couple of times."

The cops had questioned Lionel and poor mentally challenged

Gus with the same pronounced lack of diligence I'd observed first-hand. Last night, Lionel declared a holiday and went careening down the road in his Monte Carlo. His shack remained untenanted as of that moment.

I muttered reassuring nonsense and retreated to my cabin, where I powered on a fresh cell phone and made the first of two calls.

Detective Rourke answered. I asked if he was still looking into the Walker case and he said yeah. I reminded him that I'd provided a partial plate and requested to be apprised if he tracked down the owner.

"Thanks for the assist. But, see, I'm not in the habit of involving civilians in police business, chief."

"Think of me as an informal partner. Let's do lunch."

"I brown-bag it."

"Perfect. I'll fix you a sandwich. Lots of lettuce."

The line went silent for a few moments.

"Okeydokey, chief. Gimme a day or two. Take care." Detective Rourke hung up. Next I rang County and found out Lionel had been locked up on a drunk-and-disorderly beef.

There wasn't much to do after that except wait for the gears to grind in the machine. I dressed in a plaid long-sleeved work shirt, jeans, and a new pair of steel-toed logging boots. Shrugged on a plaid lumberjack coat, locked the door, and jumped into the Ford and headed for town.

FOURTEEN

I paid the cash bond and waited outside the Ulster County Jail until Lionel limped through the double doors and down the granite steps. He looked like a ball of yarn that'd gotten batted around by a tiger. Clothes ripped, eyes blacked, nose busted, the rest of him bruised up, down, and sideways. He remained in high spirits, however. I figured it had something to do with all the skin missing from his knuckles. He whistled a jaunty wartime tune and climbed in beside me with only a brief grimace of pain.

"Howdy, pardner. You must be the disturber of the peace," I said.

"Rootin', tootin' straight," he said. "I am also a raiser of hell."

His car had been impounded and the four patrons who'd given him the beatdown behind the Golden Eel stole seventy bucks and a picture of an ex-girlfriend from his wallet.

"Heck of a photo," I said.

"Swimsuit model. Linda's in Tahiti doing magazine covers as I sit here in my misery. She's doing magazine editors, photographers, and towel boys too. That's why she's an ex. Fuck, I'm out of cigs."

"Obviously, this is an emergency."

I threw the truck into gear and squired him to the Benson Bros. quick stop and loaned him a twenty. I observed through the window as he leaned on the counter to chat up the trailer park princess working the till. He emerged with a pack of Marlboro Reds and a carton of Steel Reserve. He already had a cigarette in his mouth and smoldering before he made it back across the lot.

"Time to drink," I said as we flew down the road. "You eighty-sixed from the Eel?"

"Nah, Hoss. You don't get eighty-sixed from the Eel."

The Golden Eel was a shabby conglomeration of shotgun shack and Quonset hut plopped next to the slimy bank of the Rondout. The curved span of the 9W bridge loomed overhead like the flying buttress of a medieval cathedral. On the opposite bank stretched a chain of marinas, wrecking yards, and warehouses. Across the street were vacant lots, abandoned garages, and a limestone ridge screened in heavy underbrush and beech trees. A block and a half south, Gunderson Avenue cut east and west, its length bracketed by Italian restaurants, tony salons, and bars that catered to the touristas and well-heeled locals. The north–south culture war sometimes resulted in broken bones.

The lot was crowded on this Friday night, including a squad car with two unis slouched on its hood eating calzones and chugging beer. Their bright eyes were cold.

We strolled in through the bat wings and found a recently evacuated booth. Yeah, this was a hole-in-the-wall you dared not bring the wife and kids. A smoky, greasy joint that smelled of pissed alcohol, burnt tobacco, and testosterone. The main room was low-beamed and dim as a cell, packed with off-brand bikers, longshoremen, and Catskills rednecks. AC/DC, Joan Jett, the Allman Brothers, and

David Allan Coe took turns raging from the jukebox. The scene reminded me of a hybrid of a Viking longhouse and a honky-tonk in a dystopian future after all the bombs had dropped.

I ordered Jim Beam from a buxom waitress with golden eyeshadow. Lionel went with that old standby, Cuervo.

"Got anything like this back in AK?" He licked the salt from his wrist and slammed his shots, one, two, three.

"Dutch Harbor and Seward do it Thunderdome-style." I flattened my left hand palm-down on the table so he could see the jagged scar that sliced from knuckles to wrist. "Had me a time there."

"What does a Samoan do at the North Pole? Bust the legs of the elves who try to unionize?"

"Samoans love Alaska. They've got the best gangs. However, I'm Maori. There's also some English peasantry lurking in the tall grass of my lineage."

"Same fucking question, then."

"I make awesome snow angels."

Lionel winked at the waitress. The intricate skull-and-crossbones patch on his shoulder had nearly come unstitched.

"Marine Force Recon," he said upon noting my interest. His eyes shone. "First Battalion. Been in Fallujah and Helmand. Heard the owl hoot and seen the crow fly. Those bastards last night . . . Nabbed Linda's photo, but I'd be damned if they were gonna take my colors."

The waitress brought more tequila and bourbon. Lionel offered one to the lady and us three clinked tumblers. She downed hers and patted his hamburger cheek and swayed her way toward the bar.

"*Slàinte!*" I said.

"*Shlàinte*, fuckers!" He drank and pointed with the empty at four men who'd prowled through the doors. Average height, well-muscled; two with buzz cuts, one bald as Kojak, one shaggy on the collar like myself, except he had a whopper of a Fu Manchu going. Dark shirts, khakis, and the requisite pouts of macho gunslingers and bullyboys.

"The devils appear. This is their favorite watering hole."

"You serve with them?"

"Not in the Corps. The mean-looking dude on the end—baldy? That's Teddy Valens. The asshole in chief. Green Beret. We did a hitch with a merc outfit together. Might say a disagreement over the treatment of civilian natives led to bad blood between us. He thought they should die so we could loot their shit. Me, I'm not so much with the raping and murdering. Ain't no U.S. laws to worry about in some of those theaters of operation. Cowboys and Indians all the fuck over again."

"Ah. I had you fitted for the white hat."

"Don't know about white. Gray, maybe."

"DynCorp?"

"Black Dog out of Maryland. Provides security for American contractors at a shitload of hot spots. Iraq, Afghanistan, the Congo. Valens is no nice guy. His boys aren't sweethearts either."

Watching the mercenaries strut and preen and forcibly occupy a table of college girls and their frightened college boy dates, I had to agree. These soldiers weren't sweethearts. After a bit of threat and posture, the heroic mercs let the college kids depart in peace. The girls were crying; one of the boys too.

"How is it you ended up in the slammer and those bozos walked?"

"Officer Friendly took their word over mine." Lionel sighed and rolled his head on his neck, cracked his knuckles. "May as well amble over and get to it. Round two."

"No, not tonight."

He chewed on that.

"Why are we here?"

"Recon, soldier. I wanted to take a gander at the brave fellows who jumped you. They risked their sweet asses. Four of them versus one Marine? Had to be a close contest."

"I guess question two has to be, why'd you come bail me out?"

"Leave a man in the pokey? Come on, Robard."

"Told you, call me Lionel. I got all the Robard I could handle in the Corps. Question three: you heard about Reba?"

"I heard."

"Cops came by, asked some bullshit, left on a doughnut run. They ain't looking. Not really."

"Yep," I said.

The mercs had spotted us in our nook. They were sending hard-case glares, except for Valens. He studied a drinks menu with great intensity.

I drained the Jim Beam and slipped my revolver from its oiled holster, rested it on my knee. Two of the bullyboys swaggered our way. The buzz-cut twins. They moved well. Dangerous, on principle, in the manner of jackals or coyotes.

"She *could* be on the lam."

"Virg and Jade think otherwise." Lionel eyed the approaching mercs. He bounced the shot glass in his hand. He was calm and easy.

"Hi," I said when the pair reached us and waited there puffing like confused, furious apes.

"Isaiah, meet Galt and Tucker," Lionel said with a broad, loveless smile. He kept on bouncing the glass like a knife thrower on his cigarette break.

Galt's lip was split. Tucker's nose would never recover.

"You got some licks in," I said. And to the mercs, "Ah, Tucker, your beautiful face!"

The duo gave me the once-over, then ignored me.

"Hey, jarhead," Galt said to Lionel. "Didn't we tell you to find another bar to sit your canary ass in?"

"I'm sorry, I forgot," Lionel said with mock regret. He made a show of slouching and looking at his hands.

"Of all the gin joints in the world, you bozos had to walk into this one," I said in my best Bogart.

Galt narrowed his eyes and opened his mouth, doubtless to utter a witty rejoinder.

I placed the revolver on the table, hand on the butt, finger inside the trigger guard. Yonder, Señor Valens wasn't preoccupied with his menu anymore. He couldn't see the gun, but he understood Galt's and Tucker's body language fine. His man was about to get plugged with lead.

"Bye, bye, birdie." I looked at Galt.

"Really? What, you going to smoke us right here?"

I raised the gun a couple of inches and aimed the barrel at him. I cocked the hammer.

"I'll drill you in the mouth, the way your mama likes it."

Tucker had had his fill. He clutched Galt's arm.

"Dude's mental. C'mon."

I waited until they'd retreated.

"For what it's worth, I agree about Reba. She's in trouble. Virgil and Jade know their grandkid. Besides, I had a bad feeling about her from the first time we met. Some people are fated, as Mom would say."

"Your mom said people are fated? As in, die early, go to prison, that sort of thing?"

"Some people."

Lionel didn't laugh, didn't even blink.

"We better skedaddle. My buddies got itchy trigger fingers. Shootin' is liable to commence."

I followed him out into the cool dark. The gun remained in my fist, tucked under my coat. The mercs stayed put, glaring death threats. There'd be a later, I assumed.

"None of this is your affair," Lionel said once we were in the truck and under way. "You and Reba don't get along worth a damn."

"I thought I was growing on her."

"Think again. But you're in it now."

"I am. Jumped right into this giant cow pie with both feet."

"Why? Gotta be a reason why. Man don't go to war, don't take a pickax to a mountain, without a why."

"Call it payback or pay it forward. Call it atonement. Mostly? For the first time in a long time, I get to choose."

He smiled.

"What's funny?" I said.

"Your dog tags, man. Never met somebody wearing 'em from a real dog."

Maybe it was a test, maybe he thought I'd be pissed. I let it roll off me.

"Yeah. Well, I'm at that point in life where I measure my remaining years in good dogs."

"I dig. Worked with the bomb squad. Best dogs in the world."

Lionel lit a cigarette, cracked the window to let the smoke go streaming into the night. He glanced at me and, by the dashboard glow, his expression was solemn as an Arthurian knight's from some kid's picture book. I swear, the noble little bastard flashed a halo for a second.

"I'm your man. Tell me where and when we start."

"It's already started," I said. No halo on me.

FIFTEEN

All those years in Alaska, I'd loyally served the Outfit. Let's be clear on one thing, however. I never joined the Family. I performed *work* for the Family. Mr. Apollo kept me on a more or less permanent retainer. No loyalty oath, no *omertà*. Also, no ironclad protection from rival factions or rivals within my own faction. I could be rubbed out with impunity if someone took offense. I also counted as a member of the Outfit while on the job with regard to propriety. Were I to step on someone's dick while conducting Outfit work, then Chicago had to own it.

Not a chance I'd ever get made even if I had signed the blood pact. Chief headhunter was the greatest honor an outsider could expect of an organization that ran on patrilineal lines. I always thought it enough despite a nagging worm of doubt, despite seeds of dissatisfaction ever waiting to take root in my soul, despite the abused pride of warrior ancestors. I drank, gambled, fought, and lived day to day locked in battle with personal demons. That's how it is, on the Last Frontier. Days bleed together while monsters circle and you finally arrive at a place where survival is its own reward, beginning and end, like the teeth of the ouroboros chomped upon its own tail.

The walrus massacre, my violation of Family orders, the chair, and exile . . . The world unfolded in beautiful and terrible revelations. I felt an unexpected pang of conscience, which in turn made me slightly afraid. Life returning to my extremities after a long, long sleep?

Don't get the idea this meant I was a changed man. Hardly. I was the same man, only my perspective had altered. I hadn't the slightest notion of where all this would lead. However, I knew quite well the road to get there.

FIRST THINGS FIRST.

To carry out the operation in my inimitable fashion, I needed to pay fealty to the king. Saturday morning, I dialed the number on Curtis's card, talked to some schmuck who sounded as if he were eating a sandwich.

Curtis eventually picked up and listened to my spiel.

"Be at the Sultan's Swing tonight. Seven sharp. Know the place?"

I said I'd heard of it and he gave me directions and said see ya later.

Meanwhile, Virgil wrote down a list of names and numbers of Reba's immediate family and friends. He didn't ask questions. Gave me that peculiar, cagey look and thinned his lips. I handed him two hundred dollars and said I'd need a pass on the bulk of farm chores for a while, thanks. Again, he took the rent money without pesky questions or argument. Rolled it up and stuck in his shirt pocket next to his tobacco. The wrathful light in his eyes told me that the old bird wished he were twenty years younger.

Driving out to the highway, I witnessed the trapeze artists assembling before the altar to their art for early-morning worship. I glanced at my watch, then did a spit check in the rearview.

"Oh, Coleridge, this is wrong with a capital *W*," I said to my reflection. I backed up and got out and walked over to where Meg and an infuriatingly handsome fellow acrobat were stretching on the grass. Neither of them seemed overwhelmed with joy at my arrival. It occurred to me that word of my antics at the festival had gotten around.

I cleared my throat and struggled not to fidget. Getting punched in the face was always a joy by comparison to giving a woman a free shot at one's heart.

"Do you have plans tonight?"

"Yes," Meg said. Her hair was held back by a purple band. Her uniform consisted of a cotton tee with ARMY across the front and cotton shorts. The rest of her gleamed like the wet grass.

The handsome acrobat looked on me with genial pity. His abs were rocks, his teeth were perfect.

I said, "I'm taking a drive to the Sultan's Swing around six-thirty. You got a nice dress to put on? You could come with."

She let me dangle for a bit. Finally, she quirked her lips in what an optimist would've taken for a smile.

"What are *you* going to wear?"

"I clean up okay. Don't fret."

She recited a Rosendale address and dismissed me by resuming her routine that included significant stretching and bending. The handsome acrobat's smirk vanished. He appeared terribly dismayed.

I DECIDED TO VISIT Reba's roommate. My guess, her being a college girl, was that she'd be at home recovering from a Friday-night bender. It being college, every night was likely party night.

Kari Jefferson's apartment sat atop a brick Gothic Revival house on the rough edge of Kingston. Many of the surrounding buildings were dilapidated or shuttered. Poor folks gathered on stoops or played stickball in the street or congregated in weedy yards. A lot of the men wore shirts a couple sizes too large or no shirts at all. Baby mamas pushed carriages while toddlers with dull eyes and runny noses chewed Day-Glo pacifiers. Pit bulls panted behind rickety fences, watching it all go down. Reba's Mazda sat near the corner, its doors locked. Seats and dash were clean, so I moved on.

I didn't know as much about Ms. Jefferson as I would've preferred. Twenty-one years old, she attended SUNY New Paltz and her father was a hotshot director of psychiatric services for the county. Kind of surprised me that Dad hadn't shipped her off to Vassar or Amherst. It also puzzled me that he let her hang around the *po'* folks. I climbed the tight stairwell, crunching empty party cups underfoot, and knocked on her door.

Kari Jefferson answered the door, hungover. Last night's makeup, bed head, raccoon eyes, the whole bit. She had on some guy's basketball jersey top. The jersey didn't disguise her figure. Her bunny slippers were new and plush.

"Hi, Kari," I said with every ounce of charm at my disposal. "Sorry to disturb you. My name is Eli. I'm Reba's uncle." Eli West was my favorite and most disposable alias.

The reason she was stuck in Kingston and not riding a scholarship to an elite academy came into focus as she stared at me, dimly turning the pieces over in her teeny little mind. Surely Reba had never mentioned her ruggedly sexy hunk of an uncle . . . Thankfully for both of us, Kari gave deduction up as a bad job right away.

"Yeah? Wanna come in?" Her voice rasped.

The apartment was wrecked. A guy in boxers sprawled on the bed. He snored. Probably the owner of the basketball jersey.

She stumbled around and laboriously made two cups of instant coffee and handed me a Van Gogh mug. Van Gogh's ear vanished with the addition of hot water.

I sat on the edge of a ratty couch and sipped coffee, trying not to make faces like you do when being poisoned.

She curled into a stuffed chair and tucked her legs beneath her.

"From out of town, huh?"

"Why, yes, I flew in from Anchorage." I pointed at the ceiling. "Alaska."

"Uh, oh, right, right. I'm sorry you came all the way for no reason. It's like I told the cops. Reba does this."

"Disappears?"

"Nah, she just splits. Does her own thing. She always comes back. Will this time too. You'll see." She studied me more closely. "Are you a cop or an investigator, or something?"

"Heavens no," I said. "I'm in communications. Business in New York, very boring. I got a call from my sister, and since I'm in the area . . . You know. Thought maybe I'd check it out, make Mom and Dad feel better."

Kari stared at me with an expression either inscrutable or vacuous.

I kept beaming benevolent intentions.

"By the way, how is it you girls know each other? Classes?"

"Uh-huh. We're in art together."

The way she said it struck me as peculiar. Too flaky to spin a good lie, but cunning enough to hem and haw when it served her purpose.

Unlike Ms. Jefferson, I wasn't too shabby with putting two and two together and carrying three gangbangers to arrive at the sum of "drug connection." I visualized Kari and Reba lounging around the apartment. Kari would say, *Hey, man, why don't you text that pal of yours, the banger, and score us some rock?* Or blow, or Mexican Gold, or whatever these crazy kids were into this month.

"I heard she was supposed to go partying with you the other night?"

"Unh. We were gonna meet up in town. She didn't show."

"Reba's underage. Fake ID, I presume?"

"Unh. But we know the guys at most of the places and they let her slide anyway."

Reba always wore work clothes at the farm. Fix her hair, mascara and lip gloss, a summer dress . . . yeah, she'd be a beauty who could easily pass for her mid-twenties. The bozos guarding the ropes would've fallen all over themselves. And maybe there was another layer. Her gang buddies most likely had juice with the clubs. Another item to add to my growing list.

"When's the last time you actually saw her?"

"That morning. I *think* it was that morning. Yeah. I went to work at the salon. Medusa's, off Stockade. She'd left when I got back at around one. Dunno where she went. We don't keep tabs on each other or anything."

I made a reassuring expression.

"Ever happen to see a pal of hers? Somebody outside your usual circle of friends . . . Skinny white guy about yea tall. Might've been two other gentlemen with him. Hispanic gentlemen. They're joined at the hip, so to speak."

There it was again, that shadowy hint of evasion in the tilt of her head.

"Oh, Hank? Think that's his name. She didn't introduce us. Unh, I've seen her with the other guys. The three of them are from Newburgh or somewhere."

"Does Reba keep a diary? A laptop?"

"No diary," she said. "The cops took her computer. Sucks, because I used it too. I hate logging in at SUNY."

"Make your daddy buy you a new one."

"I should! He's so stingy."

"Yeah, mine too. Why don't you write down the name of the club you all were headed to that night? Heck, why not make a list of the usual places she hangs out?"

She hesitated, her dim eyes sharpening ever so slightly.

"Pretty please with sprinkles?" I said as winningly as I knew how.

"Sure. Okay." She jotted down a handful of bar names on a piece of scratch paper. The Velvet. The Electric Peach. Tom Thumb. Bruno's. She handed me the list, cheerful again.

The girl was definitely hiding something. I'd smacked the truth out of too many fools in my day to miss the signs. Odds were, it was one of those stupid things people do, a white lie that looked bigger and uglier than the truth would've. She probably didn't want word of her association with thugs and dealers to get back to Papa.

I considered pressing the issue, leaning on her to see if she could be pushed. The guy on the bed snorted and half awoke. My cue to exit. There was always tomorrow, and tomorrow, to follow up on Ms. Jefferson's omissions. Or maybe a visit to dear old pops was in order.

I said good-bye and left.

SIXTEEN

Cherry, the barber at Do-Little's in New Paltz, did a job on my hair and beard, taming my Rasputin vibe by chopping enough of both to fill a sackcloth.

I drove my truck to Bad Wolf Car Wash, plugged in the coins, and watched soap and water spill down the windows while the radio crackled and Johnny Cash took his guns to town despite his mama's protestations. I went whole hog and got the deluxe wax and buff in hopes of transforming my chariot into a somewhat respectable conveyance to the Mobsters Ball. I even vacuumed the bench seat and hung a pine air freshener from the rearview mirror.

Six-thirty p.m. saw me rolling to a stop in front of a tidy green-and-white house in Rosendale. The lawn was hemmed by hedges and crab apple trees, roses and wisteria. Instead of garden gnomes, there was a toppled tricycle, a whiffle bat, and plastic throw rings lying in the grass. A flagstone walkway scattered with blossom petals curved toward a snug porch. On the porch was a wicker love seat and a swing.

Up the walk I went, brandishing a fistful of posies. I'd broken into the emergency trunk and put on a razor-sharp gray suit and glossy black wingtips. One benefit of working for the Outfit was I learned how to dress for, and behave in, high-toned social settings. Boss didn't want thugs in his employ, he wanted operatives, which really meant we were thugs who cut sharp—but, whatever. Thanks to him, I understood how to swim with the sharks. Certainly did feel sharky that night.

I held my breath as the door swung open and Meg Shaw stood in a spill of light from a Tiffany lamp. Her dress was ivory and sequined and it clung in exactly the right places to do me harm. White pumps and sheer stockings. Charm bracelet and a fine silver chain at her neck. Lucky I didn't knock her out thrusting the posies in convulsive reflex.

When speaking became possible, I said, "Uh-oh."

She pressed her nose to the flowers and inhaled, then tossed them on a dresser and came outside.

"Hmm. Nice shoes."

I put her in the truck and headed south. She reclined in such a way as to be near me yet not. Her coconut lotion scent clouded my mind. I tried to simultaneously keep one eye on her leg and the other on the road and not crash into the ditch. It was a near thing.

"You're speeding," she said, head tilted back, gaze on the trees whipping past.

I was most definitely speeding. She adjusted the radio dial until Freddy Fender started in with "Before the Next Teardrop Falls."

"A woman as young and pretty as yourself who listens to Freddy Fender? I'm slain."

"All the girls love Freddy Fender."

"Ever been to the Sultan's Swing?"

"Never ever. It's private. Daddy says it's full of gangsters."

"Your daddy ain't lying."

We cruised along the old highway beside the river. I'd dug enough into local history to learn that several of the yacht and nightclubs that dotted the riverbanks belonged to the mob or the yakuza. The Sultan's Swing was run by an Albany family since its founding in 1939. Sinatra and Martin had sung there. According to legend, a barge docked out back to smuggle away the bodies. God alone knew the truth of that, although what *was* known was in '75 a Jersey boss got whacked in the parking lot by a carload of goodfellas blazing away with AK-47s. Never a dull moment at the SS, where they truly did treat you like family.

I MISSED THE TURNOFF because there wasn't a sign, and also because I kept peeking at Meg's thighs. I reversed and cruised along a gravel drive until a valet in a tight jacket trotted over and grabbed the keys.

The building itself was pink stucco that hadn't been painted in a while. Lots of flowers and shrubs and candles in candle boxes. Classical music played soft and low. Wooden floors shone in the dimness. Crisp white tablecloths, real silver cutlery, crystal glassware, and the staff in slicked-down hairdos and dark suits. A young man with a tattoo edging from under his collar escorted us to a cozy window table. The table had a garden view, where a decayed cherub pissed into a birdbath.

The main floor divided into a tiered horseshoe dining area around a central dance floor. A baby grand on a raised dais occupied the heart. The dozen or so other couples were dressed to the teeth. I figured some of them for Curtis's bullyboys and -gals. Everybody smelled nice, though, and the girls flashed plenty of leg. I scanned the number of entrances and exits and estimated how many of the staff were packing heat. My own piece was safely stashed at the farm. Wouldn't have done me a lick of good here in the lion's den.

Meg took it in stride. She accepted a glass of champagne from a waiter and linked her arm in mine. I shook my head at the guy and he scrammed.

"Isn't this a kick in the ass?" I said. "So old-school I half expect Marilyn to pop out of a cake."

"Spiffy," she said.

We ordered dinner and made small talk. Her parents had retreated from Kingston, New York, to Mount Dora, Florida; her brothers lived in L.A. and St. Louis. She worked the stacks at the New Paltz Public Library. An Aries and merrily widowed. Her favorite book was *Crime and Punishment* and she'd been friends with Jade and Virgil Walker since they'd come in to lecture at SUNY New Paltz during her senior year in college.

Meg helped herself to more champagne. Her cheeks glowed. Her brown eyes too.

"I've never met a Meg before," I said. "And a trapeze artist, no less."

"Ah. It's actually Megara. Mom's a fan of the classics."

"Mine too. Possibly why I feel at home with the Walkers. I have a fondness for the heroic dudes. Hercules, Thor, Beowulf, Gilgamesh, John Henry. That crowd."

"My, my. The strongman archetype."

I spread my hands in a gesture of faux modesty.

"C'mon, just look at me."

"Indeed. Impressive that a macho dude such as yourself is comfortable with the degree of homoeroticism that permeates those mythologies."

"Hey, hey, I loved *Top Gun.*"

"By the way, I'm not a trapeze artist. I'm helping the club."

"Volunteer work is commendable."

"Two rules for dating me." She cleared her throat and sat straight. "Never under any circumstances tell me I look tired. I work fifty hours a week. Damned straight, I'm tired. The second thing you mustn't do? Don't ask me where I see myself ten years from now."

"That's easy. Shelving books at the library."

"Right on. Thank you. So. Enough about me. Why did you go after those guys at the festival?"

"Really? You're going to change the subject?"

"Mmm-hmm. The dudes at the festival . . ."

"If you had to guess," I said.

"Oh, they're nasty ones. Word gets around. Huey, Dewey, and Louie, the drug dealers. My girlfriend thinks they're bangers from Newburgh. Figures. Newburgh is a pit."

"Well, there you go."

"Okay, but you're no sweetie pie either, are you?" She glanced from my scarred knuckles to our surroundings. "Look where you brought us for our first date."

"Yeah, it's tony for sure. I hope I loaded enough dough. The silverware gave me pause. And the silk napkins."

She scrutinized me intently.

"You're Maori."

"Been on your mind?"

"I'm intrigued. A girl can be curious. It's allowed."

"Half Maori. All-American military brat. I'm only ethnic when it comes time for whoever's in charge to draw up teams or to get followed around by store detectives. Honestly? I don't dwell on it. Catholic-on-holidays kind of deal."

"Whoa! A little bitter, there."

"Less than you'd suppose."

"Ever go back to New Zealand, get in touch with your roots?"

"When I was nine. Stayed with my grandfather for a while. Grandpa was so raw, he made career gangsters look like cream puffs. Grandpa hated Dad and Dad returned the sentiment. Dad hated everybody, especially Mom's side of the family. One thing he did enjoy was the idea Grandpa would toughen me the hell up."

"Evidently, it worked."

"And how."

Luckily, the steak arrived, and by the time we'd worked through it there was sorbet and more champagne. Then a fellow in a tux began warming up at the piano. He was soon joined by a sultry brunette in a strapless red dress. The brunette sounded a lot like Helen Reddy.

After the first set, the headwaiter materialized and invited us to join Mr. Curtis and his companions at the big table. Plenty of money concentrated in one spot. Even more than I'd become accustomed to caddying for Mr. Apollo back on the frontier. Although it made sense, the East being headwaters of the American Mafia.

Diamonds and mink, gold watches and gold fillings galore. The girls wrapped themselves in fur and around the half-dozen hard cases of Curtis's entourage. These ladies were the immaculate type who charged by the hour, and the rates wouldn't be cheap. The men wore tailored suits. I figured them as captains for Team Deluca. No sign of the great man himself, but that was hardly a surprise. The Don kept Curtis around to deal with riffraff like me.

Curtis and his henchmen played the role of courteous hosts. They stood and kissed Meg's hand and shook mine while flashing overly wide smiles. Curtis introduced us around the table. Names such as Bobby the Whip, Salazar, Vinnie, and Fat Frank, some others I didn't catch. Curtis's date was Wanda, a beauty with maybe a decade on the other girls and the only one who didn't shoot daggers at Meg with her eyes.

"I have to say, I noticed you ain't touched a drop," Bobby the Whip said. Soft guy with wide shoulders and a banker's paunch. Like the rest of them, his eyes were dead glass. "I hope everything is to your liking." He struggled to remember his gerunds. I appreciated the effort.

"Honestly, gentlemen, I was holding out for the scotch."

"You're in luck, pal," Curtis said, folding his napkin and setting it aside. "I happen to have a bottle of twelve-year-old Glenrothes in the cabinet. Wanda, my angel, please entertain Meg for a minute. Man talk."

"I shall return," I whispered into Meg's ear.

The men rose and I followed them through a door into the back of the club. Last glimpse I had of Meg was Wanda scootching over to her and patting her hand while the other women exchanged glances. A school of barracudas. Instinct told me my date could hold her own.

WE GATHERED IN A GAME ROOM. Leather couches, pool tables, and a fifty-gallon aquarium teeming with sunfish and betas. The little figurine in the diving suit had toppled over. I hoped that wasn't an omen. Velvet Warhol-style posters of Frank Sinatra and thin Elvis glared at each other from opposite walls. Somebody handed me a cigar. Curtis's majordomo, Bobby Two-Shoes, stepped behind the bar, lined up tumblers, and poured the scotch.

Curtis smoothed his tie with one hand and raised his glass in the other.

"Isaiah has come a long way to be with us tonight. Rumor has it, he went to Alaska a ninety-pound weakling. Now look at the husky fucker!"

I chuckled politely with the rest of them and downed my whiskey.

Bobby the Whip was quick with a refill. He managed a sanitation facility near Albany. Vinnie operated two nightclubs in Kingston. Fat Frank did commercial real estate. Curtis owned a trucking company. Which is to say, they maintained squeaky-clean fronts for their adventures in racketeering.

"C'mon. Let's stretch our legs." Curtis nudged my elbow and led me through another door. This one let onto a covered porch that overlooked a lawn and a bunch of rose beds. The Hudson moved, sluggish and muddy, through dogwoods. Stars winked in the darkening heavens.

I smoked my cigar and waited.

Curtis was a different man here in his element. Genuinely affable and relaxed. He exhaled a smoke ring. He removed a handkerchief from his breast pocket and blew his nose.

"You want to get back into the game. What I thought."

"That's the wrong thought." I told him about Reba's disappearance, how I intended to investigate, and what I needed regarding cash and intelligence.

"This gonna be a regular thing?"

"Got to see how it goes. Think of this as a trial balloon."

"We don't like Boy Scouts."

"Then you're going to love me."

"Vitale Night don't."

"It's complicated, what we've got together."

"Word is, the Outfit higher-ups gave you a pardon."

"How does New York feel about it?"

"New York don't interfere in Chicago business. I'm only reporting the news. Apollo's got a lot of pull. You're out clean. Except, Night don't want to honor the arrangement. Word is, he's gonna move on you."

I yawned.

He studied the smoke. I bet a million calculations a second were going on behind the palooka façade.

"Vitale is fast. Quick-draw artist. I seen him work. You quick on the draw?"

"Not particularly. I like to get my hands on people."

"*Not particularly* is gonna get you in a wooden box."

"My problem."

"So, I got a problem too," he said. "This is a lovely spot. Very nice. But, you see, I got allergies. The hay fever, or what have you. It's murder. You?"

"Nicotine and alcohol keep my symptoms at bay."

"Right. You probably got a constitution like a horse. Enjoy your steak? Our chef won a prize in Italy."

"He did fine with it."

"You clean up good," he said, scrutinizing my suit. "Nice-looking lady on your arm."

"Don't get any ideas."

"I won't. Me and Wanda might as well be hitched. Seventeen years this July."

"Congratulations on making it to amethyst."

"Huh?"

"Or you could buy her a sofa. Lot of options for number seventeen. Sort of a no-pressure anniversary."

He eyed me, obviously calculating whether or not I was mocking him. His expression didn't soften, but it wasn't quite homicidal either.

"My other problem is Charles. You remember Chuck."

"Mr. Blond. Dino the Ax's prodigal nephew."

"*Prodigal* is a nice way to say *fuckup*." He puffed on his cigar and stared at the water. "Like I said, okay kid, but wired wrong for the life. He did a nickel in the pen. Ever since he got street-raised, he's been a mad dog. Completely off the rails. The other day we had this deal with the Vietnamese—"

"Hold on, Curtis," I said, raising my hand. "The less I know, et cetera."

"Sorry. Suffice to say, the gooks are pissed and I'm out forty large. All because a his mouth."

I cupped my hand to my ear.

"Hark. Is that the sound of the other shoe dropping? Chuck's in your hair and you want to wash him out. Alas, Uncle Dino wouldn't appreciate the poor job review. A more indirect approach is called for. That's my cue."

"That's your cue. So's we're clear, I don't want him dusted. Just fix it so he has to be reassigned to a more appropriate department. Like chauffeurin' or slingin' drinks here at the club. Somethin' where a cane isn't too much of a liability. Gotta be natural, though. Can't come from me or I'll have to deal with the Ax. And so will you."

"I'm too young to get the ax." Tangling with some connected doofus wasn't high on my list. On the other hand, it was necessary to get into the Family's good graces. "Fine. Two conditions. I get a call when Night lands in New York. Also, a ticket to ride."

"Hang on a second, buddy. We got a working relationship with Chicago. I can't go against the treaty."

"Understood," I said. "Don't worry."

"No kidding? I don't need to worry?"

"You don't need to worry."

"Okay. You'll get your two-minute warning when the shooter arrives. Stay off my toes, you can run your little investigation. But take care of Chaz first."

"I'll arrange something."

"Won't take much," Curtis said. "Embarrassed the shit out of him when we paid you that visit. He's a touchy guy. Been tellin' me every chance he gets how he wants a piece a you."

"Oh, that *is* easy. Unleash the hound."

"Unleash the hound?"

"Tell him I said Italians are pussies and point him in the right direction. Nature will take its course."

"We'll see." He checked his watch. "One more thing. I invited him down for dinner. He'll be here in about twenty minutes. Hope you got your game face on."

I met his gaze. Gave him the dead-eyed stare I saved for special occasions.

"Jesus," he said. "Maybe I put my money on the wrong horse."

He wasn't referring to Charles.

"Laid cash on Night rubbing me out?"

"In a big way."

"Yeah, you're going to cry when you eat that," I said.

"Y'know what, fella? I kinda hope so."

SEVENTEEN

I made an emergency call to Lionel, returned to the main room, and collected Meg, who was clearly at ease amongst the predatory fish. She tucked a napkin full of scribbled phone numbers into her handbag and accompanied me to the bar, where I promptly ordered a revolver of the cheapest booze available. It had to be cheap because I needed nastiness for the work to come. The bartender arched his brow and produced a monster of a tumbler and filled it to the rim with firewater.

"Do you enjoy thrills and excitement?" I said in a passable Wolfman Jack.

"As much as the next girl. Why?"

"Because, as of two minutes ago, I'm on the clock."

I drained a third of my glass in one long gulp, took a breath, and brought the contents down to about two fingers. Helen Reddy's stand-in had come and gone. The pianist had a decent voice, though. After a few minutes, the bartender poured again. Only a double this time. I polished it off and slid the glass away.

I winked at Meg.

"Wanna dance?"

"Do I ever."

I slipped a couple bills to the piano man and requested "Mack the Knife."

"I love this song," Meg said. We moved together, separated by a bit of space, as was proper. "You've got nice moves for a man who's knocked back that much liquor."

"Man alive, you're beautiful."

"Is that the Jim Beam talking?"

"He's coaching me a little." I gazed into her eyes and felt more light-headed than could be blamed on the booze. "I want to apologize up front."

"Okay. Better make it good."

"There's a girl missing and I'm looking for her. Nobody else is."

"Is she your girl?"

"Somebody's."

"Are you a detective? It's not what I'd have guessed."

"What would you have guessed?"

"The huge, mean dude who works for the loan shark."

"Eerily perceptive. I need something from our gangster hosts. They require a service in exchange."

"Huh. My instinct says it isn't a good idea to get in bed with this crowd. Plus, every episode of *The Sopranos* ever."

"Great instincts. It is, however, unavoidable. The getting-into-bed thing."

"Time will tell. The apology?"

"I apologize for how certain contractual obligations are going to ruin our evening. I really am sorry, because it's been a swell night so far."

"Swell? My dad says swell."

"Who's your daddy?"

"I should slap you." She moved in a little closer, however. "Are we in danger?"

"Just me," I said.

"For some reason, I'm a wee bit disappointed."

The song ended and we repaired to the bar for another round. Feeling it now, I loosened my collar.

Big blond Charles swaggered into the lounge. He did a double take upon spotting me. He cut a beeline to the head table, where Curtis and his cronies had resumed their seats. A conversation ensued, followed by jeers and guffaws, doubtless at his expense. I'd seen the routine before. The guys would be merciless until Charles took care of business as he'd boasted. Almost made me feel like a heel. Almost.

Curtis had laid a neat trap. I made a note to not underestimate the slick enforcer with the terrible makeup. He'd apparently read *The Prince* too.

It went as I expected, which was satisfactory and tragic by degrees. Charles sat amidst his so-called pals, enduring their japes, his face red as a brick. I slumped over at the bar, patently drunk and belligerent, nursing yet another glass of bourbon. Occasionally, I gave him a surly glare to fan the flames. Overkill, to be sure. In my mind, the risky part of the operation was that I'd crawled out of bed from a life-threatening illness less than forty-eight hours ago. My fuel needle hovered around seventy-five percent at best.

The instant he rose, I patted Meg's hand and moved toward the bathrooms as if by coincidence. The sway in my step was exaggerated and I didn't need to steady myself with an outstretched arm, but, you know . . .

The lavatory opened before me, long and narrow and over-bright. White tiles. Marble toilets and countertops. Van Gogh knockoffs hanging over the soap dispenser. Lavender deodorizer. Spiffy, as

Meg noted. The alcohol blazed through me and I availed myself of a urinal.

Charles flung open the door and stopped, balanced on the balls of his feet. Everything depended upon his intentions. If he pulled a gun or a knife, matters would escalate and possibly spiral out of control. The furious light in his eyes relieved me. No weapons. The big guy wanted to take me apart with his fists. He'd chosen life without even realizing he'd peered into an abyss.

"You strapped?" he said.

I showed him my empty hands.

"Okay. Okay. Yeah." He popped his knuckles and took several deep breaths. "Go for anything, I'll kill you. Understand?" More knuckle cracking.

"Oh, this is a friendly beating, then?"

He wore a blue linen suit and fedora like he'd stepped out of a 1930s wanted poster. He removed his hat and hung it on a hook. His blond hair was pulled back tight in a ponytail. Next went the coat and then he rolled his sleeves over bulbous forearms. Crummy prison tats of skulls and bullets and so forth. Didn't utter a word, didn't glance away from me as he prepared. His eyes were bloodshot; he sneered and gnashed his teeth. The boy had definitely worked himself into a lather.

I sagged against the wall and zipped my fly with an insolent flourish.

Charles raised his hands and moved on me with a crab-like stutter step, the prison yard shuffle. I caught the first punch on my arm and it smarted because the guy was powerful and he could throw, make no mistake. The second punch hooked under my guard and dented my ribs. That stung a lot worse. I got my elbows in front enough to soak the worst of it. Sounded like a mallet walloping a side of beef. One-two-three to the body, with a left hook to the temple, kapow, and my head bounced off the wall, sent pieces of tile cascading to dust. I went to a knee and he drop-kicked me in the chest. I got up fast and received a right cross to the jaw for my troubles.

Generally, drunkenness engenders a misapprehension of one's invulnerability. Bottled courage is the bane of barroom warriors around the globe. Not in my case. I applied it as a tranquilizer, a sacred medium between the civilized veneer and the primordial savage. Yes, a yeoman's dose of alcohol blunted my reflexes; it also relaxed my muscles and enabled me to roll with the punishment. It slowed my mind and kept me calm while the fires of violence built and built.

This was a gladiatorial exhibition, nothing more. The booze helped me hold on to that idea.

Charles—angry, angry Charles—remained oblivious to my metabolic transformation. Sweat glinted on his cheeks. He grimaced with concentration and dug his fist with the signet ring into my belly, then backhanded me when I lowered my guard. Whiteness filled my vision. I went slack and allowed my body to be battered and flung. There was a damned lot of me to abuse. I went deep into myself, became a leaf in a hurricane, whirling toward the eye.

My head slammed through the door as he bum-rushed me into the lounge. Reality smeared into a blur of lights and distant screams, his labored grunting, the squeak of our shoes. People cleared the way for our wrecking ball passage. After crashing through the main entrance, I pivoted and flailed at the front of his suit. Charles started from his hip and drove me off the steps with a vicious uppercut that put me on my back in the gravel.

The stars flared, lovely and unreal, short-circuiting as if they were a holographic projection. I rolled over and crawled between two cars, hidden at last from the crowd gathering on the porch.

Charles wheezed. He'd gone from exultation to exhaustion. Using someone for a punching bag isn't as easy as it appears. A couple minutes of that will tucker out the hardiest soul. He betrayed that exhaustion when instead of trying to finish the job, he waited until I struggled upright. He shoved me against the frame of an Escalade and socked me again.

I grinned through blood at him, nearly there, almost fully into it. I don't process pain as a normal person does. The more I get hit, the stronger I grow as the dopamine and adrenaline do their magic. Couple that with enough liquor to stone a rhino and it's a bad night for whomever lays a hand on me. While I don't enjoy getting beaten on, and while I've been injured in my day, no man, except for dear old Dad, has ever truly hurt me with his bare hands. I'm not certain it's even possible for anyone who isn't a professional fighter. Charles possessed talent, size, and meanness. However, he wasn't by any stretch of the imagination a pro.

I started whispering to him.

"My favorite match of all time: the Rumble in the Jungle." Another punch connected with my face. I turned my head and slipped the blow. "Do you understand what rope-a-dope means, Chuck?" His follow-up to my short ribs had nothing on it. "You've got to know your history."

His face shone blank in the houselights. His mouth gaped. He smacked me again, again, again, weaker each time; kitten soft. The strangled sounds he made were music to my ears.

I snatched his final punch out of the air, clamped his wrist, and looked him in the bulging eye.

"Show's over, chum. Sorry about this."

I clinched him and reversed our positions. I slammed a knee into his testicles, driving through for a spot near his shoulder blades as one does, then released him and stepped back. He slid to the ground and writhed. He had no air to scream, although, judging from his expression, he would've loved to. I braced myself by grasping the roof of the car and stomped Charles's left knee with the heel of my shoe. Full weight, full force, everything I had. I felt bone and cartilage mash, heard the familiar pop of a joint that would never be the same. His face went gray and his body stiffened as if he'd touched a live wire. He found his voice again and shrieked. An animal's wail that raised the hairs of my arms. I got away from him and strode across the lot to the building.

I needed a drink.

EIGHTEEN

Lionel put us in his Monte Carlo. Valets from the club would bring my truck home later. We dropped Meg at her place. She leaned over the backseat, where I lay bloodied, to thank me for the dance. Blew me a kiss and departed.

"That went well," I said.

Back at my cabin, I counted the wad of C-notes Curtis had slipped into my coat pocket on my way out the door of the Sultan's Swing. He hadn't owed me a dime. It's a compulsion with wiseguys—they throw cash around like a guy with Tourette's cusses. Shoving envelopes into pockets is habitual.

I set aside the dough and opened a bottle of booze.

Lionel hung around for a nightcap. He shook his head.

"Ain't you drunk enough? I sure ain't, but you? You're sloppy, fallin' down drunk."

"I'm so drunk, this'll put me over the top and on the downhill slide to sobriety."

We clinked glasses of Johnnie Walker Double Black.

"*Slàinte,*" I said.

"Slàinte."

The screen door kept the mosquitoes at bay. Crickets sang in the hollow. A cool breeze ruffled my sticky hair. My face hurt wherever it hadn't gone completely numb.

"That's a fancy suit you ruined," he said. "You dress like that when you worked in Alaska?"

"Caine in *Get Carter* has been my model. I used to be better about not splashing blood on them."

"You played that guy. I got there and had a few seconds to speak with your girlfriend before you and Hans busted through the wall."

"I played that guy."

"He never had a prayer."

"No."

"Why the charade?"

I appreciated the fact that he used the word *charade*.

"Whenever you think of gangs, think *Romance of the Three Kingdoms*. In the gangster universe, it's all ancient Chinese court drama. Face, protocol, plausible deniability. This is what motivates wiseguys and bangers. Pussy and money too."

"But mostly saving face."

"That's right."

He appeared to consider that for a bit.

"What now?"

"Now we pound the pavement. We talk to everyone Reba knows. Her friends, her professors. The cops. Someone knows something."

"Someone always does. Making them talk is the fun part."

"We find that red Suburban, maybe we'll find the guys who were in it. We find the guys, maybe we find the girl. Do you know anybody you can trust on a stakeout?"

"Me."

"No. Go through this list of Reba's friends. The basics—when did they see her last, did she have a boyfriend, was she in trouble, et cetera. Get ahead on your farm chores. Tell Coates what's what. I'll need you at least one day this week."

He shrugged.

"Coates is cool. He'll play ball. I also know a cat who can run surveillance."

I wrote down Kari Jefferson's address with a copy of the girl's yearbook photo and passed it to him.

"Have him keep tabs on who comes and goes. If Jefferson leaves the apartment, your guy tails her. Five hundred for twenty-four hours' work. I'll pony up extra for pictures. There's more, though."

He waited while I drained my glass.

"One fine day, a man from Chicago will come to see me. A heavy hitter. He'd love to add my scalp to his collection."

"He as good as you?"

"Better," I said. "Night is a robot. Precision reflexes, zero conscience. Women, children, dogs, he'll kill anything you point him at. Fast with a gun. Billy the Kid, Doc Holliday fast. Last time we met, I won because he didn't understand the gravity of the situation. Caught him with his guard lowered. That won't happen again."

"You're pretty fucking calm about it."

"Violence doesn't scare me. Plenty of other things; not violence."

"The ancient Chinese curse *May you live in interesting times* seems to apply here," he said.

"Bad part is—"

"That's not the bad part?"

"Vitale was spawned by a family of professional murderers. Hung their shingle out since the colonial days. Some are pros—a few do it for fun. Assume I get the drop and whack him. Then I'll be dealing with all his bloodthirsty kinsmen. My bastard grandchildren will be dealing with his bloodthirsty kinsmen."

"Huh. What are you going to do?"

"Whack him, obviously."

"Alrighty, then."

"We're going to want weapons. Clean, untraceable. I'm in the market for revolvers, no automatics. Thirty-eight snubs and .357s, preferably. Nothing cheap, nothing disposable, even though we may indeed be disposing of them. And a couple of rifles. I like Rigby and Remington. At least one .308 with a good scope. In touch with anybody who can handle that?"

"I know a guy who knows a guy. I've dealt for him on the side— only way to keep my chin above water." He shuffled his feet and glanced away, as if I'd accused him of something. "Shoveling shit alone isn't going to get me to Bora Bora anytime soon."

"Hombre, I'm not judging. If this works out, it'll be an ongoing arrangement." Of course, *If this works out* was code for *If we survive.* I sighed and fetched the money Curtis had paid me to cripple hapless Charles. Lately, it felt like I was nothing more than a currency conduit. "That enough for a down payment?"

"Done," Lionel said, slipping the envelope into his coat. "I'll visit my source and get what you need. Wednesday. Thursday at the latest. What are you gonna do?"

"I'm going for a drive into the lovely Adirondacks," I said. "Unfortunately, I must go visit my old man. Don't ask."

"Okay. Here's some news. I got tailed tonight. A four-door sedan. Brown. Five, six years old. Followed me until I turned off at the Sultan's Swing."

"Weird. I'm usually the one who gets tailed for driving while not white. Could be the Family. Deluca's boys hedging their bets. Then there's the Black Dog goons . . ."

A shadow crossed his face. He shook his head. Less a denial and more like a man rousing himself from a dark vision.

"No . . . Valens ain't tracking me. He's too lazy. Anyway, I made it for a government car."

"DEA? FBI?"

"Yeah. That's how it felt. Didn't get a look at the driver."

"Curiouser and curiouser," I said.

Sunday was no day of rest for wicked me, thus, after we finished our drinks, I fell into bed and dreamed nary a dream.

DAWN EVANS WALKER, mother of Reba, awaited me in the yard when I staggered from my cabin at the crack of 10 a.m. No doubt, she'd gotten leave from her job in Cleveland. I could tell by the way she'd planted her feet that she'd been bird-dogging my door for a while. A stout lady with tired eyes and an ironed-on scowl. Navy blue blouse and slacks. Kept her hair cropped matron-style. Reba had inherited her nose and mouth.

We shook and she had a strong grip. Nursing is tough work.

"I wanted to see for myself," she said. "*Had* to see this person who's going to find my girl." Terse and pitiless. Her daughter's mother through and through. "Well, sir, every Friday night I stitch jigsaw men up in the ER who look a sight better than you do."

Barely put together in a T-shirt and sweats, oozing blood and lumpy with bruises, to say I looked a mess would be to put a very fine point on the matter.

"It was all for the good, Mrs. Walker."

Her frown deepened as she caught wind of my boozy reek.

"That definitely sounds like something you say a lot. I'll allow that some fellows do their best work drunk. My ex-husband protested as much."

"Is it possible that's where Reba is?"

"What? No. She wouldn't run to him. Not in a hundred years."

"How can you be sure?"

"Jade told me you were on our side. Reba hung around a bad element. One of them did this. They took her." She was a rock, Mrs. Evans Walker, but her voice trembled.

"Ma'am, I wouldn't be much use if I didn't ask questions."

She exhaled and relaxed her shoulders. She didn't ask for my credentials. That surprised me a bit. Instead, she reappraised me, perhaps peering deeper than before; took my measure and accepted the situation at face value. A mother's desperation is considerable.

"I called Dante and asked, point-blank. He's a louse and an idiot. And a drunk. Can't keep a secret, can't keep his mouth shut. It's always gotten the best of him. Reba is the light of his life. If she'd come to him, he'd be crowing. He hasn't seen her, hasn't heard from her in months. She's not there. Trust me, Mr. Coleridge. She's not there."

"I believe it, then."

"Jade says you have a good heart. Says you're a lout, but a good man."

"She has my number. The Walkers have been kind. I want to help."

"You're friends with my daughter?"

"Reba hates my guts, ma'am."

She smiled; the sun breaking through storm clouds.

"She would, wouldn't she? My girl has attitude."

"To spare."

"I don't know if I like you either. Doesn't seem to be a choice. Just . . . do your best."

"I'll do my worst, ma'am."

Mrs. Evans Walker didn't smile this time. Neither did I.

———

I FIGURED THE UPCOMING TRIP might be a bit taxing on the ancient Ford, so I rented a sleek Acura in Kingston. The cell rang as I forked over a credit card and signed the papers. My new best friend, Detective Rourke, wanted to meet for brunch.

The detective waited in his brown Buick in the lot beside the Frozen Rainbow, a popular blue-collar joint that specialized in about a million flavors of ice cream. He was eating chili fries.

I pulled alongside and passed a paper bag through the window. Rourke took a gander at the cash within. He hadn't shaved lately and his jowls were gray and grizzled.

He said, "You may be onto something with the Suburban. Woman who lives across the street from your girl Reba's place remembers seeing that car double-parked in the street on the day in question. Says a Native American was at the wheel. All she knows. The Suburban came up stolen. Belongs to a duffer with property here and in Florida. Didn't even realize he'd been ripped off until I called him."

"I guess you're hunting it."

"High and low. As for the sausage-making end of it—phone records don't look promising. We're cross-referencing numbers. No evidence that she skipped town by bus, train, or jet. Nothing on surveillance, nothing on paper."

"Let me know if you get a hit."

"Don't worry, I'll be in touch. We've got mutual friends."

"That so?"

"I got a season pass to the Sultan's Swing on Uncle Curtis's tab. Need anything, you holler."

"It's a small world, after all. We're cozy as, well, pigs in a blanket."

"There's funny and then there's your act."

"Something you could help me with—Reba Walker's laptop. Her

roommate says the police confiscated it. Any useful data? Save me a lot of legwork."

Rourke gave me a blank stare.

"Nobody's confiscated anything. We did a phone interview with the Jefferson chick. Dumb as a bag of hammers."

Had Kari lied about the computer? She'd acted awfully sketchy, but ingenuous regarding that particular detail. This definitely called for another visit.

"By the way, you happen to have a tail on anybody at the Walker farm?"

"No. Why?"

"Maybe nothing."

"Better watch your six." Rourke took a big bite of fries.

"Okeydokey," I said. "Have a lucky day, Officer."

Five minutes down the road, I glimpsed another brown sedan in my mirror. The car hung way back and slid in behind a panel van. A driver and a passenger. Cops or government types, definitely. Why were they interested in little old me?

I tuned the radio to a classic '80s station and pressed the accelerator.

PART II

POLYPHEMUS

NINETEEN

Dad swore by Fairbairn and Applegate, two of the toughest hand-to-hand experts alive during the World War II era. Jim Bowie might've been the only warrior Dad respected more. He first taught me some of that rough-and-tumble around the tender age of seven. How to make a proper fist, the most vulnerable areas of the human body, where to kick a man to put him down, how to take a punch. *Because, son, you're going to get punched.* He drilled me in the art of down and dirty. The ear clap, the head-butt, the hip throw. The fish hook and Monkey Steals the Peach.

Unfold your fingers like this, son, and slash the edge of your hand across his windpipe. Somebody gets you in a headlock or a bear hug, grab his pinky and snap it off. Drop your chin and take the blow. Roll with the punch. Use your bulk to absorb the shock. You're a great, armor-scaled fish, rolling. Ignore pain. Ignore fear.

In life-or-death struggle, son, always go for the bridge of the nose, the eyes, the philtrum, or the throat. Bite, gouge, kick. Never use your hands if you can help it. Never fight fair. Son, this is CPR in reverse: stop the breathing, start the bleeding, induce shock.

He gave me my first gusher of a bloody nose and my first concussion. With love, naturally. Always with love. His pores oozed scotch as he knocked me around the backyard of whatever military accommodation was our home at the moment. As I grew older and bigger, the lessons escalated. I proved durable and received only one serious broken bone from getting slammed through a deck table onto flagstones. That incident taught me it was far better to roll or bounce.

Six years since our last encounter and yet the very notion of getting within spitting distance of him gave me acid. The coward in me hoped Mervin was traveling abroad. I would have tea and cookies with his girlfriend, Harriet, and leave a note in her care.

I glanced at my white knuckles. The vinyl on the steering wheel had torn. Sweat trickled along my clenched jaw. I pulled in at a service station and washed my face in the lavatory. Bought a cup of coffee, heavy sugar and cream, and sipped it at the window while I scanned the road for the brown sedan. A decent stream of summer traffic flashed along the two-lane. None of it my shadow. The digital thermometer over the store sign read 89 F, and the humidity was oppressive.

"Not even June and lookit this damned weather!" the clerk said when he rang me up for a bottle of seltzer. "Not even June, man. I'm movin' to Scotland. Three days of summer on the moors, man. It's all they get over there. Three days of summer. That's the life."

It didn't sound like such a bad idea. Folks in the Scottish countryside needed somebody to dole out their petrol and Crunchies, same as anywhere.

MR. APOLLO PROVIDED DAD'S new address before I departed Alaska. I'd penciled in a driving route on a map of New York State in case it ever came to this. The map did its work. Another twenty miles along the highway carried me into the heart of big country. Mountain domes heaved up from billion-years-old bedrock. I turned onto a less traveled access road at a fancy sign advertising the *Anvil Mt. Resort*. Forest surrounded me for a while. Pine, elm, and birch gradually thinned as the narrow lane twisted and climbed. A hawk wheeled on a wire beneath the sun.

I crossed a field littered with prehistoric stones and shocks of white grass. Farther on, a massive wooden gate hung ajar. Dad's house sat atop a bluff; a timber lodge that resembled the kind of place Arnold Schwarzenegger would've annihilated in a fireball back in the 1980s. The outbuildings, a garage and a barn, made it a matching set. Indeed, this was the High Lonesome and it comported handily with my father's fantasy of himself as the indomitable lord of all he surveyed.

How did his lady feel about it? Did she play the role of a fairy-tale princess cloistered in a wilderness castle? The satellite dish on the roof suggested an interest in the outside world. Maybe it was enough.

"Here you are in the lion's den," Harriet Calisto said from the porch. She gestured to a husky man in aviator glasses and a bomber jacket who'd appeared from behind a juniper hedge with a rifle at port arms. "It's all right, Franklin." To me she said, "Come on in, darling. The lemonade's cold and the vodka's colder."

The décor was what you might expect from a pulp action hero who'd invested shrewdly. Bearskin rugs and buffalo-head trophies; swords, shields, and paintings of longships tossed upon stormy seas. Antique rifles under glass. Bay windows oversaw a vista of craggy mountainside and pristine wilderness. A white wolf slept near the darkened hearth. Huge and collarless, it raised its head and fixed me with its predator's eye. Only for a few moments, sufficient to let me know I'd been made. White Fang lowered his head to snooze again, but I wasn't fooled.

Harriet poured a lemonade and vodka into a frosted glass and kissed my cheek when she handed it over. I whiffed jasmine. Jasmine was Dad's favorite scent next to leather and scotch.

"My word. It feels like forever," she said without a trace of surprise at my abrupt arrival. "You've been in another scrap."

"The guy got in a couple dozen lucky punches." The fact I'd changed into a fresh shirt and slacks didn't do much to offset my gruesomeness, apparently.

This was only our third meeting in the flesh. On the most recent occasion, she'd presided over a brief, ugly scrum that resulted in bruised jaws and a father–son divide that widened unto an abyss. You wouldn't have detected the strain from her breezy demeanor, though.

Harriet was lean and graceful in a white summer dress that demonstrated her legs to good effect. An elegant lady; mildly effervescent in the manner Norma Jean had been in her time, with a curled blonde bob and Nordic blue eyes. Twenty years my senior, her smoldering sex appeal hit like a punch to the sternum. That appeal wasn't ornamental; she deployed it like a weapon. At point-blank range, the strength of her personality crackled even more so than the charm she'd radiated in a score of thriller and crime flicks. A consummate performer, she'd switched between damsel in distress and femme fatale with ease.

Dad, that cagey bastard, knew how to pick them.

"Sorry to drop in on you."

I prowled the room, eyeing framed photographs, certificates, and knickknacks. The photos were mainly of Dad in uniform at various ports of call, often flanked by comrades-in-arms. There was one of my graying, lop-eared dog, Achilles, and a young, long-haired version of me on a beach in Cordova. I quickly averted my gaze.

"It must be important," she said. "And no need to apologize. You are always welcome, Isaiah. I hope it wasn't difficult to find us."

"You're fortunate I deactivated the claymores," Dad said. "I was expecting a parcel and didn't want to blow the delivery guy to smithereens." Likely joking, although he was also possibly dead serious.

He'd come down the spiral staircase, moving with spryness remarkable for a septuagenarian. Tall and rawboned, silver hair cropped a touch longer than regulation. All sharp angles and sanded planes, his rough-hewn visage belonged on a Greek statue. He wore a gray chambray shirt, a thick belt with a platinum buckle, and tucked his khakis into a pair of weathered cowboy boots. There'd be a knife on him somewhere, and possibly a gun.

I studied the man, reflecting upon the fact I'd wasted a portion of my late teens and early twenties plotting a variety of fantastical and elaborate schemes to destroy him for what he'd done to Mom. That particular hatred had scabbed over with time and also due to circumstances not always being what they seemed. Other wounds remained. One glance at him standing there, ramrod straight and larger than life, a sardonic smirk in place, lent my phantom pains substance. The chill in his pale eyes suggested the suffering was mutual.

"There's a face only a mother could love. At least you aren't dead yet. That's an accomplishment. *Hell* of an accomplishment, considering." He opened an oak humidor and selected a cigar. He snipped the end with a silver cutter, struck a match, and spent a few seconds getting the cherry bright. His calculating gaze never wavered. "Care for one? Dominican."

"No thanks," I said. "Funny. The last gold-plated sonofabitch I called on was partial to fancy cigars as well. A mobster down in the valley. Him, I smoked with. Not you."

"Well, son, you felt comfortable with him. A dog lies with its own kind."

"Mervin." Harriet folded her arms. Her expression was ice and fire. A warning from the goddess. "I'll leave you boys to reminisce.

It's good to see you again, Isaiah." She departed the room, the white wolf appearing like magic at her heel.

After she'd gone, Dad sighed. He puffed his cigar and turned a cold shoulder to the liquor cabinet. Odd, for him.

"I'm on a three-week overseas trip starting tomorrow. You've got excellent timing."

"Taking a flier, Dad. It's not that bad a drive up here. Either way, I'd get to ogle your lovely girlfriend. When did you kick the sauce?"

He ignored the question.

"There aren't any accidents. You always had a gift. A sixth sense. Runs in the family, you know. Both sides for generations. You and I, your mother . . . It's much stronger in us."

"I didn't come to attain rapprochement. I need something."

"Naturally." He went to a distant part of the house and unlocked an armoire. The armoire was full of rifles. He selected a Sharps .50-90, restored from its Wild West heyday and polished to a dull shine. "C'mon, boy. Let's put a few rounds through ol' Betsy here. I think better when I'm sighting in a rifle."

TWENTY

A crisp late-afternoon breeze obliged me to fetch my coat from the car. Hot days and cool nights were the rule at this elevation. It reminded me a tiny bit of home during autumn before the big freeze rolled across the land and sealed in every living thing.

Dad loaded his own black powder cartridges. He took an ammo box from his shop in the barn and we lugged rifle and bullets to a clearing. He could've easily splurged on a proper shooting range with target rings on tracks and sandbag backstops, but he kept it old-school: bottles on a fence post, a stump marked by a white blaze, the rusted hulk of an abandoned tractor. His only concession to health and safety was the mismatched sets of headphones we clapped over our ears. We didn't use a tripod either; stood there like real men, stock snugged tight to shoulder, and boomed away, one buffalo-killing slug after another. The Sharps kicked with a vengeance, adding to my collection of bruises, but I bravely carried on.

After filling a third of a number ten coffee can with spent cartridges, we left our cloud of blue smoke and moseyed down to see how we'd done.

"Shooting still isn't your forte," Dad said, poking a finger through a ragged hole I'd drilled several inches below the faded emblem on the tractor's side panel.

"*Target practice* isn't my forte," I said.

He straightened and gazed out over the ridge. In profile, his features were hawkish. The fact I'd turned out nothing like him had to rankle. It would explain some of the harder knocks of my childhood.

"Had a bet with myself." Dad continued to survey his domain. "Two-to-one, you'd never show your face around here. My flesh and blood is mighty stubborn. Champion grudge bearers to the last. But, you've come home, hat in hand. I ask myself, what calamity has befallen my prodigal son that would bring him so meek and mild back into the fold?"

"Dream on, Pop. I'm not back in the fold. I do come hat in hand."

"You wouldn't ask anything for *yourself*. No sir. You'd sooner take red-hot pokers to the eyeballs than swallow that much pride. It's important and it's for someone else. An innocent. Someone's in a bind and you've got to save the day. Even at your worst, there was always a glimmer of nobility down deep, under all that shit you've covered yourself in."

"You should have been a poet, because that's beautiful. I'm helping a couple search for their granddaughter. She vanished into thin air. There are persons of interest. No proof, thus far."

"Positive she hasn't just flown the coop?"

"She didn't wander off. Possibly she ran. I haven't crossed it off the list."

"Could be she's dead."

"It's also possible she's alive and being held."

"Did you get a ransom note? No? She isn't squirreled away. She's hiding or she's buried."

"In any case, time is of the essence, as they say."

"Why are you wasting it on a family reunion? I doubt I can shed much light on some lost civilian."

"A friend of mine is involved with the investigation. Name's Lionel Robard. He's in a jam with a squad of mercs. Black Dog employees. I want a dossier on an ex–Army NCO named Valens. Dollars to doughnuts he has a rap sheet in Afghanistan and Iraq."

"So what?"

"Make some calls."

"'Make some calls,' he says." Dad rolled his eyes.

I had no intention of letting him off the hook. Eight months after Mom died, Mervin quietly cashiered out of the Air Force. The military wanted some distance between themselves and a career officer who'd killed his own wife. My old man took many a vacation to exotic locations around the world over the next decade or so. He came into a decent amount of money as well. My siblings claimed Dad made good on various investments and was simply enjoying retired life. I had a different theory about those lost years.

"Yes, Dad, make some calls. NSA, CIA, DoD . . . I don't know what part of the alphabet soup you fell into after the Air Force. Some department, some agency, recruited you. They're always on the lookout for amoral sonsofbitches with experience. I don't care where you've been or what you did. Tap your network, make the calls."

He didn't say anything or meet my eye. I went on.

"Valens works for Black Dog. He's a prick."

"'Course he is. Those Black Dog cocksuckers commit more atrocities before breakfast than the Taliban do all week. Nobody cares about war crimes so long as the victims wear turbans."

"I care. A dossier on him and anything else you can uncover. Hell with it. Give me his known associates, and Lionel Robard too." Snooping on Lionel made me a heel, I suppose. The guilt pangs didn't change my mind.

Dad laid the rifle over his shoulder. He sighed wearily.

"This is trouble. It stinks to high heaven."

"We can agree on that," I said.

"Better have supper before you go. The gal who cooks for us knows her trade."

The sun dropped below the peaks and the shadows grew long and sharp. Gods take me for a fool if the nearest tor wasn't a skull glaring down at us. Despite myself, I shivered.

THE CHEF WAS AS GOOD AS ADVERTISED. She grilled steak with all the trimmings. There were candles and Mozart.

In the middle of the crème brûlée dessert, Dad set his spoon aside.

"This incident in Alaska—is it settled?"

"Dad, the less you know . . ." I said.

"Broad strokes is all I'm asking. Are you finished with them?"

"Dear, please." Harriet raised her brows at him. Not that he heeded her. Dad was a boar, once he got started.

I tried the brûlée. Divine.

"Dad, the question is, are they through with me?"

"Don't get cute, mister." He flashed the animal snarl I'd seen in days of yore. His eyes glinted. His hands bunched. Sizable hands and plenty scarred. Even now in the twilight of his existence, he hated to be defied. The quality that made him an excellent officer was the very one that rendered him a terrible father.

For Harriet's sake, I relented. She'd seen enough blood spilled by us, to my regret.

"Some of my old compatriots are mad as hornets. One in particular. He'll come at me, sooner or later. You can depend on it."

"Oh, no," Harriet said and put her hand to her mouth.

Rather than tossing a snappy comeback, Dad frowned at his bowl. And that was dinner, more or less.

Harriet kissed me good-bye and Dad shook my hand. They watched from the porch as I drove off into the gathering darkness. A better visit than I'd expected or deserved and the first in many years that hadn't ended with a punch-up. Almost perfect.

Except for one little detail. There was always one little detail. In this case, it was a framed photograph on the fireplace mantel. A photograph of my father and seven or eight comrades, duded up in hunting gear. An older shot, because Dad still had some pepper in his hair. So, eight or nine years back, taken in the Brooks Range on a day colored white-gold with frozen sunlight.

I'd recognized the mountains in the background. Despite the fact he'd worn a beard and pitch-black aviator glasses, I also recognized Teddy Valens, stone-faced as he cradled a 7mm rifle.

The universe contained so much I didn't understand.

TWENTY-ONE

Headlights flashed twice directly in my eyes as I eased along the access road. The mysterious brown sedan had parked on the curb near the highway intersection. Its driver pulled forward at an angle, partially blocking the narrow lane.

The kind of rude behavior that, in the words of Machiavelli, kindles my ire.

"Buckle up for safety, suckers," I said.

I switched on my brights and tromped on the gas. The Acura clocked fifty as I blew past. My left front bumper sheared the sedan's headlight with a satisfying clang. I hit the brakes and barely made the turn on two tires in a spray of smoke and gravel, all of which my friend in the other car ate. Once on the straightaway, I cranked the radio. Moments later, the sedan heaved into sight, its single headlight glaring in the rearview.

As the needle edged past eighty-five I held her steady and allowed the other car to close the gap. At the critical moment I'd learned from countless action flicks I dynamited the brakes and felt the impact of the sedan against my rear bumper. The scream of tires was deafening.

The collision swung me around and the sedan drifted by, its taillights yawing wildly. It departed the highway and bounced down into a field and stopped. Unlike the movies, there was no explosion. Meanwhile, I popped the hand brake, corrected amidst a cloud of smoking rubber, and continued on my merry way.

I'm no stunt driver, and it was only a dirty trick that happened to catch the other guy off guard. Felt great, though. And I laughed.

I STOPPED AT THE NEAREST ROADSIDE DINER and took a window booth. The beat-to-hell sedan rolled in as I sipped my third cup of wretched coffee. The car's pockmarked windshield was black with dust. Steam boiled from its radiator.

A pair of men in off-the-rack suits emerged into the spill of light from the diner windows. The driver was dark and hard-bitten, his graying hair shaved high and tight. He removed a handkerchief from his pocket and dabbed his nose. Broken, was my guess. The other man was very young, possibly a recent college grad, and super-pissed. He slammed his door twice, but the hinges were ruined and it hung there.

Both of them noticed the Acura with its smashed-in taillight. They exchanged a comment, then limped into the diner. Blood splattered the black guy's chin and had dripped onto his collar and tie. Intact, outside of a few bumps and bruises.

The young guy homed in on me. He wore glasses with round lenses that reflected the fluorescent lights. I hate it when I can't see a man's eyes.

"Hold it right there, shithead! I am the FBI!" He pointed at me as if I was supposed to be petrified by an incantation or drop dead like one of those natives who fear the finger of doom.

It worked on the rest of the joint.

The waitress froze in the act of laying out silverware. A trucker at the end of the counter gaped at the spectacle. If there'd been a piano player, he would've been hiding under his bench.

I stifled a laugh.

"You? The whole Bureau?"

"Enough, Tim," the older one said. He smiled reassuringly at the waitress. "Ma'am, federal agents. The situation is under control."

"God damn it," the one called Tim said.

The black guy slid into the opposite seat.

"Evening, Coleridge. It's a street thing. In Baltimore you don't call the police, you call 'a police.' I'm Agent Bellow. That's Agent Noonan. He's new." He paused for effect. "We are the FBI and we'd like to ask you a few questions."

"Make with the bona fides," I said.

The older guy slapped his ID on the table. The kid scowled mightily and followed his lead. He refused to sit. Crossed his arms and glared.

I scanned their credentials. Ezra Bellow and Timothy Noonan, special agents, Federal Bureau of Investigation. The Quantico head-shots were a lot slicker than the agents appeared at the moment. Noonan wore an insufferable smirk in his. Gone now.

"Hope you don't mind if I think of you two as Salt-N-Pepa," I said. Although, upon closer inspection, I realized the one called Bellow was mixed, like me. African and Persian lineage, maybe something else. His surname was meaningless; it only meant his parents or grandparents had ditched the old-world handle when they emigrated to greener pastures.

"Jesus, you've got some stones," Noonan said. "You ran us off the road. For Chrissake, he nearly killed us, Bellow. I really don't like this guy."

"Duly noted," Bellow said in his affable manner. Obviously, the dangerous one of the pair.

I affected a startled expression.

"Wait, what? That was you two back there? Gawd, I'm sorry. I thought somebody was road-raging or wanted to harm me because of my swarthy complexion. Things have been so tense since 9/11. Honestly, I was fixing to call a police and report the incident."

"Oh, come on," Noonan said.

We three stared at one another while the waitress sidled over and nervously poured a round of coffees. Bellow smiled a wide, benevolent smile.

"Bygones are bygones," he said after she'd made her escape. "Accidents happen. However, Mr. Coleridge, you will reimburse us for whatever the insurance doesn't cover. This tie is ruined, and I believe my partner might've evacuated his bowels into his pants."

"Oops," I said.

"God damn it," Noonan said.

"What do you want?" I said. "Should I call my lawyer?"

"I'd like a million dollars taped to a supermodel, and you don't have a lawyer," Bellow said. "I'll settle for a straight answer regarding your activities the past couple of days. You've made a lot of friends recently—mob captains, crooked cops, black ops mercenaries, and ace FBI agents. Reunited with your estranged father."

"To be fair, the mercs don't reciprocate my affection."

"You're searching for Reba Walker."

"Who isn't even officially missing," Noonan said.

"She's missing," I said.

"I tend to agree," Bellow said. "I checked into the details. An MPR was filed after forty-eight hours. Neither her cell phone nor debit card have been accessed in more than a week. That's grim. She inhabits a statistically underrepresented demographic in regard to governmental services, especially as it pertains to criminal justice. In other words, she's a poor nigger. Poor missing niggers are not a law enforcement priority. She turns up in a ditch, the state will send someone right away with a body bag. Until then . . ."

"Until then, there's me," I said. "And my friends."

"We can be friends too. No reason why not."

Noonan, bubbling like a mini volcano, blew his top.

"See, I don't buy your act. My partner might, but I don't. I've read the book on you, pal. Just because shit hasn't stuck doesn't mean you aren't dirty. You aren't going straight. Not a chance. Things went sideways with the Outfit, Daddy buys you a stay of execution, and now you're looking to be a player again." He bared his teeth. "Isn't that the truth? These contacts are going to help you get your foot back in the door, am I right? You left some bodies on the tundra. The Hudson's a convenient place to dump a few more. I'm sure Deluca and his scumbag family are dreaming up all kinds of uses for a thug like you."

"Gracious," I said. "I'm sensing a lot of hostility. Is this good cop, asshole cop?"

"Tim, you can't shoot him."

"God damn it," Noonan said with real regret.

"On second thought, forget about the supermodel and the cash," Bellow said. "What I'd love is a lift to the nearest motel. Our car seems to be on its last legs. Could we impose upon you, Mr. Coleridge?"

"Going to move this party to a Motel 6? Count me in," I said with more enthusiasm than I felt.

———

THE AGENTS RENTED A ROOM with two doubles at Mama Vito's Motel. It was a pain in the ass because Bellow insisted on using some Bureau voucher and that meant him and the clerk fumbling around, making phone calls, and so forth. By the book, and then some, was Agent Bellow. Made me curious about the kid-gloved way he'd handled me so far. That spoke of need. Need was an element I understood how to exploit.

Finally, the clerk handed over room keys, we got where we were going.

Bellow ordered room service and put in for a 6 a.m. wakeup call. Noonan kept his peace as he unpacked and changed from the dusty suit to polo shirt and cargo pants. A former UCLA frat boy, unless I'd missed my guess by a country mile. He dialed up a porno on the flat-screen and settled on the farther bed, arms crossed sullenly, blue images of silicone-enhanced bodies reflecting in his glasses. The kid hated me and that made me sad.

Bellow glanced at his partner, and then the television, with a trace of distaste. Beneath his mild exterior, the man was wound tight as a Swiss watch. He tossed his coat aside and rolled up his sleeves. His pistol was a 9mm automatic in a shoulder holster. He laid pistol and holster on the table, then mixed a gin and tonic from the minibar and hesitated to replace the bottles until I waved him off.

"I quit cold turkey in '99," he said, examining the glass as if for a flaw.

"Congratulations."

"My wife passed away eight months later. Kidney cancer. I started drinking again. For real this time. Haven't looked back. Well, not often." He sipped his gin. The muscles in his face relaxed. "Ah, that's the stuff."

"Congratulations anyway," I said. "People should do more of what makes them happy."

"So where were we?" He lit a cigarette. A Benson & Hedges man.

"You were telling me that this is the beginning of a beautiful friendship. All I have to do is spy on the villains to prove my good intentions. That's where this is going, right? I'm presuming you're part of the gang task force."

"Would you do it?"

"Be your fly on the wall in the House of Love?"

"Yes."

"I am not interested in becoming an FBI asset. Also known as a dead man walking."

"What did I say?" Noonan tore himself away from his skin flick long enough to spear another glare at me. "You're buddies with Deluca's crowd. Can't really blame you, though. The only prayer you've got for protection from the Outfit is to suck up to the New York Syndicate. Oh yeah, boy. We know everything, front to back. Vitale Night has pinned your photo on his dartboard. I've seen the files on him. It isn't pretty."

"Find another rat."

"We're not investigating Deluca," Bellow said. "I wanted to test the waters."

"Who else could it be?" I said.

"None of your business," Noonan said. "Ezra, don't tell him anything!"

Bellow stared at his young partner. He sipped more gin. He looked at me and sighed. His eyes were bloodshot and his nose had swollen.

"Your file is rather scary as well."

"As scary as Night's?"

"Not even close. However, what's on your record is the tip of the iceberg. No, don't deny it. Let's skip the bullshit. Apollo was careful and so were you. If we knew where to go digging with a shovel and a flashlight, it might be a different story. Thing is, I don't give a shit. Right, Tim? We've got hip boots on already."

Noonan made a face.

Bellow's lips twitched ever so slightly.

"That said, my instinct and twenty years on the job tell me you aren't here to sign on with the Deluca gang. My instinct says you're legit. *Trying* to go legit, shall we say? I applaud your ambition. Never too late to turn over a new leaf."

"But," I said.

"That is correct: but, I need—we need—you to back off. Let the wheel of justice grind. Tilt at another windmill and leave this one to the pros."

"No can do, Agent Bellow. The cops have dropped the ball. Unless you can guarantee that you're personally on the girl's case—"

"For fuck's sake, man," Noonan said. "Give the white knight routine a rest, will ya? You aren't even a detective. I mean, please."

"Easy, it's okay," Bellow said.

"No training, no license. It's a farce. Fucking ridiculous."

"Shut up, Tim," Bellow said.

"Yeah, Tim," I said, making the nix sign. "You used a swear."

"Screw this, I'm done," Noonan said. Nobody paid him any attention.

"Well?" I met Bellow's eye.

"There's no case," Bellow said.

"Ah. No case, yet you paid a visit to Kari Jefferson and snatched the computer she shared with Reba. I'm not a private eye, as your sidekick so cleverly noted, but two plus two . . ."

"We have asked questions. It's what we do. I know this won't frighten a hard ass such as yourself, but it needs saying. If you go all the way down the rabbit hole, you'll find yourself in the underworld. The tenants are very bad people. The term *people* is debatable."

"Thank you, Agent Bellow. I'll try to keep my head."

We studied each other. Two bulls at an impasse.

I would've bet my wallet that he was more than a law enforcement officer married to his badge and book of regulations. He was a father, possibly a grandfather, and Reba's situation pained him. Plain to see if you were skilled at reading body language, and I am. That told me he figured her for a goner or he was onto something big. Something big enough that if a few eggs needed breaking to make the omelet, so be it, even if it hurt.

"This the part where you threaten me if I don't keep my nose out of your affairs?" I said.

"I already did." Bellow wrote his name and number on motel stationery, folded it and passed it over. "This is the part where I say, 'Thanks for the ride, Mr. Coleridge. We'll be seeing you.'"

Noonan didn't say good-bye, but I think he flipped me the bird as the door closed.

TWENTY-TWO

O n Tuesday, Lionel took the afternoon off farm duty to squire me
around the Ulster County club scene. When it comes to pressur-
ing the rubes, two heavies are better than one. Also, after paying for
the demolition of the rental car, I'd decided to give driving a pass.

I insisted that he dress a tad sharper than was his wont. Ray-
Bans, bomber jacket, pressed jeans, and canvas-topped tennis shoes.
Meanwhile, I went with a gray suit and black wingtips that I used for
these kinds of expeditions. Classy with an undercurrent of menace.
The goal was to impress people with my status while subtly suggesting I wouldn't mind getting blood on my threads. Always better to
win battles without actually having to fight them.

According to Lionel, all signs pointed to a typically brutal northeastern summer. Hot enough to wilt a steel flagpole and thick as a
sauna, with much worse in store. Heat lightning crackled over the
Catskills. I protested that it wasn't even June and he smirked and
said something about a raisin in the sun that I didn't quite catch.

He'd put in hours tracking down Reba's immediate circle of
friends and classmates. Upshot being, none of them had seen her the

day she vanished. That information, coupled with the fact her car remained in front of the apartment, suggested she'd either voluntarily left with or been abducted by someone in or near her residence. Word had it she was sweet on a banger named Philippe. Nobody knew if they were really a thing.

I asked him to take me to Reba's old reformatory first thing. We'd proceed to the clubs later, once the sun set and the joints started hopping.

The Grove Street Academy was a bunker-style block of salmon-toned concrete on the north side of Kingston. It abutted a sleeker, more contemporary structure—SMYTH & COE HEALTHCARE. My research indicated this was a pain clinic.

Here lay a rough neighborhood of salvage yards, garages, and clapboard houses. The street side of the academy was frequently painted, but if you swung along the alley you got a view of creosote, graffiti, and security mesh windows. A hurricane fence ran along the length of the building. Teen girls in oversized sweatshirts played a desultory game of basketball in the asphalt-paved yard. They stoically regarded the Monte Carlo cruising past. A camera above a service door watched them watching us.

"Looks like a fucking Mexican prison," Lionel said.

"You know Mexican prisons?"

"One time in Tijuana," he said in a breathless voice.

We parked in the cramped front lot next to a retired police cruiser. Instead of a star, it said GROVE STREET ACADEMY on the door panel. *Fuck da Police!* had been scrawled across the trunk and only partly covered with primer.

The lobby was dim, stale, and hot. Sixties décor and no air-conditioning. Worn-out greenish carpets and a dingy tile ceiling that felt three or four inches too low for comfort. Two dusty rubber plants and a knockoff of a Jackson Pollock dripping. "Lady" by Styx piped in over the intercom.

"This must be the fabled Tenth Circle of Hell," I said.

A heavyset man in a blue jacket sat behind the counter, his face lit up by a computer monitor. The huge monitor was antiquated, like everything else so far.

His tag said MR. BLANDISH.

Mr. Blandish ceased clacking away on the keyboard. He asked who we needed and I said Director Maggie Speegle. Did we have an appointment? I told him no, this is kind of an emergency regarding Reba Walker, and also delicate, so chop-chop. He was accustomed to blunt officials and angry relatives and he got on the phone and had a brief conversation.

"Ms. Speegle's gonna see you. Sign the guest book. Security will be here in a minute." He scribbled our names on visitor badges, then resumed entering data, or surfing porn, or whatever he'd been doing when we interrupted him.

Another burly staffer with a utility belt and a walkie-talkie arrived on the scene. He got his marching orders from Mr. Blandish and gave us a cursory once-over with a metal-detecting wand. I was grateful we'd left our guns, knives, and garrotes in the car.

Our escort gave the come-along gesture. We were buzzed through a metal door and into a long, eerily lighted passage. More green carpeting and more claustrophobia.

The director's office was small and windowless, albeit tidy, with a handsome desk and a brand spanking new computer. There was even air-conditioning. The room was an oasis.

I'd done some Internet sleuthing and learned what there was to know about Grove Street Academy and its personnel. Established during the 1920s, it had first served as a school for wayward girls. In other words, girls who wore pants or got pregnant out of wedlock. After WWII, it was purchased by an ex–government contractor and repurposed into a detention-and-reformation facility and became at least somewhat profitable and one of the few such institutions to survive into the twenty-first century. The Grove mission statement used words like *pride, professionalism,* and *rehabilitation.* I shuddered to think how close I'd come to spending stretches of my willful youth in a similar building. Five minutes inside and I understood Reba much better.

Maggie Speegle's staff photo didn't do her justice. Platinum blonde hair this week, her shiver-inducing blue eyes matched her blazer. The size of the rock on her ring finger had me speculating about her husband's line of work. She kept her cadmium blue nails trimmed and smiled like she ate glass for fun.

Glancing at the photos and framed certificates on the wall I was mildly surprised none were an award for "Ballbuster of the Year." Maybe if Grove Street Academy were co-ed . . .

"And who are you supposed to be?" she said to me by way of hello. Her enunciation was precise. That's a Bard education for you.

"Eli West. Reba Walker's uncle." I flashed my driver's license. I'd been clever and brought one that represented me as Eli West. During my Alaska service, the Family's top forger had created numerous documents for me under a dozen aliases. A determined and resourceful investigator might see through the ruse.

She aimed her steely gaze at Lionel.

He cleared his throat and shifted from foot to foot.

"Uh, I'm her other uncle."

"What the Christ." Ms. Speegle massaged the bridge of her nose. Her only visible emotion was the dangerous glint in her eyes.

I gave her the news: the girl had gone missing, the family was in distress—*Obi-Wan, you are our only hope*—and so forth.

She opened the desk drawer, retrieved a pack of Kools, and lit one. She smoked, dropping the ashes into a ceramic dish that contained a lonely piece of peppermint candy.

"Ms. Walker departed this academy nearly two years ago. We have not been in communication with her since that joyous occasion. I don't believe there's anything I can do to help at this juncture."

"Even an insignificant detail might prove critical," I said. "Reba's in trouble, is what we know. I don't believe a stranger is responsible. The odds suggest a friend, an acquaintance."

"Mmm, yes. The sort of character she might've encountered here at Grove, you mean. This is an all-female institution. Unless you are speculating that a woman kidnapped her?"

"The girls have boyfriends, brothers—"

"Uncles." She arched her penciled-on brow.

"Touché," I said. "Also. There's staff. Did any of the screws get too chummy during her time here?"

"That's very thin ice, sir."

"I apologize for any offense. The question stands."

"The screening process is exhaustive. Professional oversight is diligent. Perhaps you've watched too many movies about corrupt penal institutions. Graft. Violence. Sex with guards. Hollywood sensationalism."

"Actually, all I have to do is watch the news."

Ms. Speegle exhaled heavily.

"I am sorry she is in trouble. She was *always* in trouble. Frankly, I'm tempted to concur with the police assessment. She twice escaped this facility. Before that, she frequently ran away from home. Apparently, the pattern holds true."

"Some program you got here."

"It's a stellar program. That's why it's one of only seven in the entire country. Reformatories aren't often referred to as such these days. We've earned the highest marks from the National Board of Education, numerous law enforcement agencies, the AMA, and others. No program can save everyone. Least of all, those who don't wish to be saved."

I regarded her with a freeze-ray gaze; gave it about five seconds to work its magic.

"Ms. Speegle, I appreciate that you want to protect the academy's reputation. All I'm asking for is a name. This is a real live girl we're talking about, not a delinquent, not a statistic. She rides horses and takes art classes at SUNY New Paltz. Her family is crazy from missing her. Please help me."

She carefully propped her cigarette against the bowl and laced her fingers together.

"Sad, so very sad. I washed my hands of Reba Walker long ago." She smiled with pure, unadulterated malice. "Now, get out of my office."

We got out.

MR. BLANDISH, THE RECEPTIONIST, waited outside the main entrance. He whistled as we walked past.

"Dudes. You lookin' for info on the Walker girl?"

"How did you figure that out?" I said.

"Boss called down and said not to talk with you about Reba, in case you made an end run."

I explained the situation and he glanced around furtively.

"Yeah, yeah. I'm on a break, so let's make it snappy. You wanna talk to Hank Stephens. Young punk. Worked here until last year, then he split one day. Good fuckin' riddance too. We beefed and I woulda busted his punk ass, except peeps had him covered. He mixes with a bad crowd, all I'ma say."

Jackpot. I peeled three twenties off a roll and slipped them into his hand.

"He a guard?"

"Nah, man. Asshole got a rap sheet. He did custodial here and at the pain clinic. Speegle mainly kept him around to scare the girls. Y'know, like the *Scared Straight* program."

"Send in the cons!" Lionel said.

Mr. Blandish frowned in the way folks do when they don't get a joke.

"Reba?" I said, snapping my fingers at Mr. Blandish to break the spell.

"The girl, I seen her around here sometimes. Last time, maybe three weeks ago. Came to meet Dr. Peyton. She always came to meet Peyton."

"Enlighten me, Mr. Blandish. Who is Dr. Peyton?"

"He the top dog at Smyth and Coe. Magic man; makes the pain go away."

"Reba visited him."

"Yeah, man. That who she came to see. He does pills for Grove. Anybody needs 'em, he the hookup."

"He hook up anybody on the side?" Lionel said.

"Aw, man, I don't know 'bout that." Mr. Blandish fidgeted. "Can't say nothin' 'bout that."

"Did Reba come alone?"

"No, Dr. Jefferson's daughter brought her. A sweet little brunette honey. Drives a red Porsche."

Lionel and I exchanged glances. I had a solid notion as to why Reba circled back here. It's *always* about money, drugs, or sex. Reading crime pulps taught me that much. In this case, the first and the last didn't add up. However, doctors, shrinks, and veterinarians provide the best dope around.

Reba had met Hank during her stint as an inmate. He introduced her to the wonderful world of dealing black-market medications. She'd probably met Kari as a consequence of her professional relationship with Dr. Jefferson. Kari seemed a likely candidate for criminal hijinks. Perfectly positioned in the household of a big-shot shrink and dumb enough to consider liaising with Hank and his homies a romantic endeavor.

"Where, oh where may I find our friend Hank?"

"Dunno. Back in the day, he hung at a bar over on Kite Street. Like maybe ten minutes from here."

"A name would be nice."

"Don't have a name. It's somebody's house or somethin'. When it's open, there's a cutout of Elvira in the window."

"I know the place," Lionel said.

"Thanks, pal," I said to Mr. Blandish. "Don't let the boss lady see you chatting with us or she'll send you packing."

The big fellow shuddered.

"Minus my balls."

"If you're lucky," Lionel said. "You don't look very lucky."

TWENTY-THREE

I doubled back and checked the phone booth in the foyer. No listing for Hank or Henry Stephens in the directory. The only other Stephens belonged to a Latisha M., who worked at a nail salon in Rhinebeck. Strikes one and two. I left a message for Detective Rourke with Hank Stephens's name and description. It felt like progress, if only a smidgen.

Lionel's cell phone played the opening bars of "Let the Bodies Hit the Floor" as we sat in the car.

"Calvin, my brothah." He said "Uh-huh" a couple of times and disconnected. "That's my man on the Jefferson stakeout. Says to meet him at the Spitfire, nine sharp." He started the Monte Carlo. "What's an investigation without dropping in to a titty bar?"

"First things first. Then strippers."

"As you say. The nameless bar it is."

I recognized the nameless joint instantly, having cruised by it numerous times on my journeys to and from downtown Kingston. A tall, narrow house at a three-way intersection. Flowery drapes concealed whatever lay beyond the picture window in front. Elvira's cut-out from a beer campaign Halloween promotional presided over the entrance, her barely there slinky black dress faded blue from twenty-something years of shopwindow service.

"Guess they're open for biz," Lionel said. "Good. I'm parched. That vampire lady sucked the life right out of me."

"Odd setup for a bar. Kind of resembles a speakeasy, doesn't it?"

Lionel turned his head. His shoulders trembled. I realized he was laughing.

"Oh my God. Wait 'til these fools get a load of you." He wiped his eyes and struggled to regain his composure. "I'd advise getting strapped for this one."

Ninety degrees, easy. My shirt stuck to me in uncomfortable places. I holstered the .357 under my armpit and dropped a set of brass knuckles into my coat pocket. The blue-collar bar scene was fraught with peril at the best of times. This kind of heat made mad dogs of people and sometimes the only way to settle them down was to smash in their teeth.

"You've got to be kidding," I said once we'd sashayed inside.

The bar was little more than a living room with all the regular furniture replaced by a counter, a couple of card tables, and a few stools. Half a dozen people would've constituted a crowd. At that moment, it was only the bartender, Lionel, and me.

"Is . . . Is that AUTHENTIC Nazi memorabilia?" I tugged Lionel's shoulder and pointed to a flag of the Third Reich, a spiked pot helmet, and a yellowed poster of Hitler addressing his adoring public.

"Yes . . . Yes, it is." Lionel's lips trembled as he suppressed another bout of laughter.

"So's this," the bartender said. He stabbed a fourteen-inch saw-backed bayonet into the top of the bar and left it there. Not a particularly large man, he nonetheless appeared mean enough with the scars, Aryan tats, missing teeth, and a leather vest with no shirt underneath. Considering the weather, he *had* to be tough to go with such an outfit.

"Good grief," I said, my attention focused on the bayonet.

"We don't serve niggers." The bartender pointed to a sign on the wall. It confirmed the establishment's anti-African-American policy.

"Sir, I'm not black."

"The hell you ain't, you pineapple-headed motherfucker."

"Gimme a Hoegaarden, stat," Lionel said.

"Don't serve nigger lovers neither." The bartender folded his arms.

"I think he's talking to you, Lionel," I said, *sotto voce.*

Lionel put his hands on his hips. Maybe the bartender glimpsed the butt of the Beretta, maybe not.

"One. Hoegaarden. Please."

"Fine. Keep your shirt on."

We took seats at a tiny table. Plastic toy swastikas were arranged on a shelf by the window. Pieces from a board game.

The bartender pulled a stein of white ale, sliced the foam with a knife, and came over and set it before Lionel. The hate in the man's eyes was magnificent to behold. I hoped he didn't have a machine gun stashed nearby.

"Danke, Herr Goebbels," Lionel said. He tasted the brew.

"Friend, do you happen to know Hank Stephens?" I said.

"Hank? No. Piss off." The bartender went directly behind the counter and picked up the phone.

"Good beer?" I said to Lionel.

"Pretty good."

"It's the spit that gives it a robust flavor."

Lionel lifted his sleeve to check his watch.

"Is this going to be a thing with you?"

"Whatever do you mean?"

"Well, a squad of storm troopers will be here any minute. Last time we were in a tavern, some guys almost got their heads blown off—"

"Friends of *yours*."

"Then there's the incident at the Mafia lounge."

"Business."

"We've got three or four more places to be later. I'm just asking if, before it's over, the yakuza will spray us in a drive-by."

"We'll get to them after we deal with the Waffen-SS."

"Least you got a sense of humor."

"A Samoan and a hillbilly walk into a bar . . ." I said.

"You aren't Samoan."

"No, I am not. Thank you for paying attention."

"You're welcome."

"I mean it. No one's ever done that before."

"Are you gonna get emotional?"

"No. Maybe. I want a hug. Let's hug it out."

"This guy is barely keeping his shit together," Lionel said with a meaningful glance at the bartender. "We start weeping and hugging, he's liable to come up with a Molotov cocktail and firebomb us where we sit."

"Ixnay on the hugging. But, seriously, thank you for noticing."

"Fuck off, Coleridge."

"Where do you suppose those stairs lead to?" I pointed.

"The basement. A model of the Führer's bunker."

I walked over to the stairs and peered into the shadows. "Hold the fort."

"Hey, that's members only!" the bartender said. He must have made a suspicious move because Lionel's chair fell over with a clatter. The bartender swore. "Whoa, easy, mister. How about another beer?"

I passed through a curtain at the bottom of the stairs. The basement was also cramped. Exposed pipes and cruddy plaster. There were more card tables and a shabby stage with a stripper pole. Wall-to-wall posters and *action*-shot photos celebrating the Aryan movement and the glories of white pride. These glories featured hunky dudes in leather jacking the Nazi salute and brawling with cops. Disappointing. I'd half expected to find crates of surplus military weaponry, a dungeon, Hitler's mummified corpse, or something.

When I returned, Lionel had propped his feet on the table. He'd gathered a handful of the plastic swastikas and was flicking them between thumb and middle finger, the way a kid shoots peas. The bartender appeared apoplectic.

Out in the street, tires screeched and an engine revved. A van with a four-color comic Valkyrie in a chain-mail bikini splashed on the door panel jumped the sidewalk and halted. That Valkyrie appeared lifelike enough to explode out of her top or kick the front door in. The panel slid sideways and a squad of angry white men began to unload instead. Skinheads in T-shirts with heavy-metal slogans, greasy jeans, and combat boots. They'd come to play—everyone carried a baseball bat or a steel pipe.

I counted eight. That wasn't so bad.

"At least we all like metal," Lionel said, admiring the van's paint job.

"Speak for yourself, whitey. I prefer Stevie Wonder."

The leader was a stout fellow, older than the others by a decade or so. A full head of blond hair, pug nose, crooked teeth. His prison tattoos were minimalist and confined to his beefy forearms.

Which meant he could cover them up for the day job, whatever that might be.

He walked in alone, which impressed me a tiny bit. Alexander the Great would've done it that way.

"I thought you said a nigger was wrecking the joint," he said to the bartender. "This dude's an islander. You're an islander, right?"

"Meh," I waffled with my hand. "Does it really make a difference to you what flavor of subhuman I am?"

"Maybe I'm confused. You were asked to leave this establishment."

"In no uncertain terms. Hi, my name is West. This is my buddy, Leroy. You must be the Führer."

"Name's Joe Horsley. Go by Horse. Those dudes hanging around the van belong to the Hudson Valley Chapter of the Sons of the Iron Knife. I'm the president."

"Hello, Mr. President," I said.

Lionel cleared his throat and stared out the window. He hummed "Take the Skinheads Bowling."

Horsley said, "You realize me and my crew are gonna have to put a whoopin' on you if you don't get your asses gone. Them's the rules."

"I can't leave," I said and held up two fingers. "Two reasons why not."

"Yeah?"

"Reason one: I have to know why, if it's true that you hate black folks so much, one of your brethren is cavorting with an African-American girl?" I slid Reba's photo across the table.

He flicked a glance at the photo and his jaw tightened.

"Yeah, I seen her with him. Reba somethin'. Ain't no club law against keeping a piece on the side."

"Well, that's very enlightened of you."

"Reason two?"

I leaned back in my chair so the wood creaked under my weight. My jacket shifted and he got a gander at the .357.

"I've done many dark deeds in my misbegotten life, but until today I've never beaten to death the president of a white supremacist gang. As you might guess from my swarthy complexion and unsightly scarring, it has been near the top of my to-do list."

"Hold the phone, guys," Horsley said.

I affected surprise.

"Don't tell me you want to duck a fight?"

"Uh, let's table this for another day."

"This is a confounding development. Are you confounded, Lionel?"

"A wee bit," Lionel said.

"Bob, step outside," Horsley said. "Give the crew a couple of pints on me." He waited until Bob the bartender had gone. He leaned forward with an earnest expression and said, "Look, man, this is peacock shit. The boys are tough, but I don't want to pit them against heavy hitters unless there's a damned good reason. Are you with the Manitou?"

Lionel laughed.

"We're not," I said.

Horsley sighed.

"Okay. Didn't think so. We can talk, then. All peaceful and shit."

"Makes me nervous, a Hitler-loving ex-con like yourself starts preaching peace."

"Not peace, common sense. I figured you were serious when I got the call from Bob. Nobody stupid enough to barge in here unless they're connected. I did a nickel in Sing Sing, I've seen your type before. Seen scars like you got. Always on a certain type of character.

You're raw as fuck. What do you want? Maybe we got something in common."

"Which is?"

"Hank's worthless carcass swinging from a telephone pole."

"You really hate defectors that much?"

"Bet your ass we do. Hank crossed a few lines."

Self-described neo-Nazi groups are a dime a dozen. My inspection of the place had clued me in to the fact this particular group was a wannabe faction of the Aryan Brotherhood—and one glance at the scowling, but eminently callow, goons who'd arrived on the doorstep confirmed that assessment.

"What made you think these Manitou friends of yours would send somebody over?"

"Ask me no questions about club business, I'll tell you no lies."

I decided to let Horsley off the hook.

"Fine, we'll keep it simple. Where's Hank?"

"Lot of us would like to know. I haven't seen him since he split Kingston months ago. Probably in the projects with his new homies. Newburgh, Southside." He spat on the floor and crossed his arms. I believed him. There wasn't any faking that kind of disgust.

"He got a better offer?"

"Went with the Manitou. Token white bitch."

"Ouch." Lionel gave me a I'll-fill-you-in-later eyebrow waggle.

Often, the better part of valor is pretending that you know more than you actually do.

"Hey, I got one of those. Don't knock it." I patted Lionel's arm. "Gracious, Mr. Ed. Go ahead and scream at us some. We'll skulk on out of here to help you save face."

"Thank God," Horsley said. "I had bridgework done last month. Hate to wreck it."

Lionel held the door for me on the way to the car. We received some dirty looks, but Horsley kept the troops in line.

"That dude is full of shit like a Christmas goose." Lionel started the car.

"Politician is a politician."

"Can we go look at strippers now?"

"Okay, son. Let's go see the strippers."

TWENTY-FOUR

Lionel and I canvassed the hot spots on Kari Jefferson's list of Reba's haunts.

The Electric Peach and Tom Thumb were at low ebb. I worked the bouncers, two of whom were Samoans and who saw in me a sympathetic soul. Clubs love Samoans because they are so big and scary-looking that they don't have to actually smack around too many rowdy assholes. Always better for business if one can keep the yahoos in line with intimidation rather than actual beatings. That was why I couldn't handle security jobs—I'm big, but not enormous, and there are too few opportunities for real violence.

Word had already gotten around from Deluca's crew concerning what I'd done to Charles. The Samoans made me vow to keep them in mind if I happened to ever need a couple of ballbusters. I said I would and segued right into my mission.

Plenty of staff recognized Reba by name. She had a reputation as a sweet girl with iffy friends. Alas, none had seen her on the afternoon of her disappearance. As for the Three Amigos, nobody wanted to talk about them at all. After the sixth or seventh bruiser I questioned made like a clam at the mention of Hank and company, I packed it in. Their stonewalling was confirmation enough.

The manager at Tom Thumb expressed displeasure with the lack of police involvement. He offered to let me scan security footage, but the feed only clocked seventy-two hours. I thanked him and politely declined a hefty offer to join the team on Saturday nights.

Nine o'clock rolled around. We dropped by the Spitfire on Broadway to meet Lionel's buddy, Calvin Knox.

Red and blue tracers flashed out of a neon biplane with a lace bra dangling from the wing. The doorman wore thick shades and barely acknowledged us as he collected the cover charge. Inside was clean, for a strip club. At least I didn't step on any broken glass or trip over a body. Two mostly nude women were performing a desultory bump-and-grind in tandem to a techno beat. Haze, thick with more red and blue light, lent the hall an underwater aspect. Seven or eight customers gathered near the stage. A few others occupied surrounding tables. None of them were interested in Lionel or me.

Calvin Knox waved us over to his spot along the back wall below a mural of the Red Baron's plane spiraling to its doom. Slim, black, mid-forties, with a prodigious Afro and a gold chain around his neck. He wore a high-collar silver shirt open to his navel, white slacks, and sharkskin cowboy boots. I figured the getup had to be a put-on.

Lionel made the introductions. He explained that Calvin earned his bread as a professional photographer and an ace surveillance specialist. He'd done a stint with the Associated Press as a war correspondent embedded with infantry units in Afghanistan. Lately, he freelanced the local scene.

Most of his photos went straight to New York, although he'd accepted gigs from private investigators and law firms. Lionel first met Calvin by chance at the infamous Golden Eel. They'd tipped a few brews, traded war stories, and become fast friends. Neither man held the law or rules of polite society in high regard.

A girl in platform shoes and an uncomfortably tight miniskirt took the order—vodka for the boys, cranberry juice for me. Dialing it back for the rest of the evening felt like the mature choice.

I knocked glasses with my associates. We traded the usual pleasantries, sniffing around one another as strange dogs will, until I waded into a moment of silence with the evening's agenda.

"Calvin, why did you summon us to this particular dive?"

"Patience, friend." Calvin nodded serenely. "Give me ten minutes and all will become apparent."

"If you say so." My feet hurt. I wanted to go home and crawl into bed. I also wanted to call Meg, much to my chagrin. The impulse had snuck up on me. I hate being snuck up on.

"Come on, man. Can't complain about the scenery." He cast a glance at the waitress as she tottered away.

"This place would be way cooler if they tricked it out like a World War I officer's club," I said. "Fellas in uniforms and pencil mustaches. Chicks with ivory cigarette holders and those gloves that go to the forearm. Dancers would dress in flapper costumes. That'd be classy. As it is, the motif doesn't make much sense."

Lionel downed his vodka and immediately signaled for another.

"Used to be a grill. Ribs were fucking amazing. *A-ma-zing.*"

"Billy Bacon's," Calvin said. "Yes, indeed, William Chesterfield served the best ribs this side of the Tappan Zee Bridge. Bacon wasn't shabby either. He was a history buff, especially grooved on the biographies of the famous dogfighters. Commissioned this fine art." He kept his long hands clasped behind his neck. The man radiated ease, even as his eyes continuously surveyed his surroundings with calculation born of a life spent dodging mortar shells. "In '96 or '97, Big Bill got crosswise with the Coyotes over liquor distribution and they snuffed him. He should've stuck to the ribs. I'm not kidding. They were magical."

I'd heard of the Coyotes. A bad-to-the-bone motorcycle gang, if there ever was one.

"Then it got resurrected as the Spitfire?"

"Some punk with an MBA out of Harvard tried. Got his ass handed to him and went crawling back to Boston. Nobody cried over that debacle. The worm wanted to repurpose it as a sports bar. Five years ago, a small-time real estate swindler made a move on it. Took a page from the mob's playbook. Changed the name and brought in strippers and the occasional B-list comedian. Got connected with the most powerful gang in the neighborhood. His name's still on the lease, but the White Manitou hold the marker. The Spitfire fronts nasty, nasty business."

"Drawing a blank on the Manitou," I said. "The president of the Sons of the Iron mentioned that name . . ."

Lionel swallowed his second vodka. His eyes were red.

"It's bad news, pal."

"Northeastern Native American tribal gang," Calvin said. "Buffalo, Toronto, New York, and down into Philly and Baltimore. Algonquian and Seneca run the show. That's the core, at any rate. Reality is more complicated. They're co-opting poor kids, don't matter what ethnicity. Iroquois, Mohawk, blacks, Hungarians, Latinos, an Italian and an Irishman here and there."

"A rainbow coalition of evil," Lionel said.

I got the picture.

"Green is their favorite color of all, of course."

"Green is *everybody's* favorite color," Calvin said. "Been around since the 1960s, they've blown up over the past few years. Casinos, tribal police, county clerks, politicians, all kinds of business under their thumb, all kinds of people in their pocket. What the Manitou don't control, they influence. *Major* influence, son. What they can't influence, they have a tendency to destroy."

"Who's in charge locally?"

"Locally, as in Kingston? No idea. Regionally, I'm pretty sure a suit in the Apple calls the shots. Larry Modine. Hot-shit business-man. Gives to the right charities, active member of a native heritage commission, friend of the police department."

"Pillar of the community," I said.

"It's a front—journalists have investigated his ties to the seamy underbelly. Numerous Manitou bangers have worked on and off the books in his legitimate corporate enterprises."

I scribbled these pearls on a napkin.

"Cal, whether or not this will prove useful remains to be seen. It *is* immensely informative. Anything else for Papa?"

"Keep in mind, I'm getting this thirdhand from junkies and hookers."

"Man, the day you can't rely on junkies and hookers."

"Whispers have it, there's turmoil among the leadership. Turmoil usually means a thinning of the herd. Be a raftload of corpses float-ing down the Hudson any day now."

"Makes sense," I said. "They can't go on expanding without crossing the mob. Heads are gonna roll."

"Exactly. Gangland shootings are up this past year. DEA might be turning the screws. Feds stir the pot, all hell could break loose."

"Hank Stephens went over to the Manitou," Lionel said. "This is fucked."

Calvin frowned.

"That girl of yours couldn't have picked a worse crowd if Satan hisownself was running a dating service. Human trafficking is among their favorite vices. These dudes like them young and pretty.

She's lucky if she doesn't wind up pulling a train in a crack house. Or worse. The thing you need to keep in mind is that these dudes are dangerous. Skull and crossbones on the label, bad medicine. They take trophies. Skins, skulls, and scalps. Spooks the living shit out of the Italians and all the other gangs. It's primeval."

I thumped the table with my glass.

"That isn't primeval. This isn't native tradition. The Jesuits brought that garbage across the shining sea. The English taught the natives plenty about skinning and trophy taking. These silly bastards are perpetuating a terrorist myth."

"Dude, easy. I only report the news," Calvin said.

Wheels turned in my mind. Here was Bellow's hinted warning made explicit. The Feds were after big fish, all right: the White Manitou. Thanks to the Three Amigos, Reba had gotten tangled in the whole mess.

Calvin produced an envelope. Photos revealed Kari Jefferson tooling around in a red convertible and lounging poolside. Her dad's lovely home, I presumed. The last three were pics of Kari peeking into shopwindows. Tailing her, Agent Timothy Noonan cast furtive glances over his shoulder as he did his best to appear inconspicuous. I recognized the Broadway Theatre marquee in the distance.

"Took that last one earlier this afternoon. Dunno who the white cat is. A cop. I mean, lookit those shoes. Cop shoes."

"He's a cop all day long." I paid Calvin his fee, which he counted with evident satisfaction.

"What's it mean?" Lionel said in a thick voice.

"'We shall see,' said the blind man."

"Something else might be of interest." Calvin slid over an empty pill bottle. OxyContin prescribed to Reba Walker from Dr. Peyton dated three weeks prior. "Found a whole pile of these stashed in the dumpster behind the girls' apartment. Uppers, downers. Painkillers. Antiseizure meds. I think visits by you and Five-O put the heat on little miss Kari Jefferson and she cleaned house."

"Explains what the Three Amigos wanted from her and Reba," I said.

Lionel eyed a close-up of Kari.

"Is it a stretch to think this chick is good for making Reba vanish?"

"She doesn't feel right for this. She's a dilettante in over her head."

The waitress brought Lionel another vodka as the song ended and the DJ thanked the dancer and genially cajoled the men at the stage to loosen their wallets.

I watched Lionel slam his booze.

"My friend, I think you may have yourself a small drinking problem."

"We all got addictions, brother," Calvin said.

"Hi, I'm Lionel and I'm an alcoholic, it's true." Lionel swished his empty glass.

Calvin laughed.

"And I'm addicted to what brought low Don Juan, Cyrano de Bergerac, and that hombre in the Marty Robbins song 'El Paso'— which is to say, romantic love."

"Which is to say, pussy," Lionel said.

"What about you, Coleridge? You a slave to whiskey? Blow? Poontang?"

"Ain't none of that shit controls my good buddy." Lionel's eyes were fiery. "No sir. He's got an entirely different monkey on his back."

"How about we leave off with talk of monkeys," I said.

We sipped our drinks.

"You're wondering why I brought you to Kingston's finest strip show," Calvin said and gazed at the stage. "Here comes the reason, in all her nubile glory."

"Gentlemen, give it up for the Ice Czarina, Anastasia!" the DJ said and Hall & Oates began to sing "Private Eyes."

I had an instant to consider the notion that there should be a moratorium on exotic dancers and porn stars commandeering the names of dead Russian princesses. Then, adorned in shades, crimson pasties, a white bikini bottom, and perilously high heels, onto the stage strutted Kari Jefferson.

"Well played, Cal," I said.

Lionel pulled a wad of dollar bills from his wallet.

"Oorah!"

TWENTY-FIVE

The waitress took my request and a ten-spot to send Kari over after she finished her set. Kari put on a blouse and a wrap and slipped off her high heels. She beamed a 120-watt smile and waggled her fingers in that wave girls do.

"Uncle Eli!" she said with disarming sweetness and sat very close to me while Lionel smirked and Calvin kissed her hand. She was dusted in glitter and after a few seconds so was I. "Oh, vodka!" She leaned over to check Lionel's glass. "I'll take one of those."

"Darlin', are you old enough to drink?" Lionel valiantly attempted to sit up straight.

She plucked up my cranberry juice and sipped it. The bar was dim, but I could tell she was sky-high. I showed her the picture of Agent Noonan and asked if she'd ever seen him. Or an older black gentleman.

"I dunno this one. There *was* a man in a suit who dropped by the apartment last week. Barlow? Kinda nice-looking too. For an old guy."

"Is he the cop who took the computer?"

"Yeah. He flashed a badge. What was I gonna do?" She coyly sucked on the straw. "I love your 'fro," she said to Calvin.

They gazed at each other.

"Sorry to bust this up, but it's time this young lady got home," I said. "Don't you have finals?"

"Maybe . . . And maybe I've got nothin' but time to kill," she said.

"C'mon, I'll drive you home," I said. When she opened her mouth to protest, I gave her the stern-uncle expression. "Hey, your eyes don't even have whites, you're so stoned."

"Okay," she said and pressed her car keys into my hand.

I DROVE KARI IN HER CONVERTIBLE. It took some doing to adjust the cramped seat and figure out the controls. I've always preferred trucks and big, boxy sedans from the 1980s for a reason. Meanwhile, Calvin dumped a nearly comatose Lionel into the Monte Carlo and trailed us at a distance.

It was a few minutes after midnight when I parked in front of her apartment and helped her from the car. She leaned heavily against me and at the door she tried for a kiss, which I deflected as artfully as possible. Her perfume and liquor scent made my stomach queasy. Whatever pills she mixed with alcohol couldn't be healthy. She smelled like half the girlfriends of mafiosos did after they'd succumbed to the reality of their purgatorial existence.

Back at the Spitfire, Calvin had asked her why a rich girl wanted to strip and she said, "Because it's mine." I figured that applied to the fact she lived in a shitty apartment, went to a mediocre school, and toyed with the thug life. Just another bored, rebellious child.

I said, "Kari, a little birdie told me that Reba has been to Grove recently."

"Gosh, I don't know."

"You were her driver."

Her expression flickered.

"Uh, yeah. She had an appointment with her pain therapist. What's his name . . . Private stuff. I don't push her on it. She's very sensitive about Grove."

"Okay." I'd already decided not to confront her with what I knew. Not like this. Easy as pie to grasp her elbow and squeeze. She'd cave before it got too rough. That was the old Isaiah. Reforming meant doing this the hard way.

"Hey, Uncle Eli. Don't tell my dad I dance, huh?" She squinted up at me, trying for coquettishness but accomplishing mostly sloshed.

"Don't sweat it, kid. See you around."

"Mmm-hmm." She punched my arm. "Wanna come in for a drink? I got rum an' Coke."

I stared into Kari's vapid eyes and revisited the essential inequity of the cosmos and again thought how if it were *her* missing this past week and change, every media outlet in the United States would be running the tragic story until the cows came home. I also found myself wondering if she possessed the requisite steel to kill someone, to bury them deep. Doubtful, yet I'd seldom gone wrong overestimating the baseness and depravity of human beings.

"Good night . . . Shoo!"

She shooed. Calvin rolled alongside and I got in. Lionel curled in the back, snoring. We headed back to the Spitfire to drop Calvin at his ride.

"Lionel said what you two are doing. Righteous, man. He introduced me to Reba. Had me over to the farm for a barbecue. Coulda been my kid, if things had gone another way with one of my ladies. Need anything, holler."

"I shall."

He was quiet for a few moments, obviously choosing the right words.

"Not to be the prophet of doom, but if Reba isn't lying low or turning tricks, then she's dead. Eight, nine days? That's the hard fact."

"People keep telling me she's a goner. She's *missing*, that's all we know."

"You got to figure she's history."

"Her family hasn't quit. I won't."

"Because you're so close to some kid you've known a couple of months?"

"Because I am a man of my word."

"Fair enough. What are you and L Dog gonna do if this turns out for the worst?"

"Vengeance."

"Vengeance." Calvin sighed. "I read you. My family believed in an eye for an eye. All the fighting boys I ever met live by the maxim, wound for wound, no brother left behind. It isn't my way. I can respect it, though." He drove a bit farther, then said, "Kari, our little Russian ballerina, does two sets a night. I caught her earlier act, had a couple of shots. Whatever she's popping, it makes her quite talkative. Her daddy's throwing a party at his house this Friday evening. A whole slew of fat cats bound to be in attendance. In case you're interested."

"Crashing a party now and again is good for the soul."

"Shake the tree and see what falls out. Here we are." Calvin's rig was a nondescript hatchback. "Don't judge," he said. "Work I do, it pays to blend."

"Them boots and that 'fro help you blend in too?"

"Depends on the terrain, brother. Depends on the terrain."

TWENTY-SIX

The Walkers put on a breakfast spread in the main house. Scrambled eggs, hash browns, and coffee. One of Jade's interns always smuggled home a few bags of beans when he performed relief work in South America. Jade's and Virgil's faces were drawn with grief. They smiled too broadly and with too much determination. Dawn Evans Walker greeted me with a scowl reminiscent of her daughter's.

I wolfed down my eggs and related what I knew, omitting many of the finer points. Bottom line: Reba remained among the missing while I continued flailing after leads. Afterward, with the sky still black overhead and silver along the rim, I helped Gus feed the horses and shovel out the stables.

Lionel crept in, haggard and unshaven. No "Good morning" from him. He tugged his Stetson down low over his bloody eyes to avoid Coates's withering glare, climbed aboard the tractor, and disappeared into the back forty as the sun finally broke upon the horizon. Jade brought out more coffee. Gus didn't drink coffee. However, he happily gathered the sugar cubes and hid them in his pockets. The boy saved them as little treats for the horses. I sipped another cup of coffee and chatted with him about a dead mouse he'd scooped from the water trough and how it might be safer if he laced his boots properly. Fairly typical of an exciting morning at the farm.

Detective Rourke buzzed me. He'd run Hank Stephens through the database. Twenty-four years old and the proud owner of a rap sheet with way too many of the lines and boxes filled in. Felony assault, burglary, and possession with intent to sell were the biggies. Current whereabouts unknown, although his mama lived on a plot in the lower Catskills. Known criminal associates numbered in the scores; however, two matched nicely with the thugs I'd encountered at the Fire Festival—Philippe Martinez and Eddy Yellowknife. Both men had lists of priors a yard long, both were White Manitou foot soldiers. Neither possessed a current fixed place of residence since they had immigrated from Mexico and Canada, respectively, and neither had pinged the radar in over a week. I took down the address for Stephens and wished the detective a beautiful day.

I changed into a windbreaker, fresh jeans, and steel-toed hiking boots, jumped in the truck, and headed in a northerly direction.

I DROVE INTO HILL COUNTRY. The back roads were the kind where potholes had been refilled so often that the lanes were lumpen and glaciated.

Admittedly, I sallied forth with a clichéd preconception of what awaited. This cynicism was rewarded by the gradual erasure of telephone poles and road signs lacking bullet holes and a concomitant proliferation of crapped-out shacks sinking into the boggy landscape, pre-1990s trucks with deer-horn ornaments and gun racks, and hefty yokels in coveralls congregating in weedy yards and dirt parking lots of mom-and-pop country stores and gas stations. Where my dad's domain was a majestic wilderness aerie, this particular region was populated by the shades of Burt Reynolds and Jon Voight and "Dueling Banjos."

The directions I'd snagged from the Internet proved incomplete. I pulled in at a log-and-tin building that advertised itself as a combination gun shop and liquor store. Nothing says country living like being able to stock up on bourbon and double-aught buckshot at one handy location. I did in fact seize the opportunity to buy a quart of Old Crow. I had plenty of bullets.

A bear of a man in bib coveralls wrapped my hooch in a paper bag as he listened to my questions about the whereabouts of the Stephens home. He hawked a stream of tobacco into a brass spittoon and counted out greasy change. Then he gestured vaguely and said to turn left at the intersection about four miles past his shop. At least that's what I hoped—most of his teeth were gone and he spoke with a mushy accent.

Despite the proprietor's stellar directions, it took the better part of an hour to locate the Stephens homestead. Driveways were barred by metal gates, barbed wire marked property lines, and NO TRESPASSING signs included a skull and crossbones or an American flag. Other posted warnings included mention of attack dogs and assorted firearms. The Stephenses' family road wasn't any different, except instead of a gate there was a logging chain strung from two decaying poplars and a rotted wooden mailbox with STEP ENS stenciled on the side. I parked and stepped over the chain and began trudging along the dirt lane.

It climbed steeply into the woods. Shade came as sweet relief from the midmorning heat. Yet I hadn't walked a quarter mile before sweat soaked my clothes. Clouds of biting flies circled my head.

Eventually, the road leveled and I entered a clearing of gray tree stumps and fallen-down fencing. A double-wide trailer with an A-frame attachment sat toward the middle, surrounded by rusted hulks of tractors, junk cars, and arcane logging equipment. Parked alongside the trailer, a dented station wagon with muddy windows appeared as if it might actually run.

There were several outbuildings: a shed, chicken coops, ram-shackle corral, and the remnants of a barn. Nothing left of the barn except for the far wall and posts sticking out of the charred earth. Exactly the variety of scenic backwater Americana where one might expect to find the bones of revenuers, T-men, G-men, and nosy cen-sus takers from the days of moonshine stills and tommy guns.

Two dogs skulked from the tall grass and trotted closer. Mutts, the pair of them, with mottled, shaggy fur, bright blue eyes, and sizable jaws. I continued to stroll as if I belonged and hoped these boys weren't interested in chewing me to pieces.

"Barney! Buford!" A woman in glasses and a short-sleeved shirt stepped from the trailer. The dogs came close, stiff-legged, and sniffed my proffered hand, then loped back to their mistress.

"Beautiful dogs," I said when I neared the porch. "They bite?"

"Tear your balls off," she said. "Mean as the devil, when they wanna be. Deputy sheriff kilt their sire in '09. Old Drake wouldn't let him outta his cruiser, so the shitheel rolled down the window and shot him dead." She pronounced it *daid*. "Deputy passed away last winter. I take the pups over to the cemetery so they can piss on his grave now and again."

"I'm sorry," I said and meant it.

"Clementine Stephens. Call me Clem." Dentures and gray, straight hair to her shoulders. Her shirt was an advertisement for a 1983 bluegrass festival and it hung loose on her wiry frame. Faded, holey pants and mismatched moccasins. She appeared a decade older than her actual age, which I estimated in the late-forties range.

We didn't shake hands.

"Name's West. I'm here for Hank."

"That so? Friend a his?"

"Afraid not," I said, watching her hands without letting on. Doubtless, she kept an arsenal within reach. "Don't worry. I only need to speak with him. My niece is missing and I'm asking her associates what they know."

"*You're* the one." She stroked Barney's ears. "Henry come in a couple weeks back, white as a sheet. Said a gang of Samoans came after him at the festival."

"Wasn't a *whole* gang. Me, myself, and I took a shot at young Hank and his homies. They had it coming."

"Hank's a no-account snake in the grass. Like his daddy before him. Wanna beer?"

"Okay, that'd be nice."

While she went inside, it was me and the dogs. I wasn't entirely convinced she wouldn't come back out with a shotgun. She returned with cans of Natty Light and slung one to me underhand. Warm light beer isn't my favorite beverage. Nonetheless, I popped the top and sucked it down with gusto.

She cracked her own beer and let the foam boil over her knuckles and forearm.

"My gut says to trust you. You the only man who ever come around lookin' for my boy who didn't try to bullshit his way into my good graces. Only two types shoot straight. Lawmen and criminals. You ain't no lawman, by a damned sight."

I rubbed my jaw.

"Not square enough to pass for Dudley Do-Right?"

"It ain't bad. My husband had himself a weak chin, covered it with a scraggly old patch."

"The sheriff shoot him too?"

She made a pistol with her thumb and forefinger and blew pretend smoke from the pretend barrel.

"Sheriff Cochran, or Cock in Hand as us hill folk call him, gunned down a whole passel of mountain folk durin' his reign. Feud ain't nothin' new. Our families run moonshine durin' Prohibition. The law been snipin' at us since the days of Ness and Capone. Question I got is, who *you* workin' for? The Italians? The Russians? Or one a them colored gangs?"

"None of the above. All I want is my niece. Simple."

"Simple, shit." Clem crimped her mouth like she planned to spit. "What'd the boy do to make you mad enough to squash him?"

"He and his pals were getting rough with the girl. Made the mistake of trying to get rough with me."

She looked me up and down and clucked her tongue. The dogs growled in unison, ready for their cue. She shushed them with pats on the head.

"Henry was always the idiot. I mean, none of my kids are bright, but Henry's a burned-out bulb. Took up with the Sons of the Iron Knife a while ago and Lord knows that woulda got him kilt sooner or later when they found out he's a quarter Seneca."

"You don't say." I scrutinized her more closely. The straight hair and chiseled profile made sense.

"I'm about as white as you are. Anyway, when he left 'em for the Manitou that horse guy vowed to make a belt outta his hide. Surely they want to find him as bad as you do. How it is with Henry. Makin' *friends* wherever he goes. He always tracks shit into the house."

"The Iron Knife seems enthusiastic about oppressing traitors and minorities. They have your address? Might be a smart policy to keep an eye peeled for a bunch of Teutonic dickheads going door-to-door in a van selling Avon."

She guzzled her beer, licked the slime from her arm, and chucked the can into the bushes. Both dogs went on alert, although neither moved. Well-trained killers.

"Lemme see your driver's license."

I yawned and stretched and took the opportunity to glance at the tree line. I gave her my phony ID.

She stared at it for a few seconds, then handed it back.

"You a long way from Alaska."

"Some days, it does feel that way."

"Take off your shirt and pants."

"Mrs. Stephens! I'm shocked."

"It's lonely here without a man," she said, wry as Highland scotch. "Shirt and pants. Do go lightly with that hog leg, else my man in the woods is gonna blow your brains all over the side of this trailer."

I sighed theatrically and removed my jacket, then the holster with the pistol inside and laid it on a stump. I laid the fighting knife alongside and emptied my pockets of various items. After all that, I unbuttoned my shirt. The skin between my shoulders crawled. I could feel the crosshairs of a hunting scope zeroing in.

"Pants!" She stamped her foot.

"Lady, if I had a nickel for every time somebody said that." I dropped trou and turned a slow circle for her. "I'm a boxers man. Do you want to check if I'm circumcised or are you convinced I'm not wearing a wire?"

There was a hint of color in her cheeks.

"Thanks, big fella. You all messed-up like nothin' I ain't seen in a

coon's age, but you ain't wired and you ain't Manitou. Got themselves a horrible tattoo, them scary boys do."

"Might have a secret handshake too."

"Go on and get dressed. Leave your toys where they lay. Let's
walk a piece."

TWENTY-SEVEN

Clem strolled a few paces ahead as we hiked through the field. The dogs ranged to either side, periodically disappearing into the waist-high grass.

"Watch your step, there's gopher holes all up in here," she said.

She wasn't kidding. The ground opened occasionally, revealing pits and deadfalls. I picked my way with care and calculated whether it was best to drop low and slither into the undergrowth before the sniper in the trees could get off a round or keep moving and see where this impromptu tour led.

The grass thinned and the earth softened into marsh. She moved into the shade of a weeping willow. A shovel, its blade sticky with clay, and a wheelbarrow waited next to a fire pit ringed by blackened stones. Mosquitoes whined and strafed.

"Bog ain't got no name on a map. We call it Woolly Swamp." Clem indicated where the marsh gradually descended through copses of willow and alder. Farther off, solid ground was broken into islets surrounded by scummy water. A paradise of frogs, swallows, and biting insects.

"As it happens, I'm somewhat of a Charlie Daniels fan," I said. "This must be where the bodies are buried."

"Glad we have an understandin'." She reached into her pocket and handed over three driver's licenses. The men pictured were shaven and scowling. "Eldon Turner, Robert Jakes, and Willard Crowley. Never seen 'em before they come callin' the other day. Rude sonsofbitches."

"Sons of the Iron Knife." I didn't know them either. Still, it was an easy guess.

"Ayuh. You asked if them skinheads knew where Henry lived. Answer is plain. They come up here lookin' to put a bullet between his eyes. It didn't work out so well for them. There was a fourth fella. Sent him back to town with a message to stay off this mountain."

"I hope it sticks."

"I don't give a hoot either way. No shortage of holes to put a man in around here."

Flies crawled along the lip of the wheelbarrow. I took a peek. Two lumpy burlap sacks, soaked in blood and spackled with flyblow, and a machete with tape around the hilt.

"Two bags, two heads, and one trespasser sent home with his tail tucked. Where's the last guy?"

"Them pieces belong to Crowley and Jakes," Clem said. "Turner is yonder in the woods. See where the crows are wheelin'? Follow the dry patches about two hundred paces, you can jaw with him, maybe." She waved like she was shooing one of her mutts. "Go ahead. I'll wait on you."

Two hundred paces brought me, soaked boots and all, to an alder thicket. Unfortunate Eldon Turner languished there, chin tucked to chest, arms stretched wide by ropes, legs splayed before him. Clad in a grimy T-shirt and nothing else. He'd been seated on the sharp tip of one of the punji stakes that thrust from the dirt around him.

Crows cackled and complained in the branches, hopped around out of kicking range.

I knelt and lifted his chin.

"Well, pardner, this is a hell of a pass you've come to."

Turner was mostly gone. He drooled ropes of blood and spit. His glassy eyes wobbled in different directions. He emanated that sick death reek that comes from a man after his insides have begun to come apart.

My instincts were to pick a direction and flee. I resisted and walked back to Clem.

"I've seen some ruthless acts. That Vlad the Impaler routine might be the worst."

A lie she didn't appear to believe.

"Cain't take credit. Was the Manitou that picked off them boys."

"The Manitou followed the Iron Sons here into the boondocks?"

"Ayuh. Followed 'em up here and bushwhacked 'em. Warned me to leave Turner to his fate. Said to bury him when it was time."

"Ever consider the possibility of putting the guy down yourself? Nobody needs to suffer like he's suffering."

"Bah. I asked him a question and he didn't want to answer. So let him sit." She grimaced. "Besides. Scared me spitless, that scene did. That's why my kin are on alert with their varmint guns—'case either group decides to try any bullshit. They'll get a welcome, you better believe." She stuck her fingers into her mouth and gave a shrill whistle. Her faithful hounds rustled in the grass, at a moderate distance. That decided everything for me in that instant.

I glanced to my left and took another step so we were still apart but closer than she realized. Then I reached out, left-handed, and caught a fistful of her hair and yanked her completely off her feet and tight against my body. I pressed my thumb against her windpipe. She quit wriggling, pronto. I put the willow tree between us and the direction she'd sneaked her last glance, which was where I estimated her friend with a rifle lurked.

"Call him in," I said.

She whistled again. The dogs darted close and snaffled and snarled, but she composed herself and soothed them until they sat on their haunches and regarded us with worry. Presently, a figure detached from the undergrowth and crossed the field. A gangly, young-ish man in a camouflage shirt and pants. He carried a bolt-action deer rifle.

"You think you can get out a this?" Clem said. "My boy Erik, he's aces with that peashooter. Then there's my dogs."

"Don't forget about the other guy. The one covering your trailer."

"Yes sir. And just you and no weapons. How you think this will come out, huh?"

"I'm thinking I'll kill all of you. Be a shame about the dogs. I don't care to hurt animals."

She held her tongue.

"Leave that rifle on the ground and step back twenty paces," I said to Erik. He busily sighted down the barrel, trying to line up the bore with my face. "Drop it or I'm going to crush your mom's throat. Then I'll come after you."

The kid didn't flinch. Way too stupid.

She hissed at him and he tossed the rifle aside like he'd grabbed the wrong end of a red-hot poker and moved back. I manhandled Clem to where the rifle lay, then shoved her and picked it up.

She stood next to her son. Expressionless, she straightened and dusted herself off, too proud to acknowledge the swelling bruise on her neck. The dogs whined and circled. They wanted to savage something, anything, in the worst way. I empathized.

I checked the action of the rifle.

"Clem. Are we talking or are we killing?"

"Talking," she said without hesitation. That convinced me not to shoot her yet.

"You need help?" I said. "Lay it on the table."

"I ain't seen Hank in over a week." She took a deep breath and released it. "The Manitou ain't no friends-a mine. Somethin' stinks and I don't appreciate bein' kept in the dark. No matter what that fool kid thinks, they ain't his friends either."

"Appearances to the contrary."

"That's right. I propose we make common cause."

I recalled Calvin's prediction that some sort of internal gang struggle was in the works. A "thinning of the herd," he'd said.

"Please, go on."

"I want you to find my boy."

That caught me off guard, but I kept a straight face.

"If Hank had anything to do with my niece's disappearance . . . Well, I make no promises regarding how this winds up for him."

"Whatever you got planned ain't any worse than whatever he's stepped in now. Could be your girl and my Hank are missin' for the same reason. They got crossways with forces larger than any of us."

"Okay," I said. I knew plenty about getting swept up by forces greater than myself. "What do you propose?"

"This is my bargain, city boy. Supposin' Hank didn't harm your niece—and a sawbuck says he didn't—you find him and bring him back to me. I'll make it worth your while."

I glanced at the ramshackle trailer and environs.

"Assuming he's in the clear regarding Reba, exactly how do you propose to reward me? I don't drink moonshine or smoke weed."

"My money ain't in a bank. Man like yourself must understand how it is. Get that little shit back in one piece, I'll cut you the fat off a stack of Federal Reserve notes to the tune of eight grand. For my conscience, mind you. Hank ain't worth the powder it'd take to blow him to China."

"Point me in the right direction. As I said, there might not be a happy ending."

"No hard feelin's, slick. I ain't mad. My late husband probably woulda cut my throat if'n he were in your moccasins."

She spat into her leathery palm and we shook on the deal. Then she turned and headed for the trailer and I fell in. Erik followed and I watched his shadow from the corner of my eye.

"Rough side of Newburgh," Clem said. "The Battery, last I heard. Start there, you'll catch his scent."

"The Battery. Let me guess—Manitou chapter house. Punji stakes, gats, grenades. Angry Algonquians."

"Ayuh. Can't narrow it down for you. Have to kick in some doors, I reckon. Or find somebody who knows more. The Sons know. The Eye-talians for damned sure know."

She wasn't wrong. Finding the HQ of one of the biggest, meanest East Coast gangs wouldn't be the real obstacle. Problem was, I needed leverage, an offering, something to take in to an audience besides my hat in my hand.

We got back to the shack and the massive hillbilly with dental problems from the gun shop cum liquor store leaned against a pickup. He'd laid a .30-06 across the hood and was swigging one of Clem's beers.

Gods, I wanted out of that swamp. I handed Erik his rifle and collected my pistol and other belongings.

"You're putting some heavy faith in my abilities," I said to Clem. "From what I understand, the White Manitou is practically an army."

She grinned coldly.

"I put faith in the good Lord. My dogs are scared a you. Buford and Barney ain't scared of nothin'."

"Really?" I said. "They don't seem too afraid."

"Those two are attack-trained. They'll go after man, bear, cougar, what-the-fuck-ever. I told 'em to sic you when you first come along the road. They wouldn't do it. Piss-scared."

"Gee," I said.

TWENTY-EIGHT

The hillbillies gave me a lift back to my truck. I waved good-bye as they rumbled away in a cloud of country dust.

My cell rang.

"Hi," Meg said. "What are you doing tonight? Say, around sixish?"

"Uh, coming over to see you?" I said.

"Got it on the first try. Good boy! Bye."

I stared at the phone and grinned like an idiot. It buzzed again.

"Right, this is Kline—I drove you from the airport," Kline said. "Mr. Coleridge is away on business. I am authorized to pass along information he gathered at your request."

"Hello again, Mr. Kline. Please fire when ready."

Kline cleared his throat.

"Theodore B. Valens. Aged thirty-five years. Marital status: Divorced. No children. Former Green Beret. Purple Heart. Former Golden Gloves Hudson Valley regional champ, welterweight division. Boxed light heavyweight in the Army; undefeated in twenty-six bouts, one draw, one no-contest. Security contracts for several civilian agencies; chiefly, Black Dog."

"Green, gold, purple, black. A colorful character."

"A dangerous character. He resides in Kingston but is out of the country months at a stretch. Third World tours."

"Rap sheet?"

"Not in civilian or military life." Paper rustled. Apparently, Kline was reciting from a list. "In his capacity as an independent contractor, he has been accused of a variety of offenses by foreign governments and watchdog groups, ranging from assault and rape to murder. These alleged offenses have occurred exclusively in jurisdictions not covered by U.S. law enforcement codes. Black Dog, his primary employer, has apparently contributed significant financial sums to local governments to quash these charges. At the moment, Mr. Valens operates free and clear of all legal entanglements." He hesitated. "I have also included a dossier on one Lionel Robard. Please relay your email address and I'll send you the relevant documents. It's a large file. There are photographs and audio recordings."

Damn, the old man had come through for once in his miserable tenure as a father.

I thanked Kline and rattled off my email. Then, right before he hung up, I said, "By the way, where is Mervin off to?"

"That information is classified as a need-to-know basis, sir. Good day." *Click.*

As I thought.

MIDAFTERNOON SUN BLAZED HELLISHLY when I rolled through Kingston. I stopped into a florist's next to Hennessey's Barbershop and bought two bouquets: red roses in a fancy crystal vase and mixed flowers in a cheap vase—daffodils, petunias, violets, some others I didn't recognize offhand. I proceeded to the second floor of Kingston General Hospital with the second bouquet.

Charles Bachelor didn't appear too happy to see my mug in the doorway. What was he going to do, trapped in a maze of pulleys? A plaster cast engulfed his left leg.

"Chaz!" I set the vase of flowers on the dresser alongside some wilted geraniums.

Hatred shone from his eyes. His flesh was pallid and his lips were cracked as if he'd been crawling through the badlands.

"Here to finish the job?" He slurred from drugs or dehydration or both. He glanced around. Looking for a weapon to defend himself.

I poured a glass of water from a pitcher and sat in the chair next to his bed. Was this how I'd seemed to Mr. Apollo? Wasted, ruined, helpless? A creature in need of a mercy killing, if not plain old mercy?

I offered Charles the glass.

"Drink up, kid. What do you mean, am I here to finish the job?"

He sipped without shifting his gaze from mine. He wiped his mouth with the back of his hand.

"I figured Curtis sent you."

"You figured wrong. Curtis isn't planning to whack you. He wants you to drive his limo. Or wrangle call girls. I forget. Incidentally, he's scared of your uncle. You're safe."

"Huh." Charles relaxed back into his pillow and regarded the ceiling. "Got a butt?"

"I quit. Sorry."

"My coat pocket."

I rummaged through his very nice suit jacket until I located a pack of Lucky Strikes and a lighter. I got a cigarette going and passed it to him.

He puffed away, still staring morosely at the ceiling. Occasionally, he winced.

"They got me on morphine or something heavy like that. My

head feels like a balloon. I asked Uncle Dino to dust you. Gotta admit I asked."

"He didn't grant your wish?"

"Didn't say anything. Won't take my call. So, I left a message. It's bad when they stop taking your calls." He sighed a contrail of smoke. "What it is is I screwed the pooch on that deal with the gooks. Ah, that's not even the truth. The boys had it in for me since before I got sent up the last time. I love the life, but it don't love me no more."

"You should consider a new line."

"Yeah? Dancing pro?" He took another drag.

"I'll need help."

"Help?"

"In a few months, after you mend a bit. I'm starting a business. It won't interfere with the Family."

"Mend? I'm not ever going to be right. You saw to that."

"*Curtis* saw to that."

"He gave the word, yeah . . ."

"Yes, you'll limp. So what? Get therapy, get into the gym and lift iron, it won't be noticeable. Your days of playing flag football might be done, okay? Even so, you put in the work, you'll get strong again."

"Some balls you got." His expression softened into resignation. Charles had a lot of animal in him. A beast caught in a trap will rage and struggle and ultimately submit to its fate. "Gonna say you're sorry for making me a cripple?"

"Nope."

"You aren't?"

I gave him a glimpse of the dead stare. Then I dialed it down again.

"Because I'm *not* sorry, Chaz."

He frowned.

I rose and swept the dying geraniums into the wastebasket.

"Also because you're a prick. Because I could've destroyed both your chicken legs, kicked your teeth in, or made a eunuch of you. Or done worse. Because I *have* done worse before, to other men, animals, but no more deserving than yourself. Because I went exactly as far as I had to and no further. Be grateful. For once in your pitiful, wretched existence, count your lucky stars."

He closed his eyes.

"I come work for you, are you gonna give speeches like that all the time? That'd be a problem."

"Never fear, Chaz. Mostly, I'm the silent, brooding type."

"What do ya know? That's my type. We're a match made in hell."

TWENTY-NINE

The excitement at the Stephens homestead had gotten my blood pumping while the sight of Charles languishing in his sickbed depressed me. I went home and drank a beer to even everything out. Then, it was twenty minutes of a scalding shower to cleanse myself of sweat and swamp and hospital. Too bad I couldn't obliterate the image of skinhead Turner skewered on a spike. A second bottle of Wicked Ale would have to be my consolation. Since the heat of the day promised to stick around, I dressed in the lightest T-shirt and slacks I owned.

Foreman Coates and Lionel were in conversation when I returned to the yard and headed for my truck. Coates left in his station wagon and Lionel plodded over to me. He looked better, if only by a few degrees.

"Got a delivery for you," he said. "Man, you smell purdy. New cologne?"

"Yes. Smells like Come to Me . . . I'll be back in a few hours. Catch me then."

"I'm knocking off for the day. Think I'll head to town. Run down a few more of Reba's friends."

We said our farewells and I went on my way with a song in my heart and love on my mind. Or sex, at least.

A PHILOSOPHER ONCE SAID, "Man plans and God laughs."

A blonde with a pixie cut answered the door at Meg's house. Mid-thirties, skinny chic, high-energy. Pantsuit and Greek sandals. A delicate silver bracelet and watch designed to appear much more lavish than they actually were. Her perfume wasn't bad, but she'd laid it on too thick.

"Hi, hey! You must be Isaiah. I'm Lauren, Meg's friend. We work together at the library. She's running late, so come on in. Yep, she wasn't kidding. You are definitely a big guy. Follow me. Watch your head on the ceiling, ha, ha! Want a drink? Meg says you like scotch. Sit down, I'll pour you a glass. Got to run in a minute, but make yourself at home."

This monologue was a staccato affair. Lauren situated me on a couch and continued to prattle nonstop, her voice fading out as she disappeared into the kitchen with the vase of roses I'd brought, then fading in when she returned with a glass of something peaty.

"Meg says you work at the Hawk Mountain Farm. I love horses. We had horses when I was a kid in Colorado. Arabians. I think it was Arabians. Show horses. My mom raised them. Are there Arabians at the farm? How's the scotch?" She didn't know what to do with her hands as she watched me. Red nails, perfectly manicured. She touched her hair, brushed her sleeve, gestured meaninglessly.

I thanked her and tasted the liquor while I studied the living room.

Hardwood floors and kitschy throw rugs. Floor lamps provided a pleasant accent to the china cabinet and antique coffee table. Bookshelves and lots of books. Girl liked science fiction and horror, it appeared. A simple, cozy home appropriate for a librarian. Someone had assiduously picked up all the toys, but evidence of a child's presence remained in the grooves and gouges that no amount of wood stain or Sheetrock caulk could completely erase. A stepladder and a bucket rested near the far wall beneath the wiring exposed by an unbolted sconce.

The man who owned the equipment walked around the corner and stopped dead. Average height and lean, with the knotty hands and wide shoulders of a carpenter. Shaggy hair. His rough face belonged to that of a man who spent time in the elements and then drank a double when he got home. Intemperance glinted from his narrowed eyes and the set of his jaw. A quick to war, quick to peace, heart-on-his-sleeve kind of guy. "Meg had mentioned her deceased husband was a carpenter. Oops."

Lauren wrung her hands.

"Um, right. Isaiah, Mac. Mac, Isaiah. Mac's here to change the lights. I have to go. Meg will be here any minute. Booze is on the counter. Have fun. Nice to meet you. Bye. Bye, Mac. Thanks." She snatched her purse and beat it out the front door.

Mac stared at me, looked away, then back again. Same as a dog deciding whether or not to bite. He wore a tool belt loaded with screwdrivers, chisels, and box cutters. A framing hammer dangled in his right fist. Apparently, Meg's ex-husband was alive and well. Thinking to be polite, I'd left my revolver in the truck. Silly me.

"Isaiah." He rolled it around in his mouth. Nasally. His nose had been busted many times. Faint scars etched his hairline. His knuckles whitened as he gripped the hammer. "Hoo boy. This is one on me."

"A woman's got to have her secrets, evidently."

He tapped the hammer against his leg. Dark eyes, hard as the hammerhead.

"I'm gonna grab a beer," he said. "Want one?"

I raised my mostly full glass.

He thumped around a bit and returned with a can of Coors. He sat awkwardly in the love seat across the way and cracked the beer. The hammer remained in his lap.

"Meg didn't say she was expecting company," he said after a couple of swallows.

"Nope."

A long, unhappy silence ensued.

"You're real." When I didn't take the bait, he went on. "I mean to say, you're not acting. Me, I'm scared of all kinds of shit. Losing. Becoming an alkie like my old man. Falling off a roof or getting fried rewiring a light. Arthritis. You aren't afraid, though. You're a big, bad man, aren't you?"

He couldn't have missed the mark by a wider margin.

"After what I've gone through today, you'll find it difficult to get a rise out of me. It's a character defect. Things that should frighten me don't. *Should* I be afraid?"

"Well, I dunno." Tap, tap, tap with the hammer against his thigh.

"Make up your mind, you let me know."

More silence, and this time it really dragged.

"Where you from, Isaiah?" His tone indicated he wanted to ask something else entirely.

"Alaska. All over, but mainly Alaska."

"Alaska. Always wanted to go. Too damned cold. Too damned dark. I hunt. Lots a hunting up there. Caribou, moose. Best meat, caribou."

I allowed that, yes, Alaska was cold and dark and there was indeed a lot of good hunting.

"Meg tell you she had a man?" Another long swallow.

"She suggested you were deceased. She probably meant to say 'estranged.'"

"Might a been fantasizing about my demise. Our marriage is a cold war." He smiled with a depth of rue that was shocking and then covered his nakedness with another, longer, pull of beer.

I pondered that for a few moments.

"Not divorced?"

"Nah, dude. Separated going on two years."

"Separated." My turn to roll a word around like a marble.

"Mackenzie Shaw, at your service. Carpenter, painter, dad. Dad, yeah. We got a son. He's five come August. I don't suppose she mentioned Devlin either."

Now I concentrated on my glass as if the secrets to life swam in its contents.

"I saw the Big Wheel's in the yard. Devlin. That's solid. Glad you didn't go with an *M* name."

"*M* name?"

"Mac and Meg? Precious enough, don't you think? No need to hit a triple."

Mac inhaled deeply and let it out again. He finished the beer and carefully set the empty on a coaster on the coffee table. He pointed at the flat-screen television between the bookcases.

"Bought that for her and D last year. Tired-a D watchin' cartoons on the shitty box we had since before he came along."

I sipped and noticed that three fingers of scotch had dwindled to a fingernail.

He sighed again.

"What I'm trying to say is, I'm not an asshole. Not a *complete* asshole. I care about what happens. Some of the guys she's brought around . . . I don't know what to tell you. It's complicated between

Meg and me. Man, we're not together, but that doesn't mean I don't love her. And Devlin . . . He's my little man. You know?"

I waited because I didn't know.

"Yeah, well." He blinked rapidly. "Basketball fan? Playoffs are on. I got three hundred on Miami to go the distance."

"I'm partial to Philly."

"Seventy-sixers are bums." Mac found the remote and clicked on the set. "Celtics versus Bucks. Goddamned Celtics. I'd give a week's pay to see them drop this one."

"I remember when it was Bird, McHale, and Parish beating the world. Enough to drive a Sixers fan to drink."

He tossed the hammer underhand and it clattered into the tool bucket.

"Bro. Real men don't need no excuse to drink. We just do it."

"Ah. Is that what we are? Real men?"

"Hell yeah. Got to ask?" He'd grown steadier. The blinking stopped, at least.

"Want to hear everything I've learned? You got three seconds?"

"See those guys?" Mac plowed ahead animatedly, his gaze fixed upon the screen. The sight of men in uniforms engaged in stylized conflict had magically restored him. "Those guys ain't worth a tinker's damn. Bird and McHale, they're bronzed in a museum. Ain't nobody like them playing anymore. Weak sisters rule the world now."

MEG WALKED IN THE DOOR about forty minutes later. She was glossy and made-up and appealing in a red skirt and heels. Her calves were steely as any runway model's. She carried a bag of groceries under her arm. Her expression suggested she was neither pleased nor expecting to see us menfolk kicked back, watching the Celtics torch the Bucks.

Mac leaped to his feet like his foreman had caught him on an unscheduled break. He muttered about circuits and fuses and said he'd return that weekend to finish repairing the lamp.

"Spectacular," she said. "Except, I never asked you to fix the fucking lamp in the first place."

"Don't want my son going blind trying to read his comic books in the dark."

"Devlin can't read. He doesn't look at his books here. He plays in his room. I *read* to him in his room. The lamp in his room works fine." All this she said through gritted teeth.

"Okay. I'll get this taken care of Saturday." He gestured in my direction as he departed without looking directly at me or Meg.

Then it was us chickens and a bunch of guys chasing a ball on TV.

"Honey, you're home," I said. "What's for dinner?"

"Spaghetti," she said.

"Going to show that Italian joint how it's done, eh?"

She didn't answer but went into the kitchen and made dinner while I sat with my thoughts. I had no idea what to feel about the situation. That hadn't changed when she dimmed the lights and set the pasta, garlic bread, and wine on the dining table.

"Found your girl?" she said after a while.

"Not yet."

"Sorry to hear it." She set her fork aside and lifted her wineglass. "My life is really, really complicated. You met Lauren. She's . . ."

"Loquacious."

"High-strung. My housemate. Pays half the rent. If I counted on Mac, I'd be out on my ass."

I thought of his offhand remark about laying three bills on the Heat to win all the marbles in the NBA finals.

"Seems like a good guy. Blue-collar, salt of the earth. Those types can be reckless as they are large-hearted. It's what kills them and sustains them." I wanted more alcohol but stuck with water.

She swirled wine in her glass and tilted her head and regarded me with an inscrutable expression.

"That salt-of-the-earth guy is a drunk. He's an inveterate gambler who owes goons like you money he doesn't have. He fucks around. He won't sign the divorce papers and he won't stay away even though he doesn't live here anymore. He runs off anyone who shows the slightest interest in me and Devlin. But he's handsome and folksy and sufficiently cunning to bond with the only man I've dated who's big enough and mean enough to knock him down. Don't know how much more of that large heart I can take."

"I collected comics as a boy," I said.

"Excuse me?"

"Spider-Man. Captain America. The X-Men. What kind of comics does Devlin like?"

"Know what we're not going to do? Talk about my son. Let's save that for another evening."

"Farmed him out so we could have a quiet date? Shouldn't have. I do great with kids."

"Devlin is with his grandmother. I didn't send him away so you and I could canoodle. I did it because I wasn't sure if you and Mac would . . ." She stared at her plate, then speared me with a glare. "Anyway, you think I'm going to let a person like you around my child? Think again."

"That's probably more of a third date kind of thing. Really, am I any worse a bet than a mom who sets up a kid's dad for a beating by a raging maniac?"

Her eyes glittered. I'd gotten the color wrong. They shifted from brown to hazel, depending upon her mood.

"This is about the other night," I said. "And the festival."

She nodded.

"You have the wrong idea about what I do," I said.

"I think I have a very good idea about what you do."

"On the contrary, I don't punch annoying ex-husbands in the face. Not unless they're a danger and not unless I'm getting paid. Goes double for annoying husbands who aren't quite exes."

"Oh, my mistake. What are your rates?"

I massaged my temples. The headache had come on with thunderous intensity. She brought aspirin and dropped them in my hand. I washed the pills down with the rest of my water. The heat of her as her blouse brushed my cheek was distracting.

We retired to the living room. The Cure sang, dim and sweet. *Disintegration* has rated among my favorites since junior high. I drank another glass of water. She rolled a joint and smoked it, her body curled into the opposite arm of the couch.

"Want a hit?" She extended the smoldering joint.

"I don't smoke anymore. I drink a little."

"Uh-uh, you drink a lot."

"A little a lot."

"You hurt people. At least sometimes."

"All the time," I said.

"I don't know if I like that part."

"You'd be a psycho if you did."

"Been married?"

"No. Dodged that bullet."

"Hmm. But you came close."

"I had a great love. When I was young."

"And?"

"She left me."

"Why?"

"Because she saw me for what I am."

Meg inhaled and held it, exhaled and coughed.

"What's with the rabies tags?"

"A memento. I'm sentimental every now and again. Long story."

"I get the impression it's a tragedy."

"I don't want to dissect it tonight," I said more gruffly than I'd intended.

"What's your favorite book?" Her smug expression suggested she'd scored a point in whatever game we were playing.

"I told you already."

"When did you tell me?"

"At the Sultan's Swing."

"No way, I would've remembered."

"It's your turn to spill a personal detail."

She smiled. A small thing but real.

"Wrong. I'm not the one on trial."

"Glad we got that straight. What am I on trial for?"

"Whether or not you're going to get into my panties."

"Women decide that within the first thirty seconds of meeting a dude. So my guess is, case closed. Or open."

She covered her mouth and snorted.

"The Odyssey," I said. "It's the precursor to *Heart of Darkness.* The sea voyage with all the evil kings and monsters, and screwing of sea nymphs and lonely witches. The revenge against the suitors. I was an angry kid. Revenge appeals to teenagers. I admired Odysseus, but my heart went out to put-upon Polyphemus. Trespassing Greeks eat his mutton and drink his wine, stab him in the eye, and sail off merry as you please. The other Cyclops laughed. He got a raw deal. That said, I'm still more in Camp Hercules than Camp Odysseus."

"Funny you should mention Odysseus."

"How so? Anyway, Mother Walker mentioned him recently. I hadn't thought of the old salt in an age."

She glanced away as though trying to shake a dark thought.

"You should try Michael Shea. He wrote a collection called *Polyphemus*. I think he loved the big dope too. Although Shea was a horror writer, so it's hard to say."

Meg polished off her wine and poured another glass. She set the glass aside and knelt before me and took my hand, palm up, and examined it.

"Are you a fortune-teller?" I said.

"Also an acrobat and a speed reader. Mama did witchcraft until Daddy stole her virtue. Crazy lines you have here, Mr. Coleridge." She traced my skin with her fingernail. "I dreamed of you the other night."

"Do tell."

"Don't get excited. Nothing erotic."

"Aw. An acrobat, eh? That's unusual."

She stood and shoved the coffee table against the wall. Then she bent at the waist and pressed into a handstand. Lifted her left hand from the floor and remained steady. She walked around the room on her hands, and, when that bored her, she did a series of freeze-frame cartwheels. Her body flexed in such a way that I only got a flash of black silk panties. The final revolution deposited her on the couch. She breathed normally. Her cheeks were bright.

"Well, I never," I said. "The possibilities seem endless. Dirty, but endless. How come you're a librarian and not working with, I don't know, Cirque du Soleil?"

"I traveled with a circus. Long time ago."

"The Trapeze Club isn't part of the larger picture?"

"Fell and busted my ankles, so I went to college. Now it's all in fun."

"Sorry."

"No use in that."

We sat in silence for a minute before she tilted her head and gazed at me sidelong.

"Why is Odysseus funny, you ask?" She squeezed my hand. "Because I dreamed you were on a ship, the old kind with square sails and banks of rowers, and you sailed on a rough sea the color of green glass. You put in at several islands. Upon each island, you paid homage to its king. Horrible, vile men who reposed upon thrones of bones and whose sandals were caked in the blood of their victims. Each desired to slay you, but you were wily and resourceful and escaped with your skin. The palaces, the forests, the grass in the fields, everything around you, blazed with fire. You left the islands floating amidst the black like burning jewels and sailed into outer darkness."

"Art imitating life," I said. "I've visited two kings. Haven't set any fires."

"There's still time to wreak havoc," she said. "It's running through your fingers, though. You've got to hurry. 'Cause you're gonna die, in the end."

"How do I die?"

"A woman betrays you."

She kissed my knee and then abruptly stood and moved away.

"Go home, brave warrior. My son will be here soon and I don't want him to see you here."

THIRTY

Sleep came in fits and fragments over the next couple of nights. My dreams were haunted, not by rough seas or tyrants shouting from their thrones but by images of Reba galloping Bacchus into the black mouth of a cave and men in fatigues dropping through the earth into tiger pits. Lionel cried for help and I was afraid to look over the lip of the trap. A man I recognized from a previous incarnation of myself, but whose name I'd forgotten, entreated me from his knees not to shoot him. I pulled the trigger anyway. Tony Flowers leered as I struggled to escape the iron chair. My mother's body lay, cold and blue, near the water, her lovely face disfigured by a gash from an oar, and Mervin stood in silhouette, the very figure of the Reaper. I dreamed of Achilles sliding against the loose rocks of a cliff, accelerating away from my grasp. We both plummeted into the green abyss of eternity.

Two straight mornings I awoke, sweating and panicky. These were the bad old days of my youth once again.

I kept busy during the day with numerous calls, including one to Detective Rourke. Rourke provided me with a short list of names and addresses courtesy of his pals on the gang task force. He didn't want to "know nothing about nothing." Station scuttlebutt indicated the Feds were definitely sniffing around, but that was old news of course.

I made a couple of local trips. Over to Newburgh first. Merely a recon mission to get the lay of the land and a feel for what opposition might await me in The Battery. Newburgh wasn't by any stretch a tourist attraction. The wrong side of its tracks reinforced the notion that the Great Recession of the 1980s clamped steely fingers around its throat and hung on like grim death. The rough end of Kingston seemed posh by comparison. Fifteen minutes parked in a chain supermarket lot, I counted more gang badges in the form of do-rags, bandannas, and plaid jackets than I'd seen in a year on the streets of Anchorage. No doubt, The Battery was the place to go if one desired an ass whipping or a bullet through the brain.

My second trip took me to Gardiner, a town south of New Paltz, in search of Dr. Peyton. For a hundred bucks I cadged his address off Mr. Blandish, the clerk at Grove Street Academy. Blandish informed me that the doctor had x'd out his schedule until Monday for a conference in Seattle. Peyton, his wife, and four kids, lived in a modest late-model home on a quiet street lined with similar houses. I spent an afternoon in the shade of a maple watching a cute blond kid shoot free throws into a collapsible hoop stand. Mom, harried and frowning, came and went in the family Subaru, but no sign of her husband. I concluded that he really had gone to the Pacific Northwest and wasn't lying low.

Meanwhile, life around the farm slowly returned to its normal rhythms. Horses to be fed and shit to be shoveled were things that never changed. Each day Jade dressed in her riding duds and led mighty Bacchus into the lunging ring. Without Reba's gentling touch, he'd regressed to a mythic beast, rearing and taking great swipes at Jade with his jaws. The sessions were brief and I sensed that the horse got the better of their engagements. He tore through fences but didn't wander far, almost apathetic in his defiance.

Thursday after sundown, Lionel appeared on my doorstep schlepping two duffel bags clanking with hardware. We spent a joyous hour or two breaking down and checking over an assortment of pistols, shotguns, and rifles. The question was where to stash my arsenal, as leaving it lying around the cabin was a no-go.

My compatriot walked me through his foolproof method of securing illicit weaponry—guns I wanted to keep accessible were stored in the space between the interior and exterior wall behind the Hercules painting. Everything else got greased and sealed into vacuum bags with oxygen absorbers, then slid into PVC pipes with caps screwed onto either end. We humped the collection to a hollow tree behind my shack, wrapped the works in a canvas tarp, and stashed it within.

Lionel explained he'd used a similar method to secure a quantity of semiautomatic and fully automatic assault rifles on the property. His stockpile hadn't come cheap. Ex-president Obama, a black northerner and liberal Democrat, terrified heaps of libertarians and conservatives. Conspiracy theories regarding UN databases and secret gun-confiscation programs had flourished, along with a concomitant run on tinfoil. The typical response whenever the GOP was ousted from power. On the bright side, Obama's retirement signaled an end to extortionate rates for weapons and ordinance.

"Jade would definitely not approve," Lionel said as we rested on the porch, him with a cigarette, me with a glass of cold lemonade. "'Live by the sword, die by the sword,' she'd say."

"Chop up the other bastard with your sword, is what *I* say."

"An excellent sentiment."

Emmitt, the salvage dealer, rumbled into the yard, leaning on his horn by way of greeting. The old man parked. He waved to Lionel.

Lionel slapped his knee and laughed.

"Oh, yeah! Almost forgot. I bought you a present." He went to the van and briefly chatted with the codger. Money changed hands. He returned toting a modest flat-screen television and a set of speakers. "Dunno where Emmitt scored this. Probably hot. But who gives a shit? Let's wire this puppy. I got about three tons of bootleg DVDs for you to peruse."

"No offense, but I'm not much for Bollywood porn."

"Okay, two-point-five tons of DVDs for you to check out."

BY FRIDAY MORNING the weather cooled and the easterly breeze tasted damp. I welcomed it. I welcomed *action* after the lull of preparation.

Calvin Knox's words continued to whisper in my hindbrain. Reba was definitely dead and one or more of the Three Amigos had done the deed. That they remained so conspicuously absent from the affairs of the world cemented their culpability in my estimation. How to find them and extract the truth? Via the White Manitou— and the direct route into the Manitou would be through someone the gang trusted or needed. I rolled the dice on the gang's interest in a steady supply of scrips supplied by an unscrupulous psychiatrist— Peyton. There were other ways. Ways more suited to a patient man.

Dr. Jefferson's garden party fit my purposes. One whale of a bash, highlighted in a preview on the society page of the *Kingston Star*. Local celebrities from every list would be in attendance. I made certain to put on clean underwear and my second-best suit, which was still "snazzy enough for government work," as Dad would've said.

THE JEFFERSONS WERE *nouveau riche*, and that by the skin of
their pearly whites. Wouldn't suspect the thinness of the veneer from
the aspen-girded drive, the topiary and fieldstone fences, much less
the elegant lines of their old Georgian mansion and the fleet of limos
and luxury cars arrayed in the huge white-cobbled lot. Clean-cut
boys in livery parked those fancy vehicles and toted handbags while
guests proceeded in twos toward the curving granite steps.

A functionary was probably supposed to check my invitation at
the massive oak-paneled door, but, seriously, of the countless times
I'd crashed parties over the years, nobody ever had the balls to try it.
Besides, I looked damned fine in my Brooks Brothers special. Made
me wistful I'd gone stag—Meg would've shone diamond bright on
my arm. Dangerous to think that way about a woman I hadn't even
slept with yet. Also, the lady was no trophy and would've slugged me
for even fantasizing it.

Oh, yes, I had it bad, which was bad.

I helped myself to a glass of pink champagne, albeit merely to
blend in. A one-drink limit was my vow for the evening. My preferred bull-in-a-china-shop approach might be less than useful in this
environment, if occasional prior experience of galas and high society
soirées could be trusted to guide me through the woods. This was a
vipers' pit, and, no mistake, keeping my wits was job one. Unless
someone pissed me off. Then I could booze it up for an imminent
battle. So that was the exception.

I put on a brute scowl and swaggered a bit. No takers, though.

The floors were either polished marble or covered in exquisite
Persian carpet. Furniture had been imported from exotic lands where
everything was carved for giants who adored scrollwork on every last
household decoration. The gold-tiled ceilings backed a hanging gar-

den of small chandeliers—a massive, multitiered affair glowed like the moon in the parlor where all too many suits and dresses congregated, sucking down cocktails between bouts of tittering, guffawing, donkey-braying peals of laughter. A quartet of solemn men played chamber music. I loathe chamber music unless it's performed by scantily clad lasses and the volume is dialed to zero, and I'm drunk.

Bobby the Whip, a Deluca soldier I'd met at the Sultan's Swing, bumped my arm as he waltzed by with his dame of the evening, a redhead who'd plastered on plenty of eye shadow and rouge. He winked and told me not to murder anybody if I could help it—it was a real nice party, see. I patted his arm and made no promises. I fleetingly speculated how long it'd be before I had to shoot him and a few of his wiseguy pals.

Deeming it best not to dwell on melancholy fantasies, I proceeded to mix with my betters. An attractive older lady in a taffeta gown gestured to several other women as she explained that the modern mansion stood upon the foundation of the Colonial house—a cannonball remained lodged in one of the walls to this very day! The hors d'oeuvres were tasty crab cakes, fancy crackers with dip, and caviar. Every time a waiter approached bearing a platter, I availed myself of the goodies and praised my forethought in arriving on an empty stomach.

Amidst sipping champagne, munching crab cakes, and smiling at the pretty lasses, I located one of my quarry. Dr. Neil Jefferson reposed on a divan near the cold hearth, surrounded by several men. From their receding hairlines and easy, if refined, jocularity, I took them for colleagues in the headshrinker racket. Dr. Jefferson was pushing fifty and billiard bald. He wore rimless glasses and, for reasons beyond me, a gray turtleneck. While conducting his audience, he nonetheless noted my presence. His lips curled into a momentary sneer that vanished as he devoted his attention to one of the sniggering sycophants and pretended to dismiss the spooky-eyed lummox encroaching upon his inner circle.

I'd performed due diligence. The good doctor graduated medical school in the late '80s and gone on to a distinguished and lucrative career. Fifteen years ago, his wife, Melinda, inherited a bit of money from her parents. Currently, she traveled in Spain pursuing her career as an architectural consultant. The union had produced one child: sweet dancing queen Kari. Reading between the lines of a hundred newspaper columns, I figured Dr. Jefferson to be well connected with law enforcement, and undoubtedly the darker element as well.

I set my empty glass on a passing tray. I crossed my arms and frowned the way heavies in movies do when they've come to collect a past-due debt. It had the desired effect.

Dr. Jefferson excused himself and approached.

"Hello. I don't believe we've met. Dr. Neil Jefferson. And you are . . . ?" His hand felt brittle and damp.

"The bell that tolls for thee, doc." I clamped my grip precisely enough to put a smidgeon of fear in his eyes.

"Hi, Uncle Eli!" Kari swept in and caught my elbow and stood on tiptoe to peck my cheek. "Dad, this is Reba Walker's uncle." She might as well have put air quotes around uncle. The blue dress and pearls were decidedly more conservative than the last ensemble I'd seen on her. Calvin Knox, who'd obviously been attending to the girl, was decked out in a tuxedo. He gave me a discreet thumbs-up.

"Uncle Eli," Dr. Jefferson said, comprehension dawning. "Kari says you've decided to assist in the search for Reba."

"Hi, and yes," I said.

"I invited him, Daddy." She dazzled me with a klieg-light-quality smile that said *Don't blow my cover stripping for thrills and dope.*

We'd see how it went. Everything was on the table.

Daddy dearest glanced from me to his daughter to her stylish older man with his *Super Fly* Afro and back again. Dr. Jefferson radiated a no doubt carefully cultivated aura of icy command. Just so, bracing him in his castle while his daughter and guests observed proved to be to my advantage. Cracks splintered his façade. The curl of his lip, the flare of his nostrils, suggested a slipping of control. Spasms ticked his left hand like he was trying to crush a walnut.

"Erm, how . . . nice," he said.

"Oh, oh—this is Calvin Knox," Kari said, reaching out and pulling Calvin's sleeve until he stepped forward. "He's a photographer."

Dr. Jefferson's expression revealed that he had jumped to unpleasant conclusions regarding the type of photography Calvin indulged in.

"Freelance news stories," Calvin said. He exuded an impressive combination of modesty and arrogance. "I was a war correspondent."

"He won an award!" Kari said, clutching his arm.

"Lovely," Dr. Jefferson said. "Which award?"

"The Pulitzer!"

"You won a Pulitzer?" I said to Calvin. "Do they even give those to black guys?"

"The white dude got robbed," he said.

Dr. Jefferson stroked his chin while propping his elbow in his free hand. Classic trick, that. Calvin's Pulitzer revelation hadn't seemed to impress him much.

"Fine, Eli. Perhaps you would care to join my friends and me for a drink?"

"I don't wish to meet your pals," I said. "We need to have a conversation. Private."

"Indeed?"

"Indeed, doc."

"As you will." He smoothed his turtleneck and frowned the frown of an important man tasked with a trivial yet inescapable obligation.

"Mr. Knox, help yourself to refreshments. Kari, please excuse me for a few minutes . . ."

"On second thought, she should tag along," I said.

Kari's smile wavered, then reasserted itself.

"If this is about Reba, yes, I want to hear what Uncle Eli has to say."

"Of course you do, kiddo," I said.

DR. JEFFERSON MADE HIS APOLOGIES to the other men and briskly shepherded us into his den. The books in cases were newish, lending the impression he'd acquired titles by the gross from central casting. He seated himself behind a pristine oak desk and made a steeple with his fingers to obscure his mouth.

"You dislike psychiatrists," he said, demonstrating his ability to read minds.

"I dislike lots and lots of people," I said and seated myself on the edge of the desk. I snagged a peppermint candy from the ornate glass bowl next to the chopping-block arrangement of fountain pens and a genuine human skull paperweight. "Gee, doc. I'm surprised you didn't go all out with quill and ink." I crunched the peppermint in my teeth.

"Touché. Second drawer, all the makings. Parchment, sealing wax, et cetera." He watched me intently.

"Your daughter is a stripper."

"Hey!" Kari gave an anguished yelp, smothered by her hand.

"The tension was killing me," I said. "Besides, your old man already knew."

"Daddy?"

"Yes, dear," Dr. Jefferson said.

Kari's sobs may or may not have been genuine. The rage in her teary eyes when she glared at me crackled convincingly enough.

Dr. Jefferson tutted and said, "You are quite excellent at innuendo and intimidation, sir. Thugs and lowlifes such as yourself gain much amusement from terrorizing the innocent. Is that why you came here? To embarrass and bully us? Kari, now you see why I didn't want you associating with that girl. This is the reward for your charity."

I counted to five and tried again.

"Reba is missing. The only thing I want—"

"I haven't a clue about where Reba Walker has gotten to. Nor does Kari. Dig for clues elsewhere—you've overstayed your welcome."

I sat on the edge of the desk and stared at him impassively.

"You remind me an awful lot of a guy I shot a few years ago. He too yipped and yapped with patrician arrogance. More important, he lied through his teeth and assumed I, an ignorant savage, would swallow it."

There were several ways Dr. Jefferson might've reacted. My expectations were divided among bluster and counterthreats of lawsuits, leave the premises or he'd summon the cops, or maybe a stammering denial. Instead, his shoulders sagged.

"Reba Walker likely ran afoul of criminals. She kept bad company."

"The last person to see her was your daughter," I said.

"No! Wait!" Kari wiped away tears. "I told the cops, I told you— she was at the apartment when I took off for work that day. I don't know where she went."

"Not to tell a plow horse how to pull, but perhaps you'd do better interrogating the ruffians with whom Ms. Walker associated," Dr. Jefferson said.

"Oh, that's why I'm here. Grove Street Academy and the Smyth and Coe pain clinic are pill mills." I showed him a bottle of Oxy-

Contin with Reba's name dated three weeks before. "I found bottles for five different medications. None of which she needs, according to her guardians. She's been off the program for a long time. There's Dr. Harold Peyton's name printed on the label. Odd."

"I don't oversee Grove or the clinic—"

"Dr. Harold Peyton." I waved the bottle. "A dear friend and colleague of yours. He's chowing down on caviar in the ballroom as we speak."

"Yes. Whatever you are accusing Dr. Peyton of—because we're associates—"

"Close personal buddies."

"—just because we're associates doesn't indicate any malfeasance on my part."

"Doesn't it?" I was enjoying this, his embarrassment, his dread and fear. Reformation hadn't cured my taste for tormenting assholes.

"Despite what you may believe, I'm not party to the corruption that has, allegedly, overtaken my colleague. Interrogate him, if you must. But I'd prefer you do it elsewhere."

"Nah, I don't really give a rat's ass about either of you. Your daughter is who I want. Kari ran with Reba and Reba's dubious associates as a thrill. Isn't that right, honey? For some reason, we never have an honest conversation. Doc, I hope you can prevail upon her to come clean and name names. Buy her a new car, a pony, whatever. The alternative isn't happy for anyone."

Kari dropped her hands and gaped. Comprehension shone through the dull outrage and sniveling.

"Daddy! I don't—"

Dr. Jefferson shook his head in warning. He'd assessed my demeanor and methods and arrived at an opinion about how far south this fiasco might be headed.

"Tell him so he can leave my house." He removed a pen from the block and pushed a memo pad across the table at her. "Write it down if you're afraid to speak it aloud."

I said, "By the way, doc. Might want to count your samples and prescription pads. Kari's dealer pals would never pass up an opportunity to exploit easy access to the candy store."

"Jesus Christ," Dr. Jefferson said. "Kari?"

She swayed, her eyes bright and huge and fragile as a child's. How many occasions had a subset of this psychodrama played out between them? *What do you fear? How did it make you feel? Where did he touch you? It's all right, write it down like a secret.*

I gritted my teeth and pressed on.

"Hank's in the wind. Who's your buyer now?"

"I don't know him." The light in my eyes caused her to gulp hard. "It's some guy."

"His name and his number. Right this goddamned instant." I laid it on thick—beetled brows, flaring nostrils, and spittle.

"His name is Goliad." Kari said it clipped and cold, her little-princess act in shreds. "He's a banger. Friend of Hank's. I talk to him only when I have to."

"Write it down like your daddy said."

She blinked the tears away and wrote the number on her daddy's business card. Then she looked at me. The artful sadness wiped clean and replaced by something glacial and ancient. The skull beneath the flesh.

ON MY WAY OUT OF that Gatsby-style shindig, I buttonholed Dr. Peyton as he hesitated with a pack of cigarettes near French doors that let into the garden. Apparently had returned from Seattle early. Easy to recognize from his staff photos. Fortyish, slight, dressed in a silk shirt and slacks. Knockoff Gucci shoes. From his house to his clothes, he barely accomplished a façade of making it compared to the bigger fish he swam among. No surprise he'd signed on to sell black-market meds hand over fist. I didn't require him for my plan to gain an audience with the Manitou and I doubted the gang had ever spoken to him directly. Nonetheless, I intended to make a splash.

I leaned against him and used my size and weight to casually muscle him into the darkness. My left hand maintained a solid clutch on his testicles, guiding him like a rudder. Old hat move on my part—over the course of a long and sordid career I'd grabbed more junk than a fluffer in Burbank.

I asked him for a light with a broad smile. From two feet away it would appear as if we were chummy and a little drunk.

"No more scrips under the table," I said close to his ear.

Peyton tried to answer. His throat clicked.

I gave his balls a tweak.

"No more scrips," I repeated.

"No more scrips," he said. Right or wrong, men are seldom in the mood to debate their innocence when their nuts are in a vise.

"Give me your cell phone." He did and I dialed Kari's connection with my free hand. A man, presumably the mysterious Goliad, answered on the third ring.

"Hold on a second and I'll patch you through to Dr. Peyton. Dr. Peyton of Smyth and Coe, the fella who makes it rain Oxy." I gave Peyton the phone. "Tell the nice man what you just promised me."

Dr. Peyton said, "Uh, this is Dr. Peyton. I'm done. I'm out. Please don't send anyone around." He hadn't the foggiest idea who he was talking to. He would've said anything to make the pain stop. I wondered what it said of my character that I'd spared Kari physical abuse and yet had no qualms inflicting it upon this pathetic creature. The road to redemption is paved with schmucks, perhaps?

I took his phone, shut off the power, and slipped it into my pocket.

"Disobey me and I won't report you to the cops, I'll come to your house and put a hurt on you. Four out of five doctors agree, it's tough to wipe your ass with a hook. We clear?"

"Clear . . . We're clear," Dr. Peyton said. His eyes shone.

"Mind if I borrow your phone for a day or two?"

He shook his head enthusiastically.

"Excellent. Damn, that was good for me." I released him and he slumped, clutching himself. "Enjoy the party, doc."

PART III

THE GORDIAN KNOT

THIRTY-ONE

It rained all night and in the morning the sky was black except for a funnel where the sun burned through. A giant red eye glaring down upon my cabin at the edge of the woods. I dialed the White Manitou banger, Goliad.

"Hi, gonad," I said when the guy picked up.

"Goliad." He cursed. Heavy breathing, then, "Who this?" Either he was too stupid to read caller ID or he'd decided on caginess.

"Your mystery date. What time I come to pick you up, honey?"

"What? You trippin', man? Who this?"

"The dude who cut off your supply with Dr. P."

Nothing for a few seconds.

"You trippin', punk."

"Hey, no sweat, gonad. Make your calls, then hit me back." I broke the connection and fixed breakfast. Fried three eggs and half a pound of thick-cut bacon. Coffee, black as night. I ate breakfast while the red eye in the sky closed and it rained again. Red sky in morning, sailor take warning. Already, the slow trickle of adrenaline filled my mouth with a metallic taste.

The phone beeped. Gonad's number.

"Good morning, trouble," a different voice said.

"Morning," I said. "You must be important. Let's have a sit-down. Talk-turkey time."

"Why would I agree to that? You could be anybody." By *anybody* he meant a cop.

"My name is Isaiah Coleridge. Check around. I'm legit."

He hung up. I poured more coffee and sipped it. Handing him my name without quid pro quo was a calculated risk. That said, his network would have obtained the information anyway.

My long affiliation with the mob—and the muddy circumstances regarding my current status—would give the Manitou pause before summarily whacking me, or so I hoped. The criminal organizations were locked in a cold war. I banked on the theory that neither side would escalate tensions via a casual murder unless it got voted on and sanctioned. More important, everything about me would appeal to a gang who preferred to recruit disaffected minorities.

Essentially, this was me crossing my fingers.

The callback came forty-five minutes later.

"Quite a rep you got, Coleridge. You were on-the-job for Chicago." He didn't give me the satisfaction of saying *the* Isaiah Coleridge! but I chose to assume it was implied.

"Once upon a time."

"Looking to audition?"

"Try again. I go for a better class of hoodlum. I'm looking for a girl. Dear friend of mine named Reba Walker. One of your homies knows her—Hank Stephens."

Silence suggested a gathering of wits.

"A puppy crying for attention, that's what you are," he said, still composed. "Making a scene."

"This isn't a scene."

"No?" He sounded amused.

"In the old days, I would've blasted and stabbed my way through your gang."

"In the old days, you had a posse to back your play."

"Make assumptions about the status of my posse at your own risk."

"I like you. What's the angle?"

"Tell me where to find the girl or Hank Stephens. I'll take either."

The guy chuckled. Pure evil.

"Too bad you went at our doctor friend so hard. The doc is small potatoes, but our potatoes. Pitch me the case for why you don't meet with an untimely fate before the week is out. Guy in your line doesn't have much of a life expectancy."

"First, you'll get a bunch of foot soldiers killed. Your bosses will *love* all the machine guns and fireballs going off in downtown Newburgh."

"Machine guns and fireballs? Really?"

"Ever watch that famous war movie? That's how it'll be."

"Which one?"

"The one where everybody dies."

He waited several beats. Other voices muttered in the background.

"Okay, my friend. Brashness is its own reward. Be at the corner of Hughes and Battery. One hour. Else we come hunting."

"*Two* hours," I said. I walked outside and stood under the dripping eave.

Lionel trudged along the path, his slicker splattered in mud. He chucked aside his pitchfork.

"We on?"

"We're on." I gave him the short version. "This is dangerous. They decide to whack me, they'll do anybody along for the ride."

"I'll secure firepower," he said. Happy at last.

PROBABLY NOTHING TOO TERRIBLE would happen. Probably.

Were violence a foregone conclusion, I wouldn't dream of leading us into a shooting gallery. Machiavelli once wrote about being unable to control fortune; however, a wise man digs channels to guide the flood. Thus, I got busy with pick and shovel. I put the revolver into the Monte Carlo's glove box and tucked the jade war club under the seat with my favorite Randall fighting knife. None of these items would escape notice by a remotely competent security sweep. Nonetheless, I wanted them near to hand if matters went south.

I'd dressed in my number three suit—charcoal gray, a patched-over bullet hole in the thigh. My business suit. Not snappy, not shabby. Loose enough to cover the fiberglass shiv taped to my ankle; I kept the blade because if I didn't leave a weapon for my enemies to confiscate, they'd be on their guard. From what I'd researched of the White Manitou, the rank and file were warm-up-jacket-and-sweatpants types. I pictured myself a black knight preparing to wade into the melee against peasants. If a knight meant to astound and demoralize a yokel mob, he had to dress the part.

Lionel was the wheelman. Haggard, chain-smoking Marlboro Reds; a vision of how he'd been in days of war. Water pearled against the windows and warped the universe into a black-and-white Impressionist's canvas. The interior flushed blue from smoke and stained light. I closed my eyes and relaxed by counting all the enemies I'd rubbed out. That always made me feel better.

Calvin joined us in New Paltz. Lionel had called him and explained the mission. He climbed in back and fist-bumped Lionel over the seat. I didn't bother to order him to go home, or warn him that there might be real trouble, or say he didn't owe us anything. His expression told the whole story. This guy had routinely entered war zones. A drive to the shady side of Newburgh wouldn't rattle him.

"I knew her, Horatio." He struck a match and lit a joint. He took a hit and passed it to Lionel. "We broke bread. She had an eye for photography. I let her borrow my camera for a few minutes. Still have a dozen shots she took of the farm on my hard drive."

"No shit," Lionel said.

I returned to my meditation and visualized our vehicle as seen from the eye of a crow. So fragile and insignificant amidst the thunder, the rushing wind, and the infrequent strokes of lightning. Three men connected tenuously by loose affiliation and camaraderie were headed directly into the belly of the beast on behalf of a young woman none of them called blood. I bore witness to a strange and wondrous event that felt suspiciously like a miracle. Rain dappled skull patterns upon the glass. That omen concerned me not a whit. I opened my mouth wide and took in several gulps of oxygen.

Newburgh sprawled by the sluggish Hudson River. Three centuries and counting. An imperial beauty gone long in the tooth and whose glamour had tarnished. The evil in her heart seeped through, blacked and crumbling as her warehouses, her factories, and her streets. Trees and shrubbery grew dense among benighted neighborhoods, albeit not in the manicured and tidy fashion of New Paltz but as an expression, or a warning, of the primeval wild that lurked always ready to overrun the works of civilization.

Newburgh, decaying Newburgh, collapsing back into the savage and superstitious darkness of the days when men first hacked its geometry from the forest and the marsh. Poetically fitting that the Manitou nested here, hatching plots.

We thudded across a set of train tracks into The Battery, which in the old days had been dubbed the artisan, vandal, or cutthroat's quarter, depending upon the decade. Here spread the rest of the city, inverted like a photographic negative. Abandoned storefronts with the windows smashed. Graffiti-slashed ruins of America's halcyon era. Rusted street signs. Broken glass in the street and dead vehicles. No police in view, but plenty of scrawny stray dogs. Plenty of scrawny stray kids brandishing sticks and bats as they prowled. Had this been a fork in a jungle path, skulls would've adorned a pole, proclaiming this the territory of one murderous tribe or another.

The rain slackened as we waited on the corner of Hughes and Battery. Here were the slums of the slums—abandoned lots, heaped with festering garbage, and rows of derelict brownstones. Sidewalks were crooked and split. The whole place appeared to have been hit with a mortar barrage, then left to decay.

I leaned against the hood. Calvin rested on the trunk. Lionel remained behind the wheel with the motor running. Both of them were carrying.

A door opened in the burned-out tenement to my right. *Opened* isn't quite the term—a skinny kid in a gray hoodie picked the door up and propped it against the wall when he emerged from his spot.

"Yo, roll on in," he said. He jogged toward an apartment complex half a block down and across the street. We idled along on his heels and eased through a covered accessway into a courtyard where weeds ran riot. Cars sat on blocks. Pieces of indoor furniture were scattered from hell to breakfast. Cinder blocks and assorted junk littered the walkways. Crows hopped and cawed, picking through trash and dog shit. As for the complex proper, two-thirds of the windows were blown in or boarded over. This was the land that time forgot.

Lionel parked about a hundred feet from a buckled chain-link fence that hemmed in a swimming pool. A mob gathered near the pool. Black, Latino, Indian, and a couple whose hoodies made it difficult to tell. Two of them restrained pit bulls on choke-collar leashes that didn't stop the dogs from slavering and barking. The louder was a brindle bitch accompanied by a scarcely weaned pup that cowered on her flank. Mama dog's teats sagged and swayed as she lunged. The handlers kept the beasts separated by centimeters while money traded hands amidst hoots and jeers.

The kid jerked his thumb toward the central entrance; a pair of metal doors guarded by a squad of foot soldiers. The thugs wore goose-down jackets, despite the humidity. A couple of them hefted machetes. Tattoos and scars and bad haircuts for the whole posse. They did a bang-up job looking mean.

I told my companions to wait. Neither were happy about it, but they stayed put.

At the entrance, an Indian with all kinds of piercings patted me down. His buddy ran a wand over me; got the nooks and crannies too. Nobody said anything. I followed the kid inside for my audience with the lord and master of all that ghetto opulence. Behind me, the dogs were tearing each other apart.

THIRTY-TWO

First floor of the White Manitou hideout, the Wigwam, as I'd heard Calvin refer to it, constricted into a nightmare of torn carpeting, spent syringes, and ground glass. Dark and pissy. Holes in the walls exposed wiring and pipes. An army of ne'er-do-wells had scrawled epithets and cryptic variations on the White Manitou sigil—a stylized wolf's head, jaws agape—into a grim, repeating mosaic. Here and there, figures lay on the floor or in stairwells. I covered my nose to block the reek of sewage and decay.

Against my better judgment, I boarded an elevator minus its ceiling tiles. The snaking guts of the shaft were exposed as the car rose to the fourth floor. The kid didn't speak. He faced the red-glowing number plate with his hands jammed into the pockets of his coat. I stepped out of the brassy coffin onto clean blue carpet. The inset lamps shone pure and bright. The fixtures were shiny. Walnut paneled the walls. It even smelled minty.

My guide buzzed number 456 at the end of the corridor. Another metal door, painted white and framed in baroque red scrollwork. A bust of a demonic wolf glowered from the lintel. The door swung wide and two men took possession of me. Both wore leather jackets, tight pants, and combat boots. The one in a pink-and-blue Mohawk frisked me while his partner, cauliflower-eared and flat-nosed, gave me a patented tough-guy glare. He ordered me to turn around and I recognized his voice.

I favored Cauliflower Ears with a deadpan expression.

"Gonad? Is that you?"

He didn't dignify my query with a comment.

Mohawk found the shiv taped to my ankle the other guy had missed. He smirked and made it vanish up his sleeve. He checked my ID and snapped a picture of me with his cell phone. The ID I'd given him was kind of fake, as it listed an old Alaska address.

"Man, visiting gangsters has gotten worse than going to the DMV," I said to no applause.

They prodded me into a long, well-lighted room. I took stock. Solid, serviceable furniture that had seen much use. Windows with a view of the courtyard. Bags of weed and pipes on a coffee table. Hardwood floor, which meant it'd be slippery if I had to juke or jive. Three younger men played video games on the flat-screen with the sound muted. Five more watched from couches and chairs. Everybody dressed casually, everybody drank bottled beer. I spotted three handguns and a Bowie knife.

Mohawk went through a curtain of beads in back. A minute later, he stuck his head out and signaled me to approach. The next room was much smaller and dimmer. An antechamber lighted by the biggest lava lamp I'd ever seen. Red shadows slithered across the walls.

"Isaiah Coleridge," said the man seated on a beanbag chair behind a low rectangular table of marble. Early thirties, medium build, dark hair cropped tight. Sharp cheekbones. Sharper fingernails. The light made it tricky to be certain; however, I figured him for Indian heritage. He wore a white silk shirt, short-sleeved. A pendant fashioned from jade. Rings galore. "Donnie Talon. We spoke on the phone. Pull up a rock. Have a cup of mud." He snapped his fingers and Mohawk threw down a beanbag for me.

I sat and accepted a china teacup of espresso. Strong enough to peel paint.

"Frankly, I'm underwhelmed at your projection of force. You Manitou boys are supposed to have an army."

"How's your espresso?"

"Bitter. Like my heart. So it's good." Too dim to tell if he got it.

"I acquired a taste for espresso while vacationing in eastern Turkey. There is no substitute for real, blindingly potent Turkish blend. Fuck creamer, fuck water, fuck any dilution. Toss it back and suffer the consequences as a man." He dabbed his lips with a cloth napkin. "My troops are where they are the most efficacious—performing clan business. Installing a platoon of grunts with automatic weapons around the home base is so damned extravagant. We are in a struggle with the Italians, the blacks, the Asians, the Mexicans. Boots on the ground wins the war."

I observed how the light cast his face into darkness and limned him with a crimson halo. I felt the heavy gaze of his bodyguards behind me in the shadows. Talon might be tough despite the fact he assuredly came equipped with rich parents and a trust fund. His mannerisms marked him as an elite richie of the first water in a way that poseurs such as Dr. Jefferson could only imitate. Rich, cultured, ruthless, and megalomaniacal. Dude had to be a maniac to squat here in the gothic gloom of a dead city in the hopes of expanding another man's empire. A dangerous foe, no question.

"Why fight?" I said. "Wouldn't you rather assimilate the other ethnic gangs?"

"Spend money to make money. Spill blood to get new blood pumping in."

"All very fascinating. We've business. Reba Walker."

"Reba Walker." He said her name with implied cruelty. "Your friend, huh?"

I sipped more of the cursed brew and calculated angles and force vectors and wished the shiv was still taped to my ankle.

"Eighteen. Yea tall. Brash. I'm looking for her."

"I've seen her around. You want to know if we have the girl. Fair question. She's a fine piece of ass. Nubile. Definitely the kind we send to the salt mines. The answer is no, we don't have her. We prefer our sex workers to come from the Rez or from overseas with the serial numbers filed off. Last thing we want is a concerned citizen like you, a long-lost uncle or Prince Valiant, sniffing around. Terrible business model."

I set my cup aside and folded my hands on the table. My hands are large and scarred as anvil heads.

"You don't have her."

"We do not."

"You're sure. Absolutely, positively cross-your-heart sure."

He crossed his heart with due solemnity.

"Then we come to the next question," I said.

"I don't care what happened to your niece. You, a pro hitter, wandering around asking lots of questions and interfering in business is a different story. How can we fix this? Right, there's a couple ways. One of which you won't enjoy. Since you're friendly with the Italians, I prefer not to act precipitously unless it's required. The nice way, we come to an agreement. What do you say, Coleridge? Can we make a deal?"

"Assuming you can point me in the direction of three characters who saw Reba last. Hank Stephens. Eddy Yellowknife. Philippe Martinez."

"Yes. Yes. And yes."

"Yes what?"

"Yes, I know them. Whether or not one of those worthies is cul-pable for a crime against the girl is not for me to say. The boys are in hiding. As to where . . ." He spread his hands and shrugged.

"So, you won't give them up."

"I *can't* give them up. They're incommunicado. Orders from the man himself."

This sounded suspiciously similar to how the Family dealt with internal politics, and it meshed with Agent Bellow's veiled comments and those by Calvin.

"Would the man be Larry Modine, chief of New York?"

"Well, it's not a big secret."

"I try and try to get my head around the whole deal with Hank Stephens. This is the time line I've drawn: Stephens defected from the Sons of the Iron Knife. Probably five seconds after the Sons real-ized, he had Seneca on the woodpile."

"Hank was scheduled for a lynching. He flew the coop due to necessity rather than newfound love of his heritage. We don't judge. Much."

"Right. You also liked the medical-dope pipeline he operated at Grove."

"Your 'niece' and her girlfriend were right in the middle of that action."

"Come on, Donnie. Once Hank bailed, Reba and her gal pal were the operation. Back to Hank—ancestry isn't enough for you. The Manitou demand more from recruits. An act of faith."

Donnie Talon appeared satisfied with my assessment.

"This only gets deeper for you. Understand?"

"I do."

"Doubtful. But you will—soon. The moment you walked in here, I put a leash around your neck. Every word cinches it, friend."

"Be a few more notches before I worry. Talk."

"So be it. My superiors wanted to bring in a white boy. Or I should qualify—a kid who'd pass for white."

"Equal opportunity employers?" I said.

"We can find a hundred and one uses for a honkey turncoat. However, a blood gift was the price of admittance."

"Hank blew away a Son to prove his sincere intentions? Ah, that's what that rascal Horsley didn't want to tell me."

"Hank shot his victim parked at a red light. He also dusted a passenger. The passenger was a young fellow whose daddy owns a chain of gun shops. Daddy is pissed. Daddy also has a direct line to the headman of the Iron Sons and enough money and influence to make his concerns heard."

"Whoops," I said.

"Big fucking whoops."

"No wonder the Sons of the Iron Knife are in such a tizzy. Their president lost enough face, he looks like the Phantom of the Opera. You say Hank is incommunicado. What does that mean?"

"Means he's under lock and key until we decide otherwise. A slew of folks want a piece of that white boy. We should put Hank's lily-white ass up for auction and retire on the proceeds."

"I'm surprised the punk is still breathing. Drop him in a hole and your problems disappear."

"The Mafia might do it like that. Our traditions are different."

"Tell me with a straight face that you heartless bastards don't snip loose ends when they become a liability."

"We do, as a last resort."

We stared at each other for several moments. The lava lamp burbled and made its darksome light.

"This isn't official Manitou headquarters," I said.

Talon showed his teeth.

"Perceptive. I'm not in the habit of bringing strangers home on the first date. What tipped you off?"

"Besides the lack of the aforementioned army? Not enough heads in baskets. Nobody spiked to a telephone pole in the yard. The things that make a home."

"Does it matter?"

Oh, it mattered. Excepting the obvious soldiers I'd encountered along the way, everybody else was a pretender, a thug-life hanger-on. The metallic taste came back.

"Recently, a friend had a dream about my adventures. I'm not the hero in that dream. I'm the Cyclops."

"Mr. Coleridge?"

"May I have my shiv? Going to need the shiv."

"Go home," Talon said. "When I think of a use for you, I'll snap my fingers."

I accepted the knife from Mohawk. My hands trembled. Talon's shadow on the wall bloomed and changed. A death's-head, of course. I'd passed the point of no return before I ever walked into that building.

"No," I said. "Put me in touch with our little pal, Hank. Else we can do it the bloody way. I love doing it that way."

So much worry in the crease of his brow. I loved that too.

One of the soldiers zapped me with a Taser to the neck and a fireworks show lit up my brain. I knocked the table aside in my reflexive lunge for Talon, but he moved too fast and another dose of high voltage went into me and I dropped, paralyzed.

Talon planted his foot on my chest, posing the way big game hunters are photographed with elephant carcasses.

"Such a brave man. Stupidly brave. You'd do well to cultivate a stronger sense of self-preservation."

When I could speak, I said, "It's a character flaw. I don't scare."

"Maybe I'll send you to the pits one fine day. Yes, you've heard of them? People think the pits are a boogeyman legend. They're not. We use old abandoned mines in Pennsylvania where nobody ever goes. Circus Maximus lives." He touched his leather belt. "Human flesh, don't you know. You're in the wilderness. However bad news you might be, it doesn't mean shit to the Manitou."

"There'll be a later," I managed.

"I already told you that, tough guy." He signaled to his stooges and a boot caught me in the jaw. It didn't hurt as much as they might've liked. I played dead anyhow.

I LAY COLLECTING MY THOUGHTS in the desecrated lobby. A rat lurked in its nest of wires. It watched me slowly come alive; first to my knees, then drag myself upright against the wall. Third occasion I'd been tased over the past decade or so. Occupational hazard. Seldom any fun, this felt worse than usual, although I morbidly appreciated how powerful the little devices had gotten.

Nobody tried to murder me as I exited the compound.

Calvin and Lionel remained where I'd posted them. Still on red alert. Definitely unhappy at my disheveled and roughed-up appearance. But safe and alive could be chalked up as a win in anybody's book.

The crowd at the pool had dwindled to five men standing around the fallen mama dog. She lay in blood. Her brindle had gone black as if she'd been soaked in tar. One of them knelt, a smoke hanging from his mouth, and crushed the dog's skull with two leisurely blows from a steel jack handle. The pong-pong of it rang across the courtyard. The puppy crawled toward its mama's quivering flank but came up short because of the rope leash attached to a bench. It cried mournfully and a couple of the guys laughed, and one kicked it sideways under the bench and it lay quietly.

None of the men paid any heed to us.

We got into the car and sat there, engine idling.

"Isaiah?" Lionel stared at me. "Where to?" His expression indicated he'd asked more than once.

I clasped Achilles' tags that lay, as ever, against my breast. Etched lettering had worn smooth in places.

"In my dreams, I always jump after him. I jump every time."

"What?" Lionel said.

"My old dog. He fell. He died."

He kept studying my expression, searching it for a clue.

Lazy black splotches crowded my peripheral vision. Wind whistled, as far off as the icy blackness around Pluto, and keened in my inner ear. I recalled the warmth of Achilles' fur under my hand as snow fell and the tundra stretched toward the purple-black of onrushing night. I wanted to ask Lionel if he was better or worse in his dreams. I couldn't seem to speak. My teeth ground together.

"Amigo." Lionel gripped my shoulder. He seemed as far away as the celestial chorus priming me for destruction.

I wiped my eyes with the heel of my hand. Red light flooded the compartment. I didn't know where it came from. My heart, beating faster and faster, made the redness, made the roaring in my ears.

"What are you laughing about?" Calvin said. "Lionel, what's going on? We gotta jet."

"He ain't laughing."

"Oh, fuck," Calvin said when he leaned forward to get a look at my face. "L Dog, tell me this isn't going down."

"Nah, brother. I'm with you at *Oh, fuck.* Get up here and take the wheel." Lionel popped the trunk, leaped out, and ran around back.

It took a couple tries for me to remember how to work the door handle. I felt clumsy and dislocated from my extremities. Then I was free and walking, unhurriedly yet briskly, toward the exultant dog-fighters. Sod swayed beneath my shoes with the yield of a trampoline. With every step I grew larger and more terrible.

I snagged a pair of cinder blocks from the rubble, let them dangle. The red eye in the sky dilated.

They saw me coming and hesitated three or four heartbeats too many. Disbelief will do that to a man. I stepped through a gap in the chain-link fence and chucked the block in my left hand. It sailed wide. The bangers froze into crouches. Good for me, like the slot machine of fortune coming to rest on triple death's-heads. I slung the other block underhand at a heavy guy in a yellow coat. The one who'd kicked the puppy. He didn't duck or dive, as one might logically assume. Instead, he reflexively tried to catch the incoming missile. He caught it, all right, directly in the chest, and his breath followed the thud and he pitched backward and hit the gray-green water of the pool.

I charged. Everything happened fast after that.

Behold the essence of violence. It's not about martial arts or slick John Woo gunplay. Those things don't function under the pressure that violence exerts upon its participants. Hand-to-hand combat is decided by velocity and initiative. Ferocity, tenacity, mass, and a reckless negligence toward one's own continued existence—that's what wins the battle. Except on this occasion I had no interest in winning.

I wanted to annihilate the world.

One of the smaller dudes had the right idea. He bolted toward the complex like an Olympic sprinter. Another went for his pistol, actually had the barrel swinging around, when his face blanked and he spun and fell, every cord to the mortal coil snipped. A rifle report boomed over my shoulder. Lionel, evening the odds. That left two standing. Jack-handle dog murderer and a young guy with long hair and a goatee.

If the duo had decided to split, they might've had a chance. Or at least one of them would have had a chance at escaping. Instead, they stood their ground. These two were accustomed to violence. It had been a friend their entire lives, I could see it in their chiseled faces and in how they braced themselves for the clash, loose and easy. In an instant I glimpsed every blow given and received by them, the backhands they dealt mouthy girlfriends, the beltings from their fathers, the midnight scrums in these pitiless lots of The Battery with fists, elbows, teeth. The film reel dissolved to cigarette burns and blackness because, for them, the story ended here.

As I rushed in, the man who'd killed the mama dog walloped me on the shoulder and neck with the jack handle. Fuck him, I didn't care. Goatee gave me several quick jabs to the ribs. I didn't feel any of it. I grabbed jack-handle dude by the collar, lifted him without effort, and slammed him into his partner, one bowling pin against another. Goatee sprawled to his hands and knees. He clutched a pocketknife but wasn't in much of a position to use it. I kicked him in the eye with my pointy wingtip. The force flipped him onto his back and glued him to the paved walkway.

I yanked straight down on the first guy's arm. His head snapped around like a game of Crack the Whip. The jack handle flew. He was probably finished from severed vertebrae, not that it mattered. I drew the shiv and clamped the back of his neck the way it's done in prison yards. Then I punched all seven jagged inches of fiberglass through his sternum and crunched his breastbone like an eggshell. His eyes widened and focused upon nothing. He gobbled and gagged in mute appeal to the death gods. I gave the blade a twist and wrenched it loose. I changed to an ice-pick grip and stabbed vertically down behind his collarbone the way the Romans did it. Buried it to the hilt twice. Blood squirted up into my face. I let him go. He hit the concrete and began to crawl. After a few feet, he stopped.

Splashing gradually brought me around again.

The man in the yellow jacket clung to the lip of the pool. Not a chance he'd clamber free on his own. His baggy, waterlogged clothes might as well have been cement. Twice I stamped on his fingers. He sagged back and paddled helplessly.

I picked up a telescopic pool skimmer.

"Hey, bro," he said between gasps. "Hey, man." He craned his neck as if something in the sky interested him, and flailed his arms.

I rested the end of the pole under his chin and pushed him away from the edge toward the deep green. He clung to the pole. I released my grip and waited. His head sank beneath the surface. Frantic, he mustered the strength to surge upward and breach. He pantomimed climbing a ladder. Three, four, five times. Slower and slower. His arms drifted apart and his coat billowed around him as he slid toward the bottom where white tiles sloped into murk.

Calvin had rolled the Monte Carlo over the grass to within a dozen paces of the massacre. Lionel stood behind the open passenger door, an M14 rifle braced against the frame. Meanwhile, the Manitou foot soldiers at the main entrance were agitated. Two had drawn pistols. The Indian held a cell phone to his ear and spoke animatedly. For a moment the urge to return to the building and murder everyone inside flared incandescent in my mind. I swallowed the urge.

The puppy came alive and pissed herself when I reeled her in by the rope leash. She sank her puppy fangs into my forearm. I wrapped her in my coat. She squirmed and wailed as I carried her to the car.

Calvin drove out through the covered access tunnel. The hail of gunfire I more than half expected didn't come. I cradled the pup tight, muttering inanities into her ear. She struggled for a bit, then fell into exhausted sleep. She whined in her dreams, wanting her mother. I knew the feeling.

We were halfway home before I realized I'd been slashed.

THIRTY-THREE

In the end, when I'm laid upon a slab, the scars that crisscross my naked corpse will form a road map of benighted territories. This day I'd added several points of interest and a fresh traveler's advisory.

The Monte Carlo barreled along at eighty-five and damn the traffic lights. Me in the backseat, arms wrapped around the pup. Nameless, faceless dead lay in my wake. Three, possibly four, men snuffed in a matter of thirty seconds. Not a personal record. Close, though. What set it apart from other occasions of wanton ultraviolence in my history of misdeeds? Nobody had pulled my strings. I owned it utterly.

I watched the tops of the trees drift by and thought perhaps Dad had it right. I was Oppenheimer's dread in microcosm, a miniature atom bomb. A destroyer of small things. Not worlds, nothing so grand, but individual bodies, individual lives. In little more than a week I'd crossed purposes with mercenaries, gangsters, white supremacists, hillbilly moonshiners, gangbangers, and Feds. Blood had spilled. As ever, blood was the currency of my existence. Blood was the standard.

It would always be this way. Men with guns, men with knives, men with evil intentions. My world, my tribe. My calling.

VIRGIL REDEEMED A MARKER with a cranky semi-retired veterinarian of long-standing acquaintance. They cleared a sturdy table in Virgil's workshop and made me lie across it. Jade folded towels and slipped them under my neck.

"You'll be fine, son," she said.

Dawn Walker arrived. She took a long, cold look at the mess. She cupped my cheek with her palm and cried.

The vet, a bluff iron-haired fellow with an Amish-style beard, rolled up his sleeves and got to work. He briskly scissored off my expensive tailored shirt. He felt my neck and examined my side.

"Hmm. Massive hematoma. No broken bones. Three shallow lacerations. One deep puncture wound. Nothing major got nicked. I can sew it up, give you antibiotics, but there's a risk of peritonitis. Get X-rays."

"Stitch me, doc," I said.

"Didn't expect to spend my golden years patching holes in wanted desperadoes," he said.

"I'll vouch for him," Virgil said.

The old veterinarian stuck me with a syringeload of dope and I soon became lost in the radiance of the lamp bulb above the table.

When the mists thinned and I became fully aware of my surroundings, my ribs were stitched and swaddled in thick bandages. I slumped in a plush office chair with a blanket draped over my shoulders. The vet packed his black bag and departed after admonishing the Walkers with dire predictions regarding my inevitable demise via inflammation and infection, if not misadventure.

Jade and Virgil watched me from their perch on a bench.

"Here we are again," she said.

"Did we ever leave?" he said. "You got a death wish, boy?"

"Hush. He doesn't have a death wish. He's an oaf."

"Ever see anybody metabolize anesthetic so quickly?"

"Being a lush is good for something, I guess," she said. "How do you feel, Isaiah?"

They'd given me a paper cup of lukewarm water. I sipped it to clear the rust from my throat.

"Like a million, minus nine hundred and ninety-nine thousand," I quipped through gritted teeth, nauseated from blood loss.

"Saved by fat," she said. "Like trying to stab a walrus with a toothpick. Virg would've had half his organs pierced."

"Vital ones," Virgil said.

I laughed, which proved to be a mistake. White-hot sparks burned through my insides. I caught my breath and said I'd best get a solid night's sleep to be ready for morning chores.

"Nonsense," Jade said. "I'll not have you splitting yourself wide open after the effort we put into sewing your sorry carcass together. Show some respect. You will rest at least until your innards cease oozing forth. No sass."

I opened my mouth to sass and she wagged her finger.

End of discussion.

THUS, FOR THE NEXT FEW DAYS of my miserable life, I convalesced at the farm and stewed. I made calls and went over the facts of the case a hundred ways from Sunday. I watched home movies Jade and Virgil had filmed of Reba at Christmas and birthday parties. Most were taken during her adolescence. She'd smiled more as a little girl.

Depression isn't my style. I tend to fight the blues like I fight any other opponent—tooth and nail. The dolor that colored my mood wouldn't submit so easily. The devil on my left shoulder, with his horns and tail, reminded me that I'd failed. Failed to extract Reba's whereabouts from the clues, failed to extort the information from her known associates, failed to force Donnie Talon's hand, and failed to locate that missing link, Hank Stephens. A goose egg for Team Coleridge.

Simple math. Because of these failures, the opportunity to find Reba Walker among the living had likely evaporated. I felt as if the investigation had shifted from a search-and-rescue to a search for a body.

Jade and the vet were right—the slashes were flesh wounds except for one that glanced off a rib and went in a couple of inches. Nasty and debilitating, albeit far from life-threatening as long as I didn't get infected or push too hard and burst the stitches. Fat might have helped. The jacket even more so.

Defying doctor's orders, I toddled around the farm and worked to civilize the puppy. I named her Minerva after the goddess of wisdom. Maybe she'd live up to her namesake and it would rub off on me. After bathing and combing her, I beheld a gorgeous brindle with alternating black and white paws and brown eyes. I took her to the clinic and had her wormed and vaccinated. They estimated her to be around eleven weeks old. Skinny and flea-bitten, but in good health. An alpha female, the vet said. Her initial shyness had waned and she followed me during my rounds, slept curled against the small of my back at night. Sudden noises caused her to startle. No more cowering, though. She'd growl until I patted her and promised all was well. A fierce pup who'd grow into a large, aggressive protector, if I knew anything.

Two new females. My life got more dangerous every day.

LIONEL AND I SAT ON MY PORCH after splitting a cord of firewood. Virgil came around and looked us over. He squinted and spat tobacco.

"Come on, boys." He got a fire going in the sauna. "Do you good. Get in there. I'll check on you in a bit."

I stripped and went inside. Lionel followed. Dark and cramped. The ceiling lowered over us like a coffin lid. We steamed for a while.

Eventually, Lionel spoke.

"What is it with you and animals? Honestly, dude. You're a good guy to hang with and so forth. But, damn, underneath you're cold as an ice cube. Don't get me wrong—I like that. Man needs to know his partner is a cool customer. Except, there's this whole other side. First you get riled over a bunch of walruses. Then you lose your shit about dogfighting, with predictable consequences. Ever get that pissed over actual, you know, human beings?"

"Innocence," I said.

"Innocence?"

"There's an innocence you only find in babies, old folks, and the mentally challenged. And beasts." I nearly told him about Achilles. The words didn't come. Not then. Instead I said, "Sorry about your rifle." The other night I'd staggered into his cabin with a thank-you bottle of scotch and found him taking a hacksaw to the M14. Subsequently, the pieces were scattered in various bodies of water.

He wiped sweat from his brow with a rag and told me not to worry, it hadn't been particularly valuable. We tacitly avoided the subject of Reba and stuck to bullshit. How did I feel? The weather. Minerva.

Finally, after a long silence, I said, "Was that guy your first kill?

Outside of the war?" I meant the one in The Battery who'd gone for his piece and got blown to kingdom come for his troubles.

"Outside of the war? Yeah."

"He would've drilled me if you hadn't taken him. I owe you my life."

"Come on."

"No, really. Nothing is the same as before I came east. I've lost a step. Maybe two steps." I touched the lump of bandages where it pressed through my shirt.

"Looked fast enough from where I stood. Think anybody will come after us?"

"Possibly."

"You seem cool about it."

"It won't amount to anything with the law. The cops don't care about what happens in The Battery. It's the underworld. The gang might be another matter. Those weren't Manitou bangers, luckily. They were prospects. Have to expect Talon will put the squeeze on us."

"Okay." Lionel rubbed his eyes with a cloth. "I've talked with Virg and Jade . . ."

"Are they afraid?" Regular folks had a tendency to like me until I showed my fangs.

"No, man. I think they love you. I been under fire in two fucking war zones and I ain't seen anything ballsier than what you did back there. Nah, we're trying to figure how you're still alive. Alive and walking around, no less."

"My boss, an old guy named Apollo, used to call me Mr. Unkillable."

"Got stabbed a lot, huh?"

"I'm a klutz."

The tiny door to the enclosure creaked and Virgil stooped inside with a towel wrapped around his middle.

"Sounds serious in here."

He ladled water onto the heated stones. The resultant hiss and fume of steam comforted me in a way I hadn't expected. Steam and shadow clouded the faces of my companions. The red glow of the coals made it seem as if we'd descended into a cavern, deep in the bowels of the earth, and hunkered around a primordial flame.

"I rolled a tractor in the back forty," Virgil said. "Eleven years ago this summer. Broke my legs and my back. Got my good days and my bad days. Never been the same. Fact is, time has done caught up with Jade and me."

"You, sir, are one tough sonofabitch," Lionel said.

"Used to be, sonny boy. I damned well used to be." The old man pinched my biceps with his gnarled fingers. "Now you listen, Isaiah Coleridge."

"Please, I bruise easily."

"You've been moping around. I don't like it. Neither does the missus. You've got miles to go yet."

"I'll suck it up, Mr. Walker."

He leaned forward so I could see his eyes shining red, so I could see he had my number.

"Nobody ever truly changes. Not even the heroes in the epics."

"Did my father call? That's his favorite saying."

"Shoot straight, boy. What's behind it all? Man can't go on like you are without asking himself the hard questions."

"Amen," Lionel said.

"Mr. Walker—" I shut my mouth and tried again. "Penance."

"Aha." He released me and drifted back into the murk.

Fate had tracked me across the years and four thousand miles of

Canada and the continental USA. It had finally caught up. I understood that part of the great mystery, at least.

"Can't explain it any better than that."

"Hah, you're doing fine. First honest talk since you came here. Change isn't always necessary. It's enough to dig beneath the surface and unearth another layer. Pretend you're busting rocks in the pen. Keep peeling back the layers."

I smiled uneasily.

"Addition via subtraction, eh? What happens when you run out of layers?"

"You're dead, dumbass. Speaking of death, I bet you wondered why we didn't ship you off to Kingston General when you got pneumonia after the Fire Festival."

"My mother was a traditionalist," I said.

"A traditionalist?"

"She refused to take us to a Western doctor for almost anything. She called hospitals death houses. Made us kids swill her own home remedies that would scour the bark off a tree from the smell alone. That's probably why bullets ricochet off me."

"It wasn't pneumonia," Virgil said. "Wasn't a fever born of plague. Your sickness came from the inner darkness, Isaiah. Those days and nights you spent clawing at the sheets? You were sweating out evils. No hospital could fix what's wrong. There are demons in you, battling for your soul."

"So, you were smoking them demons out?"

"That's right."

"I think you missed some," Lionel said.

THIRTY-FOUR

Detectives Rourke and Collins came for me in the afternoon.

"Get in the car, handsome. I've got free candy!" Collins gestured to me from the rolled-down window on the passenger side. With her frazzled blonde 'do and perfunctory makeup, she could've been a world-weary soccer mom in a cheap suit.

I got in back and tried not to let on how woozy I felt. The car smelled of stale fast food, Aqua Velva, and cigarette smoke.

She twisted in her seat and regarded me through the mesh partition.

"Oh, honey. Your poor face. Gets worse every time I see you."

"It's a good look for him," Detective Rourke said.

The only witness to my departure was old Emmitt. He'd parked on the road near the main house to tinker with the running lights on his van. I inclined my head at him through the dusty window. He watched us go past, a wrench poised in his fist.

We rolled through the countryside and into Kingston. They cuffed me, hands in front with my coat draped over them, and led me through the back of the police station into an interview room. The dynamic duo, me, and a table.

Rourke attached a light chain to my cuffs and looped it through an eyebolt in the table. The sort of arrangement cops had in place for ax murderers, outlaw bikers, and similar maniacs. He clamped a manacle around my ankle and shackled me to a D ring in the floor. That's when I decided I might be in a lot of trouble.

Collins placed an opened can of Coke in front of me. I remained calm. I needed to figure their angle. Shakedowns and rousts came with the territory, the same as getting punched and shot at. Or stabbed. Despite the fact these two bozos were in Curtis's pocket, they still had jobs to protect. I'd expected fallout from The Battery debacle. On the other hand, it paid to be cagey. Cops who answered to more than one master could be running any number of games.

"Isn't someone supposed to read me my rights?" I said.

"You don't have no stinkin' rights," Rourke said.

"We aren't required to give a Miranda advisory," Collins said. "Haven't you followed the Supreme Court? It was all over C-SPAN."

"You aren't under arrest," Rourke said. "The restraints are for your protection."

"Super. I'm free to go?"

"Absolutely. Once you burst them irons and break down a locked door."

We all shared a laugh at his wit. I glanced over at the long rectangle of one-way glass. Bruises, old and fresh, patterned my mug in yellow and purple with jags of autumnal brown. At least all my teeth gleamed when I smiled for the camera.

Rourke placed a manila folder and a recorder on the table. He asked me to state my name for the record.

"It defies logic," he said. "A six-month stretch for simple assault. Four months for battery. Three months for battery. Ninety days for obstruction of justice. Suspended sentences out the wazoo for, what else, assault and battery. Miraculous. In all those years, doing what you do, you didn't notch a single felony. I mean, that's kinda rare, Coleridge. Mafiosos usually got a rap sheet a giraffe could wear for a floor-length stole. Contract killers are more circumspect. I make you for a hitter."

"If you say so, Detective."

He flipped pages and shook his head.

"You've never been held accountable for the maiming, torture, and murder you committed on behalf of the Chicago Outfit and Mr. Lucius Apollo in particular. A lot of missing wiseguys in your old neck of the woods."

"Alaska is a hazardous environment."

"I gotta hunch it's a lot less hazardous with you in the wind."

"Were I guilty of heinous deeds, surely you crackerjack law enforcement agents would've swooped in and settled my hash."

"Keep running that lip, boy. You and your fifty-cent words, that college education. Despite the leg-up Apollo bought you, it's no surprise you turned out rotten. Like father, like son. Mervin killed your mama. Hit her with an oar. Left a mark on you too, didn't it?"

"Oh, sweetie," Detective Collins said. "Is that true? Did your daddy bash your mama's brains in?"

"Says so right here." Rourke tapped the folder. "Two went out onto Black Loon Lake. One came back. Papa Coleridge claimed it was an accident. Coroner ruled death by misadventure and the powers that be swept it under the rug. Must be nice to have juice with Air Force command. Anyhow, that's about the time you took up the thug life. Military brat to teen menace. Gangs, fight clubs, eventually the Outfit. Your path went downhill on a bobsled with no brakes." He bared mismatched silver and yellow teeth and flicked a glance toward the security camera scoping us from the corner.

Detective Collins accepted a pair of photographs from the folder and slid them before me. Before and after pics. The first—Dr. Peyton smiling into the lens at a family dinner. The second—Dr. Peyton's severed head smiling soullessly from an open mailbox. The White Manitou had sent me a love note.

"Mr. Coleridge, according to witnesses, you recently had words with this individual at a certain gala . . ."

"I'm sorry, Officer. You'll have to ask my attorney."

"Let the record show the subject requested an attorney," Rourke said.

"Begging to differ," Collins said, removing her shoes and setting them aside. "What the subject said was, he wanted to do this the hard way." She slipped on a set of brass knuckles. Lefty. She stared into the camera. "Do you concur?"

To my chagrin, the brass knuckles were mine.

A moment later, the door opened and in strolled Mr. FBI himself, Timothy Noonan. He leaned against the wall and sucked on a toothpick.

"Confirmed," he said. "The man chose the hard way."

"Hark, the other shoe has dropped," I said.

"I stand corrected," Rourke said. "Please, give Mr. Coleridge what he wants."

Apparently, I wanted three hooks to the body, because that's what Detective Collins delivered. It actually hurt, mainly due to the previous wounds and the fact that she put her back into it. I didn't have the heart to tell her I'd been here before with professionals.

I rested my face against the table.

"She has three mouthy teenagers," Rourke said. "Lot of aggression to vent."

"Didn't we tell you to stay away from the Walker case?" Agent

Noonan said. "Didn't we, swear to Christ, tell you to mind your knitting?"

"There isn't a Walker case." I couldn't quite catch my breath no matter how hard I tried.

Collins stood near my right flank. She hit me again. I resisted the urge to thrash or curl inward like a worm. My tormentors would've enjoyed it.

"Rourke, I'm disappointed in this turn of events," I said when I could breathe again. "We had a nice arrangement. You steered me where I needed to go. *Et tu,* asshole?"

Detective Rourke kicked back with his hands clasped behind his head.

"Coleridge, buddy, this *is* sort of my fault. When we made our deal, I didn't realize our friend Mr. FBI had waved you off. You shoulda apprised me. You really, really shoulda listened to Agent Noonan. His pockets are deeper than yours."

"Ah, you're the town pump."

"Be nice, Coleridge."

Collins slugged my kidney for emphasis.

I turned my head to meet her gaze and grinned.

"Don't look at me, bitch!" She backhanded me across the chops. A love tap. The brass knuckles cut my cheek and bounced my skull off the tabletop. So much for *honey, sugar,* and *darling.* Soccer-mom façade peeled away to reveal the blackness.

My ears rang. I didn't hear the exchange among the three of them. Noonan approached and studied the floor under my chair.

"What the hell is this? He's bleeding all over the place."

Collins tore open my shirt and discovered the sopped-through bandages.

"I told you boys—you won't get anywhere beating on him."

Rourke raised his voice. "He won't crack. I mean, my God. He's been tortured. I haven't seen scars like this since Iraq."

"Er, I think you've killed the bastard," Noonan said to Collins.

"He'll be okay." She didn't sound convinced.

"Becky, he's busted wide," Rourke said. "Guys, he get shot or what?"

"I don't know." She sounded panicky now. "Yeah, that's a lot of blood."

Nobody asked my opinion. My vision took on a fishbowl quality. The fluorescent lights pulsed in time with the blood oozing from my side. A nap would've been good.

Rourke pocketed the recorder. Even now, his flabby, hangdog expression more melancholy than upset.

"*Pear-shaped.* That's the word for our situation. Isn't quite what I had in mind, Noonan."

"Deal with the facts," Noonan said. "Officer Cupcake did a number on this creep."

"We gotta move him. My lieutenant walks in here, we're truly hosed."

"God damn it," Noonan said. "Put him in the car. We'll take a ride."

"Excuse me?" Rourke stuck a finger in his ear. "Let me clear the wax. What did you say?"

"Get him on his feet and put him in the car."

"Hang on, Agent. We'll say he resisted, there ensued a scuffle, yada yada."

Noonan swiveled his head, raptor-like, and regarded Detective Rourke.

"He's been stepping on dicks left, right, and center. Time to flush."

"Whoa, boys," Collins said. "This is escalating, like, I dunno."

"Your mess," Rourke said to Noonan.

"Think so, Detective? You must be forgetting that two-inch file on your sorry asses. It doesn't even include the latest hits, such as you passing this fucker information vital to my investigation. I own you. Both of you." Noonan removed his glasses and slipped them into his pocket. His eyes were steely. "Get him in your car. I'll follow. Coleridge, you hear me? We're going to get you help."

Rourke bent to unlock my ankle shackle and exposed the nape of his neck near my elbow. Hard not to snap his spine then and there. Agent Noonan watched closely, hand on the butt of his automatic. I bided my time. Not the best plan I'd ever formulated.

I'D BEEN IN THIS KIND OF SPOT often enough to forego the woe-is-me-this-can't-be-happening crap. We were in the underworld. Anything goes in the underworld.

Acknowledgment didn't equal acceptance. It might've appeared that I was solely preoccupied with bleeding. On the contrary, my mind spun the hamster wheel until smoke trailed from the spindle. I still couldn't dream up a way to extricate myself from the predicament of being severely wounded, cuffed, and locked in the back of a car with armed cops hustling me to an untimely demise.

Collins took the wheel. She cruised from the comforting climes of town, into the boondocks, and down a series of back roads. One thing I've learned is, in my line you don't ever want to go for a ride in the country. The trail ended at a ravine. A bullet-riddled billboard said JENSON EXCAVATION. Except for a stripped and rusted tractor, all signs of habitation were long subsumed by encroaching wilderness. An excellent location to dump a corpse.

"Outta the car, longhair," Rourke said jovially and helped me exit.

My legs wobbled. The world did a slow, ponderous spin until I leaned against the car and sucked deep breaths.

"Honey, hang in there." Detective Collins wore her sad, motherly smile again.

"Got a personal question." Agent Noonan proved a cautious sort. He stood well beyond the reach of my arms, shackled or not. "Why didn't Talon put a bullet behind your ear?"

"I'm charming?" Well, that confirmed this wasn't reprisal for my boorishness at Dr. Jefferson's party. Noonan and Bellow were aware I'd been in contact with the Manitou. I wondered what it meant. Was Noonan in cahoots with Talon? Had he expected the Manitou to execute me on the spot? Had he asked? Preposterous, fanciful, insane. Except, anything goes in the underworld.

"I've got a personal question for you too. Why are you helping Talon?" It was a shot in the dark. Color me shocked that the bullet struck home.

His pained expression reflected the convergence of a thousand points of doubt.

"Asshole, there are games within games. Feeding a predator poisoned bait isn't quite the same as helping it."

"Yeah, right. Naturally, you turn over the kickbacks to accounting."

"I wouldn't expect a thug to appreciate the artistry of nuance or deception. Or the concept of the greater good."

Ah, my oafish countenance had fooled an enemy for once.

"I *do* appreciate self-righteousness, Mr. Agent."

"Admonishment from a hit man? Rich. Occasionally, I get to set the universe right. Adios, Coleridge." Noonan nodded to Detective Rourke.

Most colors in the landscape had drained to grainy shades of gray. The situation became more surreal by the second. Cops disappeared plenty of people. What boggled my mind was the brazenness of their plot. Were they actually going to whack me after parading me in and out of the precinct station? On the face of it, the conclusion seemed preposterous. Government buildings are wired for sound. My arrival and departure had been recorded. They'd never get away with this. The devil on my shoulder snickered and reminded me that a gold badge, such as Rourke or Collins, could easily find a way to erase a little incriminating surveillance footage.

An ex–contract hitter disappears? An ex-hitter with this skin, this face? Nobody in white-bread USA would care. Reba could've schooled me in that regard.

Rourke took a cheap holdout pistol from his waistband and racked the slide. He gestured toward an overgrown path into darkness.

"Up yours," I said.

He strode over, laid the barrel against my head, and cocked the hammer. A rookie blunder. Step inside my arm's reach, you've had it. They'd cuffed my hands in front. One swift loop and a jerk, his neck would be sliced and snapped, neat as a chicken's. His pals would open fire about two seconds later. That's two eternities. Even money had me taking down Collins too before my heart pumped out the last of my blood. A pleasant thought. I've learned to take consolation where it lies.

"Good news, Detective," I said to Rourke. "Today you retire."

Gravel crunched and another nondescript sedan rolled around the corner. Agent Bellow climbed out. He took in the situation and lit a cigarette.

I laughed even though it hurt.

"Uh-oh, everybody. Act natural. Daddy's home."

"Stow the guns, gentlemen and lady," Bellow said. "Agent Noonan, come over here for a second, please. Detective Rourke, I said put that gun away or we're going to have a serious problem. Thank you."

Detective Rourke eased the hammer down. He stepped back and made the piece disappear. His hangdog expression remained in place the way it might if his favorite show was preempted by breaking news. Spooky dude. I felt a brotherly bond developing between us.

"God damn it," Noonan said.

THIRTY-FIVE

Are you dying?" Agent Bellow didn't sound concerned one way or the other, although he drove way too fast. Coincidentally, I'd spent the past few minutes waiting to discover the answer to that very question.

My shirt had soaked black. Dying? This felt nowhere near dying. However, I did estimate my blood to be a quart or two low.

"Nah. Be fine after I get zipped up again. How'd you find the party?"

"GPS in Tim's cell. Don't tell him he's bugged. Old dogs got to keep ahead of the pups by any means."

There'd been a brief argument between Bellow and Noonan back at the would-be murder site. Apparently, Bellow won. We'd left the others behind. More houses appeared as we reversed our route back toward Kingston. Death to life—again.

Along the way, I confessed my visit to Donnie Talon and the sequence of events that followed. I omitted the homicide details.

"I've worked with Tim since he graduated Quantico," Bellow said. "He's thirty-one. A baby. My day, it took fifte, twenty years for that institutional darkness to creep in. Guys like me? We all had skins on the wall and a retirement portfolio before we got so damned jaded. Now they come out of the academy like that. Evil old men peeking through the eyes of kids. Fucking terrifying."

"Dramatic timing you've got." I pressed the soggy bandages to be on the safe side.

He punched the dash lighter. When it popped, he lit another cigarette.

"Deus ex machina happens."

"Truth is stranger than fiction, granted. Or it could be you orchestrated the whole scenario. Maybe I was never in any danger of getting my head blown off. Maybe you need me to owe you one."

He puffed his cigarette.

"Would it make you feel better to believe that?"

He drove to an emergency clinic in the industrial heart of old Kingston. A sullen doctor gave me the once-over with none-too-gentle pokes and prods. Another local anesthetic and more stitches while Vivaldi sang a lullaby. I napped on the table, basking in the white light of the operating lamp. The routine verged on old hat.

Eventually, Bellow woke me, gave me a shoulder to slump against as we sallied forth.

The doc accepted a handful of cash from the agent and sent us on our merry way sans paperwork or guff about bed rest. A Syndicate doc or simply a guy jaded beyond repair by all the gangbangers and homicidal blue-collar drunks he'd tended. He did, however, hand me a paper bag rattling with pain pills and antibiotics as a door prize.

"Got anything in there for a pain in the ass?" Agent Bellow said.

LIONEL MET US AT MY CABIN. I collapsed into the easy chair and nursed a glass of whiskey and caught him up to speed with the day's events. After a bout of frantic barks and puppy cavorting, Minerva draped herself across my feet and snoozed.

"Cute pup," Bellow said. "A recent addition to the Coleridge household?"

"She hates pigs," Lionel said. He poured a glass and handed it over without meeting Bellow's eye.

"A fellow traveler," I said.

"You probably shouldn't mix this shit." Lionel squinted at my latest bottle of pills.

"I'll risk courting death this once."

"What a mess." Bellow lit a cigarette. "My balls-up entirely. I should've sent Tim back to Virginia. Or I should've brought *you* in before you went on a one-man rampage through The Battery."

"A *three-man* rampage," Lionel said, well into another drunk. "Here's the headline news, Agent. I didn't risk my ass in Afghanistan for the American way of life to have jackbooted sonsofbitches stomp in here and abduct my friends and threaten to dump 'em in the woods. This ain't a banana republic. This ain't Mexico. Or Chile. I've half a mind to load for bear and go put down that fuckhead partner of yours."

"Easy, killer," I said.

"Fair enough," Bellow said. "I didn't sign up for this bullshit either. Nonetheless, it isn't anything new. We've used questionable methods to achieve our aims since the Capone era, since Hoover and his rubber-hose brigade."

"It's a war," I said. "No hard feelings."

"You serious, dude?" Lionel rolled his eyes and poured another Johnnie Walker. He slapped the empty bottle across the room, ricocheted it off the far wall. Minerva growled and peed on my sock.

I lifted the pup into my lap and soothed her.

"Noonan was right, Lionel. This leopard's spots aren't going to change. I'm a bad guy. Been playing that role for twenty years." I looked at Bellow. "What you've got to understand, what you've got to make your partner understand, is that this time I'm on the side of angels."

"Ah, well. There's more than one kind of angel, right? Blood-thirsty crowd, the seraphim."

"I'm not going to stop unless you kill me."

"Oh, we received that signal, loud and clear," the agent said. "I apologize for what happened today. I'll square it away with Tim and Kingston's finest. There won't be a repeat performance. My word."

"We're good," I said. "Truly."

"Thank you for your courtesy." Bellow dragged a chair across from mine and sat. "Agent Noonan and I are liaising with the Gang Task Force Special Division. We're investigating the White Manitou. The details aren't important. Nearly three weeks ago, I lost contact with an undercover informant. He goes by Philippe Martinez. Last winter, my man observed Henry Stephens and Eddy Yellowknife murder a member of a rival gang. Stephens's initiation ceremony. The order came from the New York boss, Larry Modine."

"I'm familiar with the name," I said.

"Martinez also witnessed the Skype conversation between Modine and one of Talon's lieutenants. Even better, he can place several other ranking Manitou officers at the meeting. That, in and of itself, is a nice piece of evidence, but there's a lot more."

"Skype?" Lionel said. "No shit?"

Bellow ignored him. He'd gotten plenty of practice with Agent Noonan.

"Martinez knows of a dozen murders, twice that many dope deals, and a metric fucking ton of heists and hijackings. As I said, we've built this case going on two years. Pure poison for Modine.

Unfortunately, word leaked out to the head honchos that the Bureau is watching. They don't know about Martinez, or so we hope. Chatter we've intercepted doesn't indicate he's been compromised—but they have suspicions regarding a mole. Those sonofabitches will root him out eventually. Meanwhile, in the absence of solid intelligence regarding our operation, the gang responded by ordering a whole slew of their crew to go underground."

I nodded.

"Donnie Talon said as much. You'll get a gold-plated commendations pinned to your chest if you take down this Modine character, eh?"

"Medals don't interest me, Coleridge. I'm more concerned Manitou management may decide to cut its losses and ice these guys who are in hiding. See, the local chapter answers to a kind of tribal council. Powerful bastards you'd know if you read the business section or society page. Modine or one of the other elders snaps his fingers and heads roll. Lots of heads. Labor is cheap in the Manitou hierarchy. The chiefs don't bat an eye to spend lives. By our count, there are nineteen bangers in limbo with the sword of Damocles hanging over them."

"Nineteen. Huh. Be a real bloodbath." The world would be a better place for the pruning. I didn't say it aloud.

"Our saving grace lies in the fact that these guys don't all work directly for Modine. Better still, Modine is at odds with a couple of other bosses. I figure that's why he hasn't dared to make a precipitous move. The clans take frequent potshots at each other."

"The gang version of a filibuster," I said. "Same deal with the Outfit."

"About the size of it. As you might imagine, the Bureau has a singular interest and that is in retrieving our informant and debriefing him. My stake is personal." Bellow leaned over and scratched Minerva behind the ears. "Commendations don't mean squat. I know Martinez. He's a tough guy, a criminal. He's also got a wife and kids. A dog."

I smiled at him.

"A dog? In that case . . ."

"He's a friend and I want him safe." Bellow exhaled a plume of smoke. "Maybe now you understand why we asked you to keep clear of this thing. God knows what'll come of your visit to the Wigwam. You really stirred the pot."

"Why didn't you pull the guy out before? He's got the goods on Modine and others. Isn't a murder rap enough? Why wait?"

"Short answer? The Bureau is greedy. They want Talon too. Talon is slick; we could never pin anything on him. Martinez tried to get close. Got himself assigned to the man's entourage. Talon was never around when the dirty deals transpired. I swear, my mother was right when she said Satan looks after his own."

"We're gonna find Reba," Lionel said. "Sorry if that interferes with your snipe hunt."

"It's not a snipe hunt," Bellow said. His eyes narrowed and he scowled. The most emotion I'd seen from him. The bland mask snapped into place again. "This man's life is in imminent danger. You've got Reba, I've got Phil."

"Any leads?" I said.

"Martinez vanished the same afternoon as the Walker girl. His handler received a text from him around one p.m. Message said shit had hit the fan and he was dropping below the radar with his boys Yellowknife and Stephens. Suggested this relocation might be at gunpoint. He intended to reestablish contact asap. Last we've heard."

"He could be dead. Him and Reba have something in common there."

I didn't think his worry creases could deepen, but they did.

"Yeah. I'm exploring all possibilities. The best outcome would be, if they're alive, Reba is with them. The real wild card in this is Donnie Talon. I haven't ascertained his angle. Thirty-three, married, two children in a local private school. Son of a prominent businessman of the Algonquian Nation. His father owns controlling interest in several casinos. Father seems clean, though. Donnie may have originally joined the Manitou as an act of youthful rebellion. Had to bust free of paternal bondage and trust fund drudgery."

"I empathize. Alas, Donnie seems to be the worst of both worlds." Bellow puffed on his cigarette.

"All we know is, he's spent time in the pen for the usual rackets—extortion, money laundering, and assault. Boss Modine likes the kid's style and has fast-tracked him up the food chain. Talon is a major player; he's pro expansion by any means necessary. I get the idea he'd love to seize the throne."

"There's no doubt in my mind," I said.

"Yeah? Modine might be sorry he's given the lad such a big hatchet. One last bit—Talon, Modine, the whole lot of them, spell trouble. Even Deluca treads lightly around these guys. The Manitou is checked only by a fractured hierarchy and internecine warfare among its local clans. This is a vicious organization, Coleridge. They practice the kind of brutality you see in war-torn regions of Africa, Mexico, South America, and the Middle East. Think of the slaughter in Juárez. The skinning and beheading, the acid vats."

"Punji stakes. I read you, Bellow. I've seen it at close range. And Dr. Peyton's murder—"

"Let it lie. You pressured Peyton to give up a name, I'd guess. Am I close? Don't much care either. He got into bed with the wrong crowd. Case closed." The agent sighed with a world of weariness. "I don't have much to report about your girl either. We combed her computer. Double-checked our info with the local PD. The last call on her cell was made before noon on the day she went missing. Went to the farm, but no actual message."

I took a breath and dove in.

"Agent, about your undercover informant. Who is aware of his existence?"

"Me, my direct supervisor, and the guy above him. Tight loop."

"Nobody else? Your partner?"

"I'm old, not senile. Especially not Noonan."

That explained a thing or two. Noonan would've blown Martinez's cover in a hot second. I wasn't sure how to break the news to Bellow about his partner or whether it served any purpose to do so.

We sat in silence for a few minutes. Agent Bellow rose and said his good-byes. He promised or threatened, depending upon one's point of view, to be in touch.

Lionel propped his boots on the table and drained his glass.

"Think the Manitou slagged the Three Amigos?" His unvoiced corollary being, if so, Reba might've been eliminated as well.

"I suspect it wouldn't end with those three. We'd hear about it if the purge were under way."

In my experience, syndicates took pains to keep purges and bloodletting secret from the public. A housecleaning of this scale would be a different matter. Bodies were bound to surface. Until that happened, we still had time. Less and less, though.

THIRTY-SIX

I slept in a haze of pain and sluggish, half-formed dreams. Meg called the next afternoon and I gave her a severely edited version of my adventures.

"See you in an hour," she said. "Hang tough, I'll bring you a sandwich."

Good as her word, she sauntered in an hour and a quarter later with a picnic basket of chicken salad sandwiches and a four-pack of beer. She'd pawned her son off on the housemate.

"Hmm, cozy," Meg said upon crossing the threshold of my humble cabin. I couldn't determine whether or not she meant the comment sarcastically. She'd honed ambiguity to a needlepoint. She wore a paint-spattered tee, sweats, and tennis shoes. A touch of lipstick and the faintest whiff of perfume.

"Minerva, this is Meg." My puppy crept from beneath the table and sniffed Meg's ankle.

"Hi, Minerva." She gave Minerva a piece of chicken. They were fast friends after that.

I ate a sandwich and washed it down with a beer. My head swam between beer, blood loss, and Meg resting her knees against my thigh on the bed. Darkness filled in the windows. She lit a candle and came back and sat a little closer.

"The thing about you that turns me on . . . You're a wolf that walked off the pages of a Grimm's fairy tale. You might be capable of anything." Her hand touched mine. "Why'd you do it? Take on a gang like that? Crazy."

I considered a typically wry answer, then I looked into her eyes. I also considered admitting that I would happily torch The Battery and shoot a hundred lowlife bangers as they ran out in exchange for one more afternoon wandering the tundra with Achilles. I kept it simple.

"I miss my dog."

"Heck of a dog."

"He was. They all are."

"Yep." She leaned into me. "Good grief, Coleridge, you love to mix it up, huh? Can't get it out of your system." Her index finger traced the battered contours of my face. Her other hand went into my shirt, rested warm against my belly.

"Why, you want to go a couple rounds?"

Meg laughed and raised her arms and slipped off her tee, then helped me with mine. Her eyes widened when she beheld my stripes and scars, the bloody shroud around my waist.

"You'd get whipped again. Not good for your ego. It might be the only thing keeping you alive."

"My ego is the only part of me that isn't bruised." I kissed her. She tasted salty from the beer. My heart beat heavily. That great black wind whistled in my mind, far off across the ice. The cabin, our shelter, dwindled to a point of light in the vastness of an indifferent universe.

"It's okay," she said, hot into my mouth. "I'll let you win this one."

More like a draw. That was fine by me.

THIRTY-SEVEN

My favorite cop called with breaking news. The red Suburban had been found torched on a vacant lot in Highland. Forensics had the vehicle sitting there for at least ten days. No bodies, but Reba's purse, cell phone, and wallet were among the cindered remnants.

After an uncomfortable pause, Detective Rourke cleared his throat.

"Chief, that episode the other day wasn't personal. No hard feelings, I hope."

"Business is business."

"Smart man. We'll move the Walker girl up on the docket."

I thought of the past two and a half weeks, the many hours Virgil and Jade spent on the phone, their countless trips into town to paper telephone poles with missing-person flyers. My lip curled.

"Terrific. Treat yourself to a bear claw while you're at it."

I walked past the main house and saw Jade and Dawn through the window. The women sat on the couch, holding each other and sobbing. I hung my head.

———

TWO DAYS PASSED. My amazing capacity to regenerate didn't fail me. I felt better and stronger, physically. Ready to take it to the street again. Well, maybe the sidewalk. I swam in the pond and squeezed the squash ball and took long walks with Minerva. Ate and slept.

Inside my head, things weren't so copacetic. Icebergs scraped a valley through my brain. The extended downtime meant too much time to dwell upon certain mysteries that had perplexed me. Boredom and idleness make for a particularly bad combination in my case.

"What is it between you and Valens?" I said to Lionel. The dossiers hadn't revealed as much as I'd hoped.

Midday sun steamed the green earth. We'd trekked into the pasture to repair a break in the fence. Actually, Lionel performed the labor while I stood around and observed.

Lionel lit a cigarette. He pushed back his Stetson.

"Valens is my enemy."

"Yeah, yeah. You locked horns. Not what I'm asking."

"Then ask."

"The odds of you landing here in his stomping grounds . . ."

"Got ahold of my jacket? Yeah, you did." He blew smoke and glanced toward the trees. "Thought we were busy enough hunting Reba. This ain't got a damned thing to do with that business."

"Funny how things are all connected. Or tangled in a web."

"Tell me, Hoss. You the only one allowed to have secrets?" He waited for what I might say and when I said nothing, he scowled and wiped the sweat from his cheek with his sleeve.

"I cashed out of the Corps after Helmand. Did a tour with Black Dog. That went to shit pretty quick, so I came home and bummed around. Went broke. Caused a ruckus here and there. Wound up in Toledo, where I slept with a married woman. Did a spell in lockup for beating down the husband when he objected. Coulda been worse. He had a star in his pocket. Woe is fucking me, the streets of Toledo are cold in winter.

"Kept traveling east. Cops rousted me while I was living in my car in Kingston. Somebody on the street mentioned this place. The Walkers have that Mother Teresa reputation, y'know. I offered my services as a handyman and found a home."

"When did Valens approach you?"

"Last fall. Ran into him at the liquor store. Took me out to dinner and laid it on the table. Wanted to bury the hatchet between us. Asked me to join his crew. Made me an offer I couldn't refuse, but I *did* refuse the fucker. He let it go." He was holding back. I recognized his cadences. Not precisely lying except by omission.

"Nothing since?" I said.

"Besides having his squad beat the dog shit outta me? Nah, Hoss."

Lionel Robard represented precisely the kind of man corporate headhunters, such as those behind Black Dog, preyed upon. He possessed sniper skills, combat experience, and toughness. He'd also isolated himself from society in a meaningful sense. Valens could swoop in as the savior with a lucrative job and a ready-made family. Many soldiers would succumb to the pitch and consent, in time, to any damned filthy mission. But not Lionel. Not so far.

Valens, doubtless on specific orders from Black Dog HQ, would persist via a spectrum of approaches to subvert resistance and, if that failed, escalate. Whenever I looked at Lionel, I couldn't help but consider *The Manchurian Candidate* or *The Boys from Brazil*. In a good way, mainly.

That left the puzzle of Dad's involvement. Why had he sent the data on Valens if he didn't plan to admit their former association?

Sentimentality? No way. Guilt? Possibly. Or, maybe it was a double fake move—pretend to juke left, then actually go left, kind of gambit? Dad loved mind games. His overture might conceal a trap or be precisely the olive branch it seemed. I doubted the mystery would resolve itself anytime soon.

Lionel crushed the butt of his cigarette underfoot.

"Someday, when we're even with our chores, I'd enjoy getting to the bottom of Black Dog's game."

"Never fear," I said. "We'll sort them out. It's on my to-do list."

"That list gets any longer, you're gonna need a secretary."

THIRTY-EIGHT

No matter the outcome of my time on this world, the death of my mother will always remain unfinished business. Whether by guile or brute force, none of my attempts to resolve the mystery have borne fruit. That failure haunts me down through the days of my life. It is a shadow that follows me.

A few months after my twenty-second birthday, I got royally pissed on Glenrothes and convinced a pair of goon comrades to escort me across Anchorage to my old man's place off Elmendorf. Back then, he didn't bother with a nice home on a vast plot. Condos and town houses suited his itinerate lifestyle to a T.

In any event, I hadn't seen Dad for about two years and a friend whispered in my ear that Mervin had blown back into town after a lengthy trip abroad. Finally, the golden opportunity to avenge Mom.

We were real brave fellows. Me, built heavy as a middle linebacker, the slender waif of the three. Each of us already a hardened killer despite our youth. The old man might as well say his prayers because he had a three-part curb stomping in his near future.

Drunk, seething with a young man's perfect rage, I swaggered into the front yard of the crappy town house and called Dad out. Four a.m. and the neighbors called the cops. The boys in blue rolled up but didn't know what to do with my crew, as we were widely known to work for the infamous Mr. Apollo. Ironically, had Mr. Apollo known me and the goon squad were raising hell in front of Colonel Coleridge's house, he would have skinned us alive.

Dad stalked into the street, remarkably composed for a silver-haired dude who'd spent half the night drinking and screwing. He wore a bathrobe and a pair of boxers with little U.S. flags on them and unlaced combat boots. Wiry and leather tough, maybe half the steroid bulk of my partners. Those days I benched four hundred pounds for reps, did fifteen to twenty wind sprints every morning, and ate five pounds of red meat for dinner. This was going to be a massacre.

A pair of Dad's whores lounged in nightgowns on the steps, sharing a cigarette, greedy-eyed as ravens. He told the cops to get back into their cruiser, he'd sort these stupid cock knockers himself.

The bigger of my two friends didn't appreciate being referred to as a cock knocker and made a precipitous move. He specialized in clamping his lobster claws on his victims and shaking them until their bones separated. Dad kicked his left knee backward. The kid's shrieks caused every light along the block to snap on. My other friend had boxed. He tried his luck with a haymaker. Now, this dude fought heavyweight in statewide tough-guy competitions, even took third place at the nationals in Vegas when he was nineteen. He hit you, you were in a coma.

The boxer hammered Mervin directly between the eyes the way it's done to steers down at the slaughterhouse; made a dull thump that curled my toes in empathy, and I'm not certain how it didn't break his neck. Dad fell to his knee. Made it easier for him to drive his fist into the guy's balls. My boxer pal went down for the count.

Arrogantly, I let Dad gain his feet before I went at him, elbows, knees, and teeth. Stupid, stupid.

Sunrise bled all over the Eklutna Flats and brought me awake to pain. My body felt as if it had been tenderized by a giant mallet. Dad rolled me out of the back of the truck and I got a mouthful of sand upon hitting the beach face-first. I crawled toward a driftwood log. He followed me, a wooden kayak oar in hand.

"Always on about your mom. You a giant mama's boy, ain't you?" Whack with the oar across my shoulders. "You a giant girl's blouse, ain't you?" *Whack*.

The old man had it right, damn his eyes. Seven years since Mom didn't return from their moonlight row across Black Loon Lake. Seven years since the homicide detectives, the newspaper articles, the battery of rumors, the eventual subsidence and sympathy for my bereaved father from his Air Force cronies and all the good ol' boy ass kissers who owed him allegiance. Seven years of fighting in street gangs, and then college on Apollo's dime, which I now repaid every day by stooping, bowing, and calculated acts of violence. All through it, I'd thought of Mom and feared Dad. This was to have been my graduation from that fear, the confrontation that slew the boogeyman and put paid to a childhood of unjust misery.

Once again, the gods had their laugh.

I'd love to say I gathered myself, gained a second wind, or summoned the eye of the tiger and rose from the mat to teach the grizzled bully a lesson. Unfortunately, that's not how it went. Blinded by agony and humiliation, I kept crawling while Dad harangued me and occasionally clobbered me with that oar.

In the end, I collapsed and he rolled me over and laid the blade of the oar against my throat. He leaned on it while I thrashed.

"You have chosen the way of the animal." He gazed upon me with pity and hatred. "Not entirely your fault. You've got Satan in your blood. My people are drunk coal miners. Your mama, well, she was a dark-hearted woman from an evil line. Her ancestors ate the brains of their enemies. The worst of them still do. No chance you'd possess a scrap of humanity."

I choked and watched the white-and-red sky dim to black. He swung the oar overhead, poised to split my skull and end it for good and all. The way his eyes went dead, the way his mouth twisted into a snarl, no question he meant to murder me. I spat a stream of blood at him. He lowered the oar and gazed at me with disgust.

"Had they trawled the lake, they would've found that derringer I bought her for Christmas on the bottom. She took me out there to kill me. Jealous of some floozy I took to bed. I only meant to slap the pistol from her hand, but she ducked into the stroke. Complete accident."

I remembered the night she'd stabbed him with a cleaver when he got too rough, and another time she took a halfhearted potshot at him with that very derringer and blew a hole in the wall. She tried to ice him over the fact he'd painted the town red with a burlesque dancer he'd met at a USO show. Mom's temper was legendary.

"The bitch had it coming." He hurled the oar away and fell to his knees at my side. Tears froze in his eyes like flecks of crystal. He cradled my head and wept and snarled. "It's too late for you, son. I love you anyway."

I awoke with a cry on my lips and the phone beeping a warning.

Goliad, aka my cauliflower-eared friend with the White Manitou, said, "The man wants to see you. Be at the Rainbow in twenty. He's gonna buy you any breakfast you want."

THIRTY-NINE

Donnie Talon and his henchmen rendezvoused with me at the Frozen Rainbow café. A short meeting—I barely had time to dip into a chocolate milk shake.

"I've decided to help you out, Coleridge."

Talon wore sunglasses, a bear-tooth necklace, and a powder-blue sport coat. He appeared older in broad daylight, a few white streaks in his glossy hair. Only thirty-three. Full-time villainy had consequences. Still, it felt strange seeing him in such a mundane setting. No brimstone, no horns, no black cape. He picked at a BLT.

"You've decided to help yourself," I said.

"Careful, be careful. It's a terrible mistake to presume I can be manipulated. Dr. Peyton lost his head over your arrogance. Next time, it might be someone close to you. The sad part, at least for Dr. P, is that you had no need to jump through hoops to get with me. A man of your talents could've written his own check."

He waited for me to respond. I exercised the better part of valor and sipped my milk shake.

"I would've thought you'd appreciate the gesture. The Manitou is still the underdog in the eternal turf war. Admittedly, most of what we do, the symbols, the mutilation and torture of our foes, is pure theater. I didn't grow up with a strong tradition. I attended exclusive private schools, white schools. My friends were white. My mother was a Presbyterian." He hesitated, watching my reaction.

I gave him one.

"Just because I'm half Maori doesn't mean you need to unburden yourself. We're not bros, we don't share a struggle."

"Don't we? Perhaps not. Perhaps the hollow materialism of American culture has absorbed your soul. Hard to accept. There's hatred in your eye. The only men with that kind of anger are men who believe in a cause. It grieves me to see a warrior of your caliber succumb to entropy."

"Hang around long enough, you'll get used to it."

He shook his head.

"As a man, I've chosen my own traditions, the ones that will serve me and my comrades best. The Manitou are pan-tribal and trade in fear as much as anything else. I greatly admire the Mohawk ruthlessness, their historic reliance upon what most consider barbarism and cruelty. Civilization is soft. It responds well to the knife and the spur. Stellar audition at the Wigwam nonetheless. I can't stop thinking about the mayhem you committed. Makes me want to call you brother . . . makes me wonder if you might not be precisely the bad-to-the-bone sonofabitch I need to get one over on my enemies."

I pushed aside my glass and held his gaze.

"Look, Donnie. I'll tell you the same as I told the Italians—I'm not interested in working. I left the job permanently."

"Fooled the shit out of me and those four punks you iced. From where I'm sitting, you are larger than life and on the scene. I've got plans for you, friend. Deny it as you will, but you're one of us in your heart."

"Everybody has plans for me," I said.

He smiled, perfectly white with only a hint of yellow on his incisors.

"A conversation for another day. Meanwhile, we tidied up after your visit to The Battery. You owe me for dry cleaning."

I would have preferred to kick the table over, pin him and his cronies against the rear of the booth, and drill all three with my revolver. The revolver remained in the glove box of the truck. I smiled back at Talon and pretended to be reasonable rather than desperate.

"Point taken. How might I settle my tab?"

"It won't hurt a bit. You're going to extract a scumbag from his hidey-hole and deliver him to justice. The three gentlemen you seek, your Three Stooges? Three Amigos? After exercising due diligence, their location has come to my attention. Secluded shack in the country. Cozy. Heavies are standing guard, in case the boys get the crazy notion to call out or, heaven forfend, fly the coop. The soldiers answer to . . . well, not me. They won't let you waltz in and take anybody. For that matter, the Amigos probably won't be happy to see you either. Might call for brute force."

"I don't get it."

"Get what?" he said.

"Why me? Why not an anonymous call to the Feds? Those yahoos would swoop in with a tactical team before you could say Janet Reno."

"Because I don't trust the FBI, Coleridge. I trust you."

This had been his play all along. He'd known from the jump that Martinez sang like a bird for the authorities. Should Martinez happen to testify against Modine in a certain federal investigation, there'd be a vacuum in the Manitou leadership. Talon was the type to abhor a vacuum. He'd reacted as all master villains do: he gathered information and bided his time until the right moment to strike.

And here I came, lumbering along, to fill the bill as potential fall guy. Manipulate me, traveling rōnin extraordinaire, into carrying out his light work while he maintained an alibi if it went sour. Smooth as Satan indeed. Uncle Apollo and my dad would've shaken his hand with pleasure.

He took my silence as consent.

"Deliver Martinez into federal custody. I cannot sufficiently stress the importance that he makes it to trial."

"And his buddies?" I sipped my milk shake with an unflappable air.

He grinned and transformed into the Prince of Darkness, well and true.

"I do not give a shit about the others. Because of ongoing federal investigations, there are a dozen guys chilling in safe houses. It's making the honchos more nervous than you can imagine. Several of them are not content to wait for this to blow over. A purge order is in the pipeline. Once that gets whispered in my ear, I don't have a choice." He glanced at his watch. "You've got forty-eight hours, give or take. Machinery is in motion. Today, you sit before a humble prince. Should certain stars align, next we meet I'll be a king."

"Okay, Your Majesty," I said. "The girl?"

"She's not with the Amigos. Sorry." He dabbed his lips with a napkin. "I'm certain the truth will come out when this is over."

"Yeah."

"Don't be glum, Coleridge. This is better than going on *Oprah* when she's in the mood to give away cars. It's what you've wanted."

FORTY

When shit hits the fan in my life, it's usually a truckload. Today had not proved an exception thus far. My side ached. Everywhere I glanced, I beheld a constellation of woe and travail. The death's-head of the universe grinned at me, either in sympathy or contempt.

I returned to the farm and plotted my next move. As the first order of business, I fetched a bag of guns and brought it into the cabin. Lionel walked in as I laid an array of weapons on the table, cleaning and loading or whetting, as the case demanded.

He lit a cigarette and listened to the rundown.

"Your cleaning those rifles is a coincidence, of course. As you're half dead from stab wounds and incidental injuries, no way you'd be planning a commando action. I sorta hate myself for suggesting it, but . . . This is where we turn it over to the cops, right?"

"That would be nice and simple," I said.

"Why aren't we going to do the nice and simple thing?"

"Because Talon has us on the hook for the homies we iced at the Wigwam."

"Oh. He's going there? What a sweetheart."

"Screw Talon and his gun to our heads. He isn't why I'm going in."

"Like what I'm hearin'."

"I need the Amigos alive for questioning. This may be our last chance to find Reba. The cops can't be trusted. None of them." I winced to hear my words echo Talon's own.

"No shit, Columbo. We already knew that after they tried to smoke you the other day."

"This goes deeper than a crooked action or them panicking after their Gestapo tactics went sideways." I spun the cylinder on my .357 Magnum, then loaded the bullets. Hollow-point and flat-nose alternating, three of each. "Donnie Talon is under federal surveillance. Yet he and I had tea and cookies at Ye Olde Soda Shoppe not forty-five minutes ago. No switching of cars or covering of mouths with the menu. The whole damned thing was relaxed as a picnic. C'mon, man. I've seen all the crime movies. What does that behavior tell you?"

Lionel took a drag.

"Talon knows when and where the tail will be."

"Elementary, Dr. Watson."

"Sonofabitch. Noonan and Bellow?"

"Noonan is definitely a toady to greater forces. Bellow is clean."

"Don't be too sure. Birds of a feather, man."

"Listen, I think I've got a handle on this mess. Talon is making a power play. It's a delicate balance for him. My hunch is that certain forces in D.C. want Modine like Ness wanted Capone. By the book, hellfire and brimstone Dudley Do-Rights. I'd say Bellow fits the description."

"I'll buy that."

"Other parties don't subscribe to a zealous pursuit of justice. These persons are quite pleased with the status quo of fat bribes and the devil-you-know philosophy. The pragmatic business as usual as long as they get paid. Sounds like Noonan and whoever Noonan reports to in D.C. These latter parties wouldn't care for Martinez testifying against Modine and upsetting the apple cart. I'd bet my bottom dollar Noonan is supplying Talon with intelligence. He basically admitted it the day he ordered Rourke to smoke me."

"Uh, if Noonan is pro-Modine, why would he help Talon?"

"The good ol' double cross. He feeds Talon junk. It's a roundabout way to protect his interest in Modine and keep tabs on Donnie boy."

"Think Talon knows Noonan is conning him?"

"Talon would assume treachery because that sort of suspicion is in his DNA. Besides, I can tell you from bitter experience— organizations use dirty cops and dirty Feds, but they never trust them an inch further than necessary. This is a game of Chinese checkers for Talon. He's got to play it cool and outfox not only his boss but his boss's stooges at the Bureau. That's where you and I come in. I'm a longtime bad guy; plus, he's got the Wigwam dirt on us. He's gambling that these factors make us reliable."

"Lot of moving parts," Lionel said.

"Talon talked about machinery. It's not perfect. Nothing is. Still, the bastard is ballsy. He can't pass up an opportunity to spring Martinez and take down Modine. All without lifting a finger."

Lionel lit another cigarette. His lips curled into a sneer.

"Thought I left this shit behind. Shoulda figured the government is in the business of picking what crime bosses prevail in their territorial pissing. This is what the CIA does in Afghanistan, Pakistan, Where-the-fuck-ever-stan. They pit the tribal chieftains against one another and back the winner. How the British Empire conquered the world."

"Did you expect it to be different? Warfare is warfare. The Justice Department takes the long view. Some criminals they collar. Some they kill. Some they promote because it will help them bust or kill the others. It's a business."

"Wanna bring along Cal?"

"No way. He's still shook over The Battery."

"Okay. Good. I didn't want to drag him in again."

I slid the revolver into its holster.

"The Shakespearean maneuvering between gangsters will keep. Reba *won't* keep. Martinez won't either. We have to act."

"I'm down, Hoss. But let's not be fall guys."

"Too late. We can still fall right."

DESPITE MY POLICY OF SPEAKING nary a discouraging word to Lionel, forty-eight hours wouldn't be nearly enough to plan and execute a professional operation. Such a tight deadline meant storming the joint blind and praying to the gods for a lucky break. Not an example of best practices, according to my personal manual of extermination.

I sorted through Kline's dossiers and made the hard choice.

Teddy Valens and his crew occupied the second bucket-of-blood tavern I investigated—The Iron Sights. One of the windows remained boarded up from the last drunk who'd gotten pitched through it. I arrived around 2 p.m. Didn't get much deader than that. One of those tacky joints with out-of-state plates and beer posters for wallpaper.

Valens sat in a dim corner drinking beer with his Fu Manchu buddy, Wes Hawkins. Ken Galt and Steve Tucker were shooting pool, both of them dressed in muscle shirts a neck size too small. An old drunk in coveralls slumped at the bar. The bartender stared at me as I loomed in the doorway. Basketball on the tiny corner screen. Odors of cigarette smoke and impending violence.

There we were.

"Hey, sailor," I said to Tucker. He choked up on his cue stick.

Everybody tensed when I unbuckled my holster and laid it on the table. The knives followed. I showed them my hands and introduced myself.

"I remember you," Valens said. "You're pals with Robard."

"Yep, and you're bosom buddies with my dad."

"Huh. *That* Isaiah. Must take after your ma, 'cause you don't look an itty bit like your pa. How is the old man?"

"Mean as a snake."

"Sounds right. Love that guy. A real soldier. Not a fan of Black Dog, sadly. He told you where to find me, huh?"

"No, one of his cronies did. Dad can't be bothered. Damndest thing. He acted as if the name Valens meant zip to him." I'd pondered on the subject. The more I weighed the evidence, the more I questioned what Dad had left out of the dossiers he'd instructed Kline to send my way. "He's got a hundred photos cluttering his mantel. One happens to feature your mug."

"'Course he did," Valens said. "We were close, once. I was the son he never had. It embarrasses him in his twilight years. Like you, we had a falling-out."

"He didn't mention it."

"He don't like to admit mistakes. Your pop put distance between us after an . . . incident in Iraq. Bad press all the way around. Could also be he's trying to make amends, reconnect with his long-lost eldest boy. Throw you a bone. No skin off his ass." He stood and made an elaborate point of studying me. "I can't figure out what the fuck you're supposed to be."

"My girlfriend is a librarian and you've probably never met one of them before. She thinks I'm a dangerous animal from the Black

Forest. I take a hoof to the mug here and there before I bring down my prey."

"Superstar badass," the one called Galt said.

"What can we do for you?" Valens said.

"Maybe he came here to shoot us," Galt said. "I recall you stuck a heater in my face last we spoke."

Valens shook his head at Galt.

"Thirty seconds. Whatever you need to get off your chest, mister."

"Three pieces of business," I said. "One, I'm getting set to hit a target and need equipment. Kind of materials you soldier boys play with." Nobody spoke. They exchanged glances, except for Valens, who kept his eyes on mine. I continued. "Second, forget about Lionel. You mess with him, I'm involved. That will be messy, bank on it. Last, one of you bozos swiped a pic of his girl. Give it up."

The tension in the room climbed a notch. Tucker and Galt grinned, getting wind of blood.

"Are you high?" Tucker said. He stepped toward me, stick gripped at port arms, looney tunes smirk widening into a fright mask.

"Belay that," Valens said. Cold and sharp; an NCO barking at his troops. "Coleridge. As a favor to your daddy, I'm going to let you walk out the door under your own power. Our beef isn't with you. It's with your cowardly friend."

"You are mistaken. I don't keep cowardly friends."

"The one who sent you here to fight his battles. I expected better from Robard. Wouldn't have dreamed he'd pull this weak shit."

"He hasn't a clue. I left him home because I don't want anybody to get ventilated. By *anybody*, I mean you guys."

"Really. Color me curious."

Without giving away details, I outlined my problem with the Manitou safe house.

Valens sipped beer. His stony expression didn't alter.

"Gonna be hairy. I wish you luck. Can't help you, though."

I considered arguing, decided against it.

"Worth a try. There's still the matter of that photo."

The men laughed, except for stone-faced Valens. He knew the score.

"Look, boys," I said. "Last thing I want is to throw down with your squad. I'm not leaving without that pic."

"Yeah?" Tucker said. His eyes glinted with joy. "You'll have to kick my ass first. Wanna shot at the title? Please say yes."

I rolled my neck.

"Wait! Wait! Wait!" the bartender said. "Take it outside, would ya please?"

Tucker led the way through a back door to a horseshoe pit. He peeled off his shirt and flexed. Muscular and supple, an Army tattoo over his heart. My ribs ached even more from watching him strut and preen like one of those fighting roosters that gamblers bring up from South America and tape razor blades to their spurs. For a man like Tucker, maiming and killing was second nature.

According to the jacket, Valens's crew split its leave between boozing at the local watering holes and punching one another in the head or firing a lot of rounds down at the range. Tucker's flattened nose and scarred knuckles confirmed the report. Presumably, rape and pillage occurred at the margins.

I leisurely unbuttoned my shirt, removed it, and folded it neatly. Stalling for all I was worth as the other men gathered around the pit. When I crushed Tucker's balls and snapped his neck, would the rest pile on or whip out their guns and put me down permanently? Depressing, either way it went. Bruises, contusions, freshly scabbed lacerations, I was a mess, no two ways about it. Already, my breath came heavy and labored. Sweat rolled down my body.

"He's a sunset," Hawkins said from the shade of a dogwood. "Sergeant, for Chrissake. Fucker is bleeding."

I *wasn't* bleeding, although the fresh bandages around my ribs were stained dark. The sunset comment was dead on, however. I'd seen myself in the mirror that morning. Enough bruises covered my torso that it resembled an abstract painting done in purple, yellow, and brown.

"Coleridge, what are you doing?" Valens said.

"Fixing to put this knuckle-dragger out of commission."

"That's one possibility. However, larger picture, you can't prevail. You understand, right? I assume your pappy did not sire a retard. This is an unwinnable scenario."

"My profession, there aren't many people you can trust. Fewer you can call friend." I unclenched my fists and glanced from man to man. "Lionel Robard is my brother-in-arms. I have no choice here."

Valens studied the ground for a few moments. He cut his hand at Tucker.

"Stand down. Give the man his photo. Come on in for a drink, Coleridge. You win. We'll powwow about your banger problem."

FORTY-ONE

I couldn't be certain whether the FBI had us under the microscope, so I erred on the side of caution. Around sunup, Lionel and I flattened under a tarp in the bed of Jade's Toyota. She tooled around New Paltz, dithering at the bank, post office, and feed store. She parked at the supermarket and gave me a grim nod in the side mirror as we slipped away.

Valens had left the dark blue van at the edge of the lot with the keys on the tire. The gear I'd purchased lay neatly stacked in back near the panel door. Full tank of gas and the radio dialed to a country-and-western station. In went our duffel of weaponry and we were under way.

After a few minutes on the freeway, Lionel snicked the top of his Zippo and lit a cigarette.

"Hate to look a gift horse in the mouth. Hate to do it." Then he did indeed look at me, smoke curling from his nostrils.

I fished the snapshot of his girl from my breast pocket and passed it over.

"You didn't exaggerate. She's a beauty. Too bad she's fucking her way across the South of France."

He wore a set of amber-tinted shooting glasses that disguised his expression. The muscles of his jaw twitched. He turned the photo over in his fingers, then dug out his wallet and slipped the pic inside.

"Kill anybody?" he said after a couple of miles.

"We reached an amicable agreement." I winced to recall sliding that lunch box full of cash across the table to seal our treaty. It represented a loss of more than half my remaining stake from the Outfit. Blood and money. I'd certainly sprung leaks since setting foot in the Hudson Valley.

"Valens is a mad dog."

"Won't argue with you. He has that gleam in his eyes."

"He burned a village to the ground near Kabul. I was there, man." He hesitated, as if chewing the words and swallowing them. "We came to blows. A bad scene. Real bad scene."

I kept quiet.

He shook his head and stared at the countryside.

"Long as you realize, one way or another, this'll come back to bite us in the ass."

"I'm under no illusion that we're all high-fiving chums. It's a truce, nothing more. The mercs are providing materials, fire support, and extraction. I also convinced them to get off your case for a while."

"Fire support?" His jaw clenched again.

"We won't see much of them, amigo. Valens sent two of his boys. They've got their task and we've got ours."

"We need them to do this?"

"To do it right, yeah, they're necessary. You're the expert when it comes to kicking in doors. If it's a trap or if things go bad, those eyes in the woods might be the difference." I waited a beat, then laid it on him. "This isn't about you. It's about Reba and her family. You'd eat ground glass if that was on the menu."

He got all stony.

"Let it ride, then. Just let it ride."

THE CABIN NESTLED ON A WOODED RIDGE in the Catskills, northwest of Saugerties. An old hunting shack owned by the family of a member of the White Manitou. Survey maps I borrowed from Virgil indicated one road in, mostly impassible come winter. The nearest town had become largely deserted during the Recession. Neighbors were few and of the hermit variety. Gunshots echoing along the draws wouldn't attract much attention.

I passed the turnoff and hid the van behind an abandoned gas station we'd selected the evening prior. It'd be a two-mile walk cutting straight across through the woods. I left the key in the ignition. One of Valens's soldiers would be along to valet the van back to us at the cabin if the mission succeeded.

"Good theater for a killing ground." Lionel zipped his camo windbreaker and stuffed extra shells into the pockets. He'd painted his face to resemble a death's-head to counter my own conservative tiger stripes.

"Much as it pains me to say, let's keep the killing to a minimum." I dressed in loose, dark clothes, gloves, and hiking boots. Throwaway garments. Both of us bulked up with Kevlar. I keyed the collar mic on the walkie-talkie Valens had provided. "Hercules and Aeolus at staging, over."

"Roger," Hawkins said through a swirl of static. "Eagle Eye 1 in place, over."

"Eagle Eye 2 in place, over," said Tucker.

"Going dark. Radio check in thirty. Hercules out." I shut down the radio, transferred the necessities into a mesh backpack, and shrugged it on. I carried the twelve-gauge pump in my left hand.

"Hercules. Ain't we grandiose?" Lionel poked my biceps. His mood had brightened upon examining the goodies provided by the Black Dog team. He too carried a shotgun and slung a grenade launcher over his shoulder.

"What can I say? It's the nickname the Outfit gave me."

We moved away from the road and into the woods. Fortune smiled upon us. Partly cloudy with a high in the seventies. The trees blurred in the creeping shadows of sunset. I fell in behind Lionel and let him navigate through the dense undergrowth. He traveled, loose of limb, head on a swivel, his gait precise.

It didn't take long to reach our destination.

A rutted dirt lane angled to our right and we paralleled that until Lionel settled on a catbird seat behind a deadfall about fifty yards from the cabin. Smoke wisped from the stovepipe chimney. Two SUVs sat in the yard, one with Massachusetts plates. The building had electricity and plumbing. I would've loved to know how often they split apart to resupply, or whether someone brought supplies to them, or if they were hooked to a phone or Internet. The latter struck me as doubtful—guards would carry cell phones; no landline necessary.

I checked in with Tucker and Hawkins. The two were nearby and ready to snipe if it came to that. Hawkins reported at least three hostiles, but no movement in the past ninety minutes.

Lionel broke off a hunk of jerky. He rolled over in his nest of dead leaves and pine needles and stared at the sky through the canopy.

"I tell ya. It's like I never left the Corps."

"Spent a few nights this way?"

"You said it. A whole lot of nights. And you?"

"Camped in the Brooks Range when I was a kid. Dad insisted. As for the Outfit, jobs are usually a walk-up or a drive-by. We didn't storm any bunkers. City slicker gangsters don't appreciate nature. Too many mosquitoes."

"So you're sayin' gangsters are pussies."

"Your run-of-the-mill wiseguy doesn't care to stray far from the bar, is all."

"Why didn't you enlist? You'd have been a machine."

"Dad," I said.

We fell silent and listened to the forest. Birds chirped. Branches creaked as a breeze riffled through them. Lights came on in the cabin windows. Occasionally, figures moved around inside. The front door remained shut. A fox screamed in the near distance. Another answered, much farther into the trees. The clouds rolled back and a sprinkle of stars shone through the canopy.

Around 9 p.m. Lionel tapped my arm, raised himself into a crouch, hesitated for several seconds, and then disappeared with nary a snapped twig. I ate jerky and sipped water from a canteen and waited. Longest forty-five minutes I could recall. He rematerialized opposite the direction I'd anticipated and hunkered beside me.

"Three hostiles. Three friendlies. I spotted an Uzi on a table."

"Man, how close did you get? Under one of their bunks or what?"

"Close enough. The gang looks bored. Three weeks holed up in a shack with no cable is cruel and unusual punishment. Saps are watching VCR tapes of *Fantasy Island* and *The Love Boat*."

"Harsh. These guys must've annoyed a VIP to get exiled to Siberia."

Lionel turned in such a way as to disguise the lighter flare and fired up a cigarette.

"In a few hours, they'll feel the thrill again. Nervous?"

I didn't dignify that with a response.

"Kidding, Hoss," he said. "I got that covered for both of us."

WE MOVED AGAINST THEM as a bloodless dawn glow filtered through the canopy. SOP assault tactics. Whoever slept would be in the depths of REM, stuck to the flypaper of dreams. Those awake weren't likely to be alert.

Lionel covered the back door and I took the front. Hawkins and Tucker were ready to derail any reinforcements coming along the road.

"Going live in five seconds, over," I said into the mic. I counted down five and fired the grenade launcher. A canister of CS punched through the kitchen window. The next one went into the bedroom. I dropped the launcher and cinched my gas mask. I immediately approached the cabin, shotgun at the ready.

White smoke seethed from the busted windows. Lionel reported he was at the target and ready to breach. I told him to go on three. By then, I'd mounted the porch and moved to the left of the door. Wood splintered on the opposite side of the cabin followed by a metallic thump and a flicker of bright light as he detonated a flashbang grenade.

The front door flew wide and a shirtless Hank Stephens lurched out and down the steps. I hit him in the middle of his back with a beanbag round. He accelerated in a Superman pose, arms outstretched, and skidded on his face.

Two closely spaced rifle booms erupted inside.

I ducked through the doorway. Pea soup fog dripped and coiled. A man lay motionless near a counter. A man groaned nearby. Somebody else scuttled on hands and knees, making for an exit. I clubbed him with the shotgun butt.

Lionel emerged from the murk, sidestepping with alacrity. He swung his shotgun around and fired at a shadow toward the rear of the room. Sparks arced upward from the barrel of an automatic rifle as its owner flew backward and slammed into the wall. Bullets pinged through metal and glass and tore across the roof. Then everything became still except for the rasp of my breath reverberating in my ears.

"You okay?" The mask distorted Lionel's voice, sharpened it.

"A-OK." I took a moment to lean on the counter and suck air. It might have been healing, but my body wasn't pleased with the calisthenics.

Lionel prowled the cabin ascertaining no more bogeys lurked and gave me the thumbs-up. I signaled Hawkins and Tucker with our success.

"Extraction in twenty," Hawkins said.

FORTY-TWO

The secret is this: things are seldom as complicated as they seem upon first blush.

Whenever I reach the end of my endurance, when I'm lost and confused and can't decide what to do, I do what Alexander did with the Gordian knot. Pull out my sword and chop through all those tangled threads to get to the heart of it. What's at the heart of any man-made mystery, no matter how convoluted, is sex, love, or money. Usually money and everything that comes along with a fat stack of folding green. The sages weren't kidding when they declaimed it as the root of all evil. Sex and love aren't far behind, though.

The Three Amigos were the knot and Donnie Talon had handed me the cleaver.

We zip-tied the heavies and left them behind the cabin. The Amigos sat, Indian-style, in the front yard. They were bruised and battered, eyes swollen, noses leaking. Yellowknife and his greasy ponytail were only vaguely familiar from a glance I'd had of him when he visited the farm once. I recognized Martinez as the one who'd tried to drag Reba away during the night of the Fire Festival. Sallow, callow, ex–white supremacist Hank Stephens definitely wasn't so tough with his wrists zipped together and terror in his eyes. Blood streaked his cheeks from where he'd skinned them plowing dirt with his face.

Neither Lionel nor I had removed our gas masks and we loomed over the trio like a pair of storm troopers. There were subtler methods, to be sure, but time was most definitely not on our side. I wanted to be long gone before more gangbangers or the FBI arrived.

Lionel gave me the high sign. He went around back to have a word with the Manitou heavies.

"We were sent to ice you punks," I said, enjoying the cowing effect my voice had on the Amigos. "Maybe that doesn't have to happen. Maybe one of you is going to sing and I'll let you fly away."

That elicited a burst of whining and pleading.

"Why? What'd I do?" Hank said.

"Shut your mouth, white boy," I said. "You know too much, Martinez. As for you, Yellowknife . . ."

Yellowknife had a few years on his compadres. All three were nasty little pieces of work, but his eyes were the hardest. He'd done much and seen even more. He sneered; afraid, yet not ready to crack.

"Gonna shoot us, then shoot us," he said. "Otherwise, say your piece and get out a my face."

I kicked him in the ribs and felt them crunch. He writhed in the dirt, unable to breathe. I meant it as a message to the other two rather than a rebuke of Yellowknife. I also hid the fact that delivering it hurt me almost as much as it hurt him.

"Reba Walker. Where is she?" I stared at Martinez.

Martinez's expression remained one of blank fear.

"I dunno. At her apartment. How would I know she's at?"

"Try again. Nobody's seen her since you three punks went into hiding. We figure you helped her disappear too."

"I dunno, man. That bitch is just a connection. We fuck around. I always keep a piece on the side."

I unfolded a skinning knife. The blade made a nice loud snick.

"Been a while since I castrated anybody."

He squealed and pleaded while Hank sobbed. Yellowknife continued to moan and squirm in the dirt. A symphony of misery. All in all, it was going quite well, I thought.

I DRAGGED MARTINEZ AWAY FROM the others and said, "Give me the story or sing falsetto forever more." Then I poked him in the calf with the knife. That wasn't strictly necessary. However, I recalled the punch he'd dealt Reba at the festival and had to resist the impulse to take it further.

He opened his lips and babbled.

On the day Modine had sent various Manitou subordinates into hiding, Martinez tried to secure some pills and pussy for the trip into the Catskills. Yeah, so much for his being a married family man doing the FBI a solid. He admitted to picking Reba up at her apartment with a little sweet talk and implied menace. She'd come along more or less willingly, at first, and they'd driven into New Paltz to score weed from a dealer who ran a head shop. Somewhere along the line, Reba caught on to reality: her gangbanger buddies were going underground at some shanty in the hills with her as the proposed entertainment. Jade and Virgil knew their granddaughter. Reba might be rough around the edges. She smoked some pot and hung around a dark element. That didn't make her a bad kid. It only made her a kid, period. She told Martinez to shove it where the sun didn't shine.

A screaming match ensued. It culminated with Reba exiting the vehicle at a four-way stop on Springtown Road. She'd been so pissed and frightened, she left her purse lying on the seat. About then, some

Manitou heavies pulled alongside and ordered the Amigos to board a company SUV. The red Suburban was taken elsewhere and torched. Reba ducked in to the trees until the dust cleared. She went her way, shaken and raging but unmolested.

Hank eagerly corroborated the account, and I was reasonably confident that Yellowknife would have as well, if he could've done more than gasp and clutch his middle.

I didn't want to believe Reba had been stupid enough to tag along with them after what they'd pulled at the Fire Festival, yet I did. Kids, especially tough kids with soft hearts and chips on their shoulders, make terrible decisions. You can set your watch by them. In this case, she probably hadn't felt much choice in the matter with the Amigos knocking on her door and bum-rushing her to the Suburban like coyotes herding a lamb. If only I'd been on my feet at the time. I understood Lionel's anguish. He hadn't intervened, hadn't saved her, hadn't understood that she needed saving.

Where had she gone after jumping from the Suburban? I did the math. No purse, no cell phone, no pals in New Paltz. The intersection on Springtown Road lay roughly four miles from the Hawk Mountain Farm. Easily within walking distance. Why hadn't she trudged to the farm? Had she fled to parts unknown in fear of her boyfriend? I doubted that. Someone had gotten to her before she reached home. Possibly the Amigos were lying. I sincerely doubted that. My gift for reading people, for sensing their true intentions, convinced me these three morons were too piss-scared to lie themselves an alibi.

Next suspect: Kari Jefferson, the ditz with a heart of spite. If her own alibi of being at work at the salon weren't airtight, I might've reached for the improbable idea that Reba had called her from a friend's house, that there'd been a subsequent argument and Kari committed violence against her roommate, dumped the body in a landfill or a swamp or the slow-churning Rondout. It didn't jibe, didn't fit, no matter how much I tried to make it so. Where did that leave me? It left me wanting to smash the Three Amigos into a fine powder.

Galt arrived with the van. He wore a red balaclava and a bush hat pulled low to disguise his eyes.

We put on a show for Yellowknife's benefit, and by extension all the other assholes present.

"You two punks are in for special treatment." I lifted Hank by the collar and chucked him into the van, followed by Martinez. I said to Yellowknife, "Later, Eddy. Watch your back." I climbed in and pulled the doors shut as the van rolled.

Yellowknife didn't move from the fetal position as we rounded the corner and lost him in the trees. I like remembering him that way.

HANK STAYED QUIET during the dusty, bumpy ride up the mountain to his mama's shack. I marched him at gunpoint along the driveway right to his doorstep, where Clem and the dogs awaited.

"Hope you baked a cake, Mrs. Stephens," I said.

Clem didn't shed a tear or hug her prodigal son. She handed me a mason jar packed with cash. The lid had rusted tight.

"That's Henry's trust fund. Tad more than we agreed on. Reckon you earned it."

"Thanks, ma'am. Are you sure I can't take him off your hands? He's going to bring trouble down on your family. The Feds want him on a murder rap. The Iron Knife and Manitou aim to collect his head. Might get hot around these parts."

She spat in the dirt.

"Trouble ain't nothin' but weather. It comes and it goes. Hank, get your sorry ass in the house."

I tucked the jar under my arm.

"Adios, Mrs. Stephens."

"Farewell, slick. We're done. Don't be comin' 'round this mountain anymore."

"Wouldn't dream of it." I hoped I was telling the truth.

THE BLACK DOG MERCS LEFT Lionel and me with our prisoner in the side lot of the Bellwether Motel a mile outside of Kingston. Martinez sat, bloodied and crazed, on a cement backstop. A steady glare from me sent gawking passersby onward with a lively step. Nobody got around to calling the cops, though. I made a note of that.

Agents Bellow and Noonan showed a few minutes later. Noonan stuck his hands into his pockets and refused to make eye contact as he lagged behind. Bellow was grayer and more rumpled than ever, as if he hadn't slept since our last encounter. He shook my hand and then knelt and spoke briefly with Martinez. I stepped off a bit to give them privacy, and also to sidle near Noonan.

"Awkward, huh?" I stage-whispered.

He twitched.

"Fool. Fucking idiot. At least Modine is conservative in his evil. Talon is too ambitious. He's got dreams. Dreams for him, nightmares for us."

"That's your problem, Mr. Fed. I don't play those reindeer games."

"Oh yes, yes you do. Talon belongs to the Blood Path. Never heard of it, eh? Well, why would you? It's a cabal, a secret society within the Manitou upper echelon. The hardest of the hard, the most vicious among the vicious. These are the skinners and the head takers. The slave traders. Lords of Darkness. They don't want to parley with or assimilate the other gangs. These hidden masters will settle for nothing less than a pogrom." He grimaced bitterly. "So, yes, Coleridge, you will play this game. You've already been used as a piece."

"We're all pieces, Timmy. I chose the hat over the iron."

Bellow called to Noonan and told him to put Martinez in the car. He walked over to me. No, he hadn't slept in days and his cologne merely masked the reek of booze.

"You crazy sonofabitch." He said it with zero affect. "Phil says you stabbed him."

"Did Phil mention he slugged a teenage girl and tried to drag her into a car by her hair?"

"You turned Stephens over to the hill folk. It could take an army years to dig the little bastard out of there."

"Get digging."

"Coleridge—"

"I had a deal with the so-called hill people. My policy is to honor deals with the working class."

"What am I supposed to tell my supervisors? Wait, never mind."

"Good. Now we're square for Noonan's antics—y'know, trying to orchestrate my demise, et cetera."

"What about this raid? If Martinez had gotten killed . . ."

"I couldn't warn you beforehand. I'm sorry."

"Why couldn't you tell me?"

"How do I put this delicately? As we've established, your partner is a shitbird. Also, he's up to no good."

Bellow glanced over his shoulder at Noonan, who skulked around by the car.

"Tell me something new."

"The fix is in. He's marching to a different set of orders from you. *His* handlers want status quo—Modine in power and Talon in check."

"The more I see of Talon, the more I wonder if maybe that isn't the smarter play."

"Can't help you there. Lesser of two evils is still evil. What I do know? Be wise or Martinez won't make it to any trial." I made a pistol with my index finger and put it to my head.

"I said, tell me something *new.*"

"Okay. Watch your step or *you* may not make it to retirement. My advice? If it comes down to you or Martinez, take a walk."

He lit a Benson & Hedges and smoked it. I didn't think he intended to speak again, but he did after a while.

"They disappear the girl?"

"If I thought so, he wouldn't be breathing." I relayed what I'd learned while interrogating the Amigos. "We'll canvass the neighborhood. Maybe we'll get lucky."

"Strange. I'll come at Martinez hard when we debrief. Best of luck, Coleridge."

"Agent, you have a girlfriend, a favorite hooker, anyone?"

"Yeah."

"Go get a good dinner and a lay. And get a full night's sleep, will you? You're dead on your feet."

"Ha. The irony is what's killing me. Look in the mirror, sonny."

"Difference is, I'm made for the abuse. Darker it gets, the better."

"Good to hear. Because it's going to get a hell of a lot darker."

FORTY-THREE

For three days, the residents of Hawk Mountain Farm canvassed the neighborhoods along Springtown Road. We knocked on doors, rang numbers, and circulated the word via social networking on the Internet. Calvin worked his magic and a reporter took down the story and it ran in the Kingston rag alongside a picture from Reba's senior prom.

Nothing.

Bellow called to say he'd put the screws to Martinez and Martinez stuck to his story: Reba left the vehicle of her own accord and walked out of their lives forever. I thanked him and fell into a sleep not unlike death.

I dreamed of moving through a series of pastures in pursuit of our herd of horses. Each gate was ajar or there were holes in the fences. After a while, I lost sight of them except for Bacchus, who cantered a few arm lengths beyond my reach. He stopped at the edge of a blackened plain that went on to the bloody howling heart of the cosmos. He turned in profile and reared and his eye shone white as bone. His whinny pierced my heart with an icicle.

I awoke to thunder rolling over the valley and the drum of rain against the roof.

Minerva whimpered in her sleep and pressed against my ankles. What did I have, what did I know? Reba had been a mediocre student in high school and better than average in college. She smoked grass and consorted with bangers and committed minor mischief but hadn't become a hard case despite her tough talk. She loved horses and possibly Lionel and refused to speak to her father. Her favorite band was Sublime. Her mother loved her. Virgil, Jade, and Lionel loved her. Bacchus loved her, if he could be said to love anything.

What did I have, what did I know? Everything and nothing. I'm not a detective, I'm merely a man with less exacting scruples than most.

A white stroke of lightning sizzled and doubled in the window glass. Dreams, nightmares. I don't consider them supernatural weather vanes. Dreams and nightmares are not predicative in the same sense as omens or precognition. They are the mind's sandbox wherein scenarios are sketched and enacted, wherein puzzle pieces and kaleidoscope fragments are ever turning, ever colliding, as they are drawn toward some concrete impermanence.

I walked through a downpour into the barn and flipped on the lights in that dark and cavernous space. I moved as if my body yet remained submerged in dreamtime. All that transpired unspooled with a sense of leadenness, the sensation of sinking into quicksand. I shortly discovered what a part of me had known for a long time.

But again, I'm no detective.

In the confusion of her disappearance, exacerbated by the antics of the Three Amigos, and further compounded by the charming disarray of the tack and tools, no one noticed, until I pawed through the errant bridles and dusty crops and unused leathers, that while a dozen riding helmets hung from pegs or lay discarded upon gray shelves, none belonged to Reba.

I realized with a knot in my gut we'd been fools. She had indeed returned to the farm that fateful day.

YOU ARE A TEENAGER. You have made a number of spectacularly bad choices throughout your young career. You've done time behind concrete walls due to these choices. You are smart enough to know that going with the bad crowd will bring you to ruin, but you're a kid. Your parents are absent and the only other people you trust are either away at work or distracted caring for that huge sick lug with his own checkered past.

Those bad friends from that bad crowd pressure you and you bail in the middle of the road and walk. Steam boiling from your ears, embarrassment burning your cheeks. By the time you reach the farm, you've calmed sufficiently to do what comes naturally and you sublimate your fear and embarrassment into action. Rebellious action. No one notices your disheveled arrival on that hot spring day.

You grab a helmet, but don't even bother to saddle Bacchus. No bridle, no bit. You take him from the corral and you ride. Riding Bacchus is the only time in your chaotic life that you truly feel in control. He is real, he is heavy, he is a caged and ill-tempered beast who responds to you, who listens and obeys. The two of you gallop out of the yard and down the Rail Trail, your favorite route. No one noticed your arrival and no one sees you go.

Bacchus returns, lathered, wild-eyed, bereft of his rider. The only person to take note is Gus, the stable hand. Hayseed Gus is a bit slow; the Walkers took him on as a favor to foreman Coates, who is the boy's uncle once removed. Gus's IQ hovers in the upper sixties.

He isn't capable of adding two and two. He merely assumes the big gelding has gotten loose yet again and remands him to the corral without pausing to question why the gate is unlatched.

You are gone without a trace and everyone who loves you, everyone who cares, hunts for clues in the wrong direction.

THIS IS THE THEORY I LAID before Jade, Virgil, Lionel, Dawn, and foreman Coates at the breakfast table. After a stunned silence came a burst of frenzied activity. There were calls to the police and preparations for a fresh search. Not me, though. Not me.

I zipped up a windbreaker and found the trail about half a mile past the farm proper and began walking north. Massive old-growth sycamore, maple, and pine churned around me and littered the path with shorn twigs. Leaves and detritus funneled as if into the gold-black throat of the next world.

Later, I learned that Virgil and Jade organized two dozen riders to sweep along the foothills of Hawk Mountain. By dusk, the Ulster County Sheriff's Department had coordinated a search-and-rescue operation in conjunction with personnel from local volunteer fire departments and dozens of private citizens. A small army of men, women, horses, and dogs descended upon the region.

Reba's fate would've revealed itself eventually. My involvement merely sped the inevitable discovery along. That only seems fair since my presence on the Hawk Mountain Farm contributed to her death. Had Jade not been tending to me in my delirium after the Beltane festival, she would've spotted the girl and prevented her from galloping off to her doom. Reba would still be in the world.

Night fell and the storm grew stronger. Starless, and utterly black. At last came the dull and shapeless glow of firelight through the trees. I moved toward the fire, for here was the thing I'd sought unknowing at every crossroad and hollow during the endless hours of daylight.

Old Methuselah, the itinerant potter and scavenger Emmitt Rogers, lolled in a drunken stupor. His weathered features were decayed granite in the orange and sparking glare of the bonfire. He dressed in moth-eaten fatigues and his beard was snarled and matted. His panel truck provided a lee from the wind, its hood pointed at a track that speared through knee-high weeds toward the distant highway.

Smoke boiled off into the outer darkness. I emerged from the pall and strode toward his roost. The universe spun like the cylinder of a revolver and the barrel oriented on him. Even the storm froze mid-roar. He cast aside a can of beer and raised his hands in supplication.

"You're different. From all the other times we've met, you're different tonight." His eyes blazed with tears. He tore at his hair and gesticulated. "I've dreamed you'd come here. You're Death."

The exhaustion of inevitability, of futility, that a man feels when caught in the teeth of a bore tide, crushed down upon me. None of this was chance; not in the vast, incomprehensible scheme of things. I hadn't sought Emmitt, hadn't consciously considered that his squat might place him in a prime position to have noticed Reba and Bacchus when they'd galloped along the trail. I'm not a detective, I'm a bulldozer. Yet, here we were in Pluto's drawing room as the stars flared to their deaths around us in trajectories plotted before the Catskills or Adirondacks heaved up from the primordial muck.

It had to be this way. It *had* to come to this. It's why the universe had placed the revolver in my hand.

"What have you done, you sonofabitch?" I may as well have been speaking to myself.

PART IV

ACHILLES

FORTY-FOUR

Spring gave way to summer.

Lionel hadn't exaggerated. The swelter and humidity almost did in this Alaska boy. At least once a day, and hourly during haying week, I swore to defy Mr. Apollo and sneak back to the wintry environs of my youth and shack up in an igloo. Meg sweetly, albeit ruthlessly, derailed that particular plan with home-cooked meals, a certain mischievous light in her eyes, and the threat of handcuffs. I persevered until the Hudson Valley went from green to gold and red and stole my breath.

The stretch from June to September was an open wound that closed over a tiny bit every day. Seldom had a night passed that I didn't dream of Reba Walker and her ride into oblivion.

Agent Bellow was the first person I called after Emmitt led me to Reba's cairn in a clearing not far from his campsite. The body was in bad shape, but I recognized the *13* tattoo. I'd kicked Emmitt's legs from under him and driven him to his knees. I rammed the barrel of the gun into his mouth. He didn't resist. Mad from guilt, he welcomed a bullet as a mercy. I almost obliged him by squeezing the trigger. Instead, I rang Bellow and waited for him to find us out there in the dark.

Emmitt confessed to Bellow. He explained how Reba staggered into his camp, blood pouring from her temple. Apparently, Bacchus had startled and thrown her into a tree and then bolted for home. Emmitt made her comfortable on a mat. Tended her skull fracture with knowledge gleaned from two tours in the jungles of Vietnam. His efforts were in vain. She raved and ranted and then fell into a coma and never regained consciousness. Eighteen hours from start to finish.

The veteran possessed a lengthy criminal record, much of it related to scuffles with the police, but also a couple of domestic battery charges. He acknowledged that he should've brought her to the authorities and that he should've sought help, but he lived in terror of the law. When Reba passed away, that terror consumed him, reduced him to a gibbering wreck. Over the years he'd dropped enough acid and smoked enough dope that he was probably already on his way before that awful incident. He buried her with the useless, shattered helmet on her chest, and awaited the gods to punish him.

The funeral took place in Kingston. Virgil read the eulogy; he quoted Joseph Campbell's bit about participating "joyfully in the sorrows of the world." And Calvin stepped up before the crowded hall of mourners and sang Reba's favorite song, "Summertime." Good thing I brought a handkerchief. Damned dust in that church kept getting in my eye.

Jade and Virgil had hugged me at the reception and gruffly warned that haying season was how they separated the men from the boys on the farm. I didn't know what to say, so I nodded and let it lie. The Outfit had taught me the value of keeping my trap shut. What worked in the underworld proved as applicable to real life.

"A fucking Shakespearean tragedy" constituted Lionel's sole observation regarding Reba's death. He plonked a bottle of Old Crow onto the table. He and I got epically drunk and didn't speak of it again. Not in words, at any rate.

ONE AFTERNOON, Lionel, Meg, and I sat on the porch of my cabin. Minerva snored at my feet, twitching her ears to fend off the gnats that swarmed from the nearby pond. I'd spent the day mucking the stables. Dusk approached and the cold beer might've been the nectar of the gods, for all its sweetness.

Meg shook her head at her watch and said she had to book. Mac was dropping Devlin at the house in half an hour. She kissed me and ran to her car like a jet pilot scrambling for her F-16. Despite our dating frequently since spring, I had yet to meet the boy. She'd dropped hints lately that such a meeting might be in the works. Any day now. Now that she'd warmed to the idea, my feet were inexplicably chilly.

Lionel sipped beer. He'd gotten a couple ahead of me, as usual.

"Does she know what you did for a living before you came here?"

"The whole truth and nothing but?"

"Yeah."

"She thinks she understands."

"Ain't the same."

"The kindest act we can render is to keep our true selves hidden from our loved ones. Our job is to snow them a little. Be the good and honorable person they can hold on to."

"Can't shine a woman on forever."

"You're right. We wind up paying the piper, one way or another."

"Does that mean you're going to hang up your *pistolas*?"

"It means I'm doing my damndest to make sure she doesn't catch on to what a sonofabitch I really am for as long as I can."

"Well, good luck with that."

"Hey, how about this weather?" I said. "And in other news, I hear Larry Modine of NYC was recently indicted on forty-seven felony counts, including murder."

"Donnie Talon is probably so happy, he can raise his shorts without using his hands."

The corpses of nine White Manitou gangbangers had appeared in various rivers and landfills over the past few weeks. The grapevine had it, a few more were buried deep or sunk to the bottom of the bay. A leadership change hadn't saved them in the end.

Contemplating mortality, I felt the urge to get a stone off my chest.

"I ever tell you about Achilles?" I ran my thumb over the dog tags. "He fell off a cliff. That's how I lost him. I tried to grab him when he slid. Had ahold of a bush and leaned way over, nearly caught his paw as he scrambled to get back to me. But, nope. Looked into his eyes as he went."

"Rough way to lose a dog."

"One-in-a-million accident. I was hunting a captain who'd crossed the Outfit. Tracked him into the mountains and weather set in. Freezing rain. I didn't know the area. Things went wrong. Icy rocks, moving too fast. Stupid, stupid."

"How old was Achilles?"

"Almost seven. Died three weeks short, around Halloween. It gets cold early up there. I didn't even have to shoot the captain. Bastard got exposure and died of hypothermia. My first job."

"All kinds of deaths," Lionel said. "The dog, the guy, the innocence inside the kid you were before you climbed into those mountains. Fragile stuff. I keep trying to breathe life back into myself. Keep hoping a good deed here and there will make a difference after what I did overseas. Doubt it, though."

"Here's to old, loyal dogs." I rapped my bottle against his.

He chugged the last of his brew, rose, and slapped my shoulder.

"See you in the mornin', Hoss."

I watched the stars burn through the darkening heavens. His words took me back to my last visit with Dad and something the old man told me during a quiet moment.

For once, I admire what you're doing. It's a doomed gesture, alas. The girl you're searching for is probably dead. You're no hero. You are your father's son. You've seen too much, got too much of the bad blood in you. The world is a traveling slaughterhouse. It's rolling through space at sixty-seven thousand miles per hour. Earthquakes, volcanoes, tidal waves, and deep freezes. Extinction events. Insects devour one another by the gross ton. Animals are red of tooth and claw, and men commit genocide with bigger and better weaponry every few generations. You, son o' mine, are the edge of the blade that cuts through everything in its path, guilty or innocent alike. You can't resist what it is in your nature to do.

Excellent point, Dad. Only a fool believes he can prevail against what has been bred into blood and bone. I had no intention of fighting it.

BY SEPTEMBER, I'd decided to winter at the farm.

Pitching hay and shoveling manure wouldn't suffice to keep body and soul together, however. Nor to satisfy the pit that had opened within me when Dawn Walker had glanced over her shoulder at me as she climbed into the car that would take her to the airport. I'd met plenty of widows, widowers, and bereaved children. This time, it hit home, sank in deep, and left a scar. The shattered look in her eyes branded itself into my memory. It haunted me.

Money greases the gears. To do what needed doing I required more of it and on a semi-reliable basis. Infrastructure was the order of the day. Much of that autumn was spent securing the network and laying the foundation of my new Hudson Valley enterprise. A piece of cake, really. What, with my scintillating résumé and Mr. Apollo's good word on my behalf? I'd called in favors from associates in Alaska, who'd give me local points of contact.

The question wasn't one of whether I could speedily acquire lucrative work. No, it was a matter of setting prices and conditions and deciding which lines to cross. Fresh slate, I reminded myself. Or, if not fresh, at least lightly scribbled.

Requests came in steadily. Early one week, a young patent holder needed consultation regarding violent threats her ex-partner had made; midweek, I took a meeting with a tavern owner in the Adirondacks about a biker gang that enjoyed busting the place up and stiffing him on the tab; Friday, I did lunch with a rich recluse who thought a secret admirer wanted to kidnap him. The paranoid geezer turned out to be right too.

There'd be a vetting process until I got a feel for the trade. A calibration of lethal force versus delicacy and discretion. Fixing wasn't quite as straightforward as my previous existence as a hitter. Every day presented a new problem, an unforeseen complication. Definitely the kind of work that merited hazard pay.

The only detail that mattered? I didn't have to do anything or kill anyone that I didn't really want to.

Famous last words.

FORTY-FIVE

Halloween Day I received a message from Curtis. He told me when and where to meet him. He also said he was sorry.

I calmly set aside the phone and stared out at the pasture where the horses meandered. A cool, bright morning, the sting of winter yet hidden away. The clouds appeared to have been painted against the sky. Meg and I were supposed to spend the evening in New Paltz watching the Halloween parade followed by supper at Anatolia, the best Turkish restaurant in the valley. It occurred to me to call her and cancel, to apologize for myself and a lifetime of missteps that had led to this crossroads. Instead, I patted Minerva's belly.

I put on a suit and combed my hair and went to find Lionel.

He straightened from stacking bags of grain.

"I don't like that smile, Hoss. Or that suit. I saw 'em once before."

"This? I'm not smiling."

"Yeah." He hadn't cried at Reba's funeral. For a horrible moment, I thought he might finally crack then and there. He coughed and lit a cigarette. "Headin' out?"

"I've got to take a meeting."

"Huh. Can you skip it?"

"Not this one, my friend. Do me a favor. I might be gone a while. You'll look after Minerva?" I handed him Achilles' tags.

He made a fist and held it at eye level, the chain dangling.

"Any other dumb questions?"

"There's a box buried under that big rock behind my shack. See it gets to Meg."

"If you're gone a while."

"If I'm gone a while. Adios, Lionel."

"I ain't saying it. Nope." He turned his back.

On the way to the truck, I paused and breathed in the farm. Took a long, lingering look at the barn and the house and the smoke rising from the stack. Whatever bitterness I felt regarding Reba's death, whatever awaited me down the road, this had been a good run. The best I'd ever had, perhaps.

Destiny had decreed this a day of reckoning. Time to beard the lion.

CURTIS AND A HALF DOZEN OF HIS CREW occupied the Sultan's Swing. Bobby the Whip, Salazar, Fat Frank, and a half-dozen hoods who'd probably come up from New York special. The joint sat closed and shuttered. Inside, the lights were dimmed. I, the gangsters, and a handful of waitstaff were it. One of the waiters locked the door behind me. Another confiscated my weapons. I sat at the table with Curtis at the head. Bobby the Whip poured me a healthy dose of scotch. I didn't recognize the taste except that it was a smoky Highland malt, aged sixteen to eighteen years.

Curtis puffed on a cigar. Royally at ease for a man presiding over an execution.

"Got any requests?"

"T-bone. Rare. Another one of these." I drained my glass.

"Get the man his steak." Curtis snapped his fingers. "And another scotch." He waited for my meal to arrive and then watched me eat. "You're fixing. It's a going concern, I hear."

"Braiding pony manes? Terrific. There's a trick to it. I'm catching on."

"Chuck's moonlighting as your gofer."

"Bit more to it than that. He cooks, he cleans, he drives."

"Limp and all, huh?"

"Limp and all."

"You understand this ain't personal?"

"It's okay, Curtis." The steak arrived and I cut into it.

"Big day today. How you holdin' up?"

Somebody chuckled nearby.

"Isaiah don't get scared. Not a drop of sweat, not a single tremor. Not even when the Grim Reaper grins at him. Don't you New Yorkers know anything?"

Tony Flowers moved from the shadows and sat across from me. "Hi, big fella. The more things change . . . Larger than life and twice as ugly." He'd brought a friend, the heroically muscular goon who'd worked me over in the basement in Nome.

I held my knife loosely and nodded.

"Ah, Tony. I wish you hadn't made the trip. Nice to see you anyhow."

"Duty calls. Besides, I'm freezing my balls off in Nome. It's already winter there!"

"This is a vacation, then. Get some sun, see the sights—"

"—Pull out your fingernails. I kid, I kid. Deluca is extending courtesy. Not a clue why he wastes it on you, you big, stupid pineapple."

"Tony!" Curtis said.

"Sorry, sorry." Tony Flowers held his palms out in deference.

"What I meant to say is, soon as you finish your steak, we can hit the road. Vitale's waiting and we got a plane to catch tonight."

"There's no rush, take your time," Curtis said.

Tony F leaned over and took my knife and cut a wedge of steak. He chewed.

"Oh, oh! Oh my God." He stabbed the knife vertically into the steak as a threat of violence to come, braced his hands on the table, and lowered his face close to mine. "A taste of heaven before you slide down the chute into hell, huh?"

I snatched the knife and drove it through the meat of his left hand and well into the tabletop.

After a long, disbelieving pause, Tony Flowers shrieked in English and Italian.

"Motherfucker! You dirty cocksucker motherfucker!" was the gist. The façade of avuncular bemusement completely peeled away to reveal the beast we all knew and loved. His pet goon glowered at me, lacking the conviction to make a move.

Curtis wiped tears of laughter from his eyes.

"Settle down, Tony. We're all friends here."

The goon helped pry Tony F free and Bobby the Whip wrapped the wound in a fancy cloth napkin. The napkin soaked through in a hurry.

"That's okay, dead man. That's okay, you fuck. Vitale's gonna settle this bullshit real quick. He's gonna let the air out a that fat head of yours. You're dead, motherfucker!"

"Oh, Tony Torquemada," I said. "Now there's the real you, choking on your own spit. In another life, I can kind of see you burning heretics at the stake."

He gnashed his teeth.

"Come on, gents," Curtis said. "Enough screwin' around. The Ferryman awaits."

FORTY-SIX

Curtis meant what he said. The lot of us boarded a rusty barge called *Persephone's Hand* and chugged upriver. Gulls wheeled above the boat, riding a stiff breeze that tasted of mud and moss. The chop stung when it sprayed the deck. The boys smoked cigarettes, except for Tony F, who slumped in a deck chair and mournfully regarded his limp arm wrapped in a bloody towel. Nobody said much.

This wasn't the Outfit's traditional method of settling a score. Historically, I would've taken a shotgun blast to the face as I sat at a red light or gotten a bag over the head and been transported somewhere private for an evening of torture and murder like they'd planned back in Nome. The Outfit were a bunch of macho characters, but duels and such bullshit didn't often happen in the Syndicate. Business and professionalism were their watchwords.

As I'd told Lionel, the Nights are a different breed. Vitale had been gently urged to lay off. Stiff-necked to a fault, he—his honor—demanded satisfaction. Blowing me away in an ambush wouldn't do. Oh, no. I'd bested him in Alaska, instilled doubt as to his murderous prowess. He desperately needed to set the record straight before this audience of his colleagues. He had to make an example of the infamous Isaiah Coleridge. Nothing less would do.

We moored alongside a skiff at a rotting dock on a no-name bend in the river. From there, my entourage escorted me along a trail uphill past an abandoned warehouse and through the woods. Leaves crunched underfoot and spread red and brown among bare trees. Eventually, we came to a meadow. Picnic tables were scattered across the pebbly earth. Two wheelbarrows, shovels, and a pickax served as a reminder that this was a killing field.

Vitale Night and several Deluca wiseguys were present. He alighted from a table and nodded at me. His black suit cost a lot more than mine and he wore a gray homburg.

"Natty as usual," I said.

"Is *that* what you want to be buried in?" He spoke in a rasp. His collar hid most of what I presumed to be a nasty scar from the reconstructive surgery.

The other men took up posts on either side, standing around, trading smokes, or parking themselves atop the picnic tables. They gave us plenty of room.

"All right, Vitale. I've done my part. Your show now." Curtis handed the smaller man a Glock in its holster. Hospitality and professional courtesy dictated that the local boss provide the visiting hitter armament and logistical support. Vitale Night and Tony Flowers were notorious felons. They dared not travel across the country packing heat.

Night examined the automatic. Dry-fired it to gauge the trigger-pull weight, bounced it in his hand a few times and whipped it toward an imaginary target. Imagining me, doubtless. An intuitive shooter, he punched the barrel forward rather than taking deliberate aim. Same as my method, except I wasn't half as smooth. He checked the magazine and slapped it home. He removed his coat and strapped on the holster so it rode high on his hip for a right-hand draw. Brisk and perfunctory as an accountant balancing his figures.

Fat Frank returned my .357. I holstered it under my armpit.

Curtis lit a cigar.

"Vitale, you good?"

Night handed his homburg to Tony F's goon. He smoothed his silk vest.

"I am indeed." Each word emerged scarred and bruised. Night rolled his neck and shook his arms. He paced a tight circle, eyes on me the whole time. Behind him, Tony F clutched his wounded hand and blew a kiss.

Curtis squinted at the sun descending toward the tree line.

"Better get this over with. *'Let be be finale of seem. / The only emperor is the emperor of ice-cream.'*"

"A Stevens man?" I said. "A tip of the hat to you. Here, I thought you were a bunch of illiterates."

"Wanda likes Stevens. *I* like ice cream. C'mon, you bozos. Kill each other, already."

I moved to the center of the field and stood twenty feet apart from Night, straight on and bowlegged like Old West gunfighters at high noon. We would've preferred to stand at right angles to each other. Neither of us wanted to look like wusses in front of the assembled hard cases.

Night kept his hands relaxed and slightly away from his body. Hard for me not to dwell on the fact that he'd dusted at least forty guys in his time.

"Go ahead, Coleridge. I'll give you a jump. Put your hand on the butt of your pistol. Easy, very easy."

"Thanks." I carefully did as he advised and waited.

He glanced at the silent crowd. The vaguest trace of a sneer crept over his lips.

"Whenever you feel froggy—"

I started my draw before he finished his thought. I'm not the fastest gun. Faster than the vast majority, though. I didn't stand a snowball's chance in hell.

He had the Glock cleared and its barrel oriented on my torso before I even dragged the .357 free of leather. *Snap! Snap! Snap!* The Glock's hammer made the same impotent sound it had when he'd dry-fired earlier.

I holstered my revolver.

To my left, Fat Frank looped piano wire around Tony Flowers's neck and took his head partly off with a single convulsive sawing motion. Tony's sidekick lacked a neck to garrote. Bobby the Whip stuck a pistol to the goon's temple and popped him.

Vitale Night tossed his useless weapon into the weeds. He croaked a brief, awful laugh and lit a cigarette.

"Damn. It's like that?" After no one spoke, he gestured toward Curtis in disgust. "For him? For that palooka nigger, you shed Family blood?"

"Not for him," Curtis said. "This is business, Vitale. Nome obituaries are going to be hopping this week. Last night, a local business owner and two associates suspected of dabbling in the ivory trade were found deceased on an isolated beach twelve miles southeast of Nome. The police are treating the deaths as a homicide."

I reached behind my back where I'd tucked the jade war club into my waistband and brought it forth.

"The hit has been out on you and your crew since I reported your extracurricular activities to Mr. Apollo. The mooks in Nome were warned and warned that poaching brought too much heat for too little reward. Apollo got tired of talking to a brick wall."

"It's true," Curtis said to Night. "*You* were told to lay off. Chicago wanted to put you down with the local ivory buyers. Mr. Apollo said no, not unless you crossed the line and went mad-dog."

"Here you are, foaming at the muzzle," I said.

Vitale Night eyed the club. He took a long drag of his cigarette, tossed the butt, and flicked open a pearl-handled switchblade. Held it expertly, dangling it before his midsection.

"Let's see the color of your guts," he said, cold and composed. He sprang toward me with sickening alacrity.

I accepted a shallow slash along the muscle of my shoulder as I pivoted. The cut seared white-hot, but only affected me in the ecstatic fashion that comes once you've been wounded so often pain transforms into an eager companion. My heart beat faster. I swatted him and shattered his knife hand. He twisted, teeth snapping at my nose, and I rammed the knob of the club into his belly. He fell to his knees. I hammered his clavicle and it pulped and his arm dangled.

Vitale Night hissed and stiffened every muscle in his body. His eyes were wild beyond reason. I moved behind him, caught his tie in my fist, and jerked upward while driving my knee into his spine. When I finally released tension, blood leaked from his mouth with a bubbling sigh and he toppled facedown into the weeds.

Fifteen, maybe twenty seconds to complete the entire macabre scene.

Deluca foot soldiers dragged the corpses away. The captains and lieutenants checked their watches. They stubbed cigarettes and shrugged on coats and shook hands the way guys do after a particularly excellent lodge meeting.

"There lies Bad, Bad Leroy Brown," Curtis said. He touched my sleeve and winced at the red seeping from the seam. "You got gashed. That suit's done. Frankie, take him back to the shop and get this cleaned up." He produced a handkerchief and wiped his fingers fastidiously. "Happily ever after, huh?"

"Vitale has relatives," I said. "Anyway. Thanks, Curtis."

"Thanks for what? We didn't see nothin'. We don't know nothin'. Keep your nose clean, big boy. Your fixing enterprise steps on any of our toes . . . Well, I don't gotta harp on it, do I? For the love of Mary, no hitting."

"Forget it. I've moved on from that."

"Yeah?" He glanced pointedly at the bloody grass.

"I don't have to kill anybody I don't want to."

"So you've said."

"This time, I wanted to."

FORTY-SEVEN

Between calling Lionel to let him know I'd survived, a hot shower, two rolls of bandages wrapped around my chest, and obtaining a fresh suit from Bobby the Whip's Big & Tall selection, I turned up late for the Halloween parade along Main Street in New Paltz. Thankfully, Meg had downed a celebratory shot of Cuervo and was in a forgiving mood. She'd dressed as Batgirl. Housemate Lauren accompanied her as the Black Canary. Neither costume left much to the imagination.

"Reel your tongue in before you make a scene," Meg said into my ear as she landed a smooch.

"Happy Halloween, Isaiah," Lauren said, bright as a chipmunk on speed. "What are you supposed to be?"

"Mack the Knife." I doffed my brand-new gray homburg and bowed slightly. The equally new pearl-handled switchblade lay heavy in my pocket.

"*Psst!*" Meg said, smirking. "Isn't that hat a bit small on you?"

We sat on the terrace of Broody Jack's and watched the ragtag army of ghouls, goblins, and sequin-studded princesses move past while puppeteers manipulated lumbering dragons and ogres by wire and solemn witches in oversized conical hats held aloft paper lanterns to light the way. The ladies sipped margaritas. Black coffee for me. A chill descended from the stars, but Meg shared her cape. She asked me how the farm had been. I said I'd sliced myself while hoisting a new part on the tractor and laid a barn burner of a kiss on her to change the subject.

After the stragglers rounded the bend in a final hail of kazoo shrills and drum thuds, Lauren excused herself. She had a hot date with friends to catch a rockabilly band in Woodstock.

"So, Anatolia for dinner, drinks, and maybe more?" I said to Meg as we stepped onto the sidewalk.

"Actually, I'm thinking let's skip the restaurant for tonight."

"Whatever you say, Ms. Gordon."

"The ex has a thing in the city. He asked if I could take Devlin early."

"Absolutely," I said with as much gallantry as I could muster. "Your rain checks are always good with me, baby."

She laughed and patted my cheek.

"No, sweetie. I meant, we should have dinner at my place. I told Devlin you know your stuff when it comes to comic books. He's raring to meet you." She hesitated. "We've dragged our feet long enough. Correction: I've dragged *my* feet long enough. Time to bite the bullet and make this official. We are kinda sorta official, right?"

"Raring to meet me," I said.

"Yep."

We made it most of the way to where I'd parked when she finally glimpsed my face in the shine of a streetlamp.

"Oh, wow. Are you okay? You're sweating."

Indeed, sweat dripped down my jaw and neck. My shirt had already soaked through.

"I'm super-duper." I struggled to sound brave.

"You're green around the gills." She stepped closer and rose on tiptoe to peer at me. "Oh. My. God. Isaiah Coleridge. Are you scared? Don't lie!"

I swallowed and showed her my thumb and forefinger an inch apart.

"Maybe a tiny bit nervous."

"Jesus, you great, enormous lunk." She kissed me. "It's going to be fine. Devlin doesn't maim most of the guys I bring home."

"In that case," I said.

"Fret not, killer. I'll protect you."

"Lead on, then."

The moon busted through the clouds. For a moment I expected to behold a skull hanging there. Only Luna, full and yellow, riding low on the horizon.

Meg took my clammy hand in hers. We walked into the night.

ACKNOWLEDGMENTS

Thank you to my agent, Janet Reid; my editors, Sara Minnich and Alexis Sattler; Tony Davis, for his invaluable copyedits; and John Langan, for his invaluable advice and support.